HERE COMES THE SUN

The Summer of '69

By

Russell Paul La Valle

W & B Book Publishers, Inc.
USA

W & B Publishers

For information:
W & B Publishers
9001 Ridge Hill Street
Kernersville, NC 27284

www.a-argusbooks.com

ISBN: 9781635541700

This is a work of *fiction*. All of the characters,
organizations and events portrayed in this novel are either
products of the author's imagination or used fictitiously.

Book Cover designed by Stephen Bliss and Russell Paul La Valle

Printed in the United States of America

Some generations are close to those that succeed them;
Between others the gulf is infinite and unbridgeable.
"The Scandal Detectives"
F. Scott Fitzgerald

Being young is a desperate business. . . .
"The Ski Bum"
Romain Gary

We are stardust
We are golden
And we've got to get ourselves
Back to the garden.
"Woodstock"
Joni Mitchell

For

ROBIN—always there, always true

and

JASON—forever leaping into my arms

FORESHOT: 1969

Four years later, there was a summer. There was a sun you felt on the base of your spine that suggested a vulnerability—as though it were a link to an ancient lower order. Somehow, things had spun away and swept through a moment of refracted time when a rough beast had dragged itself up from the waters, and now its ghost stood under a febrile sun, dripping and bellowing out at the land. But it was a good warmth, and it gave you the feeling it was a time of opportunity—vast and untouched and complex—breathing and pressing into the spaces around you, nudging up, begging to become a part of your story. One of those thousand wobbly somethings of summer that never seem quite certain of their own existence and that rarely come of anything.

The summer of 1969—a time squeezed out of the tubes of science, abundance, war, protest, and song that tried to make us forget the fantastic boom of the universe and its reckless journey to nowhere . . . and everywhere. A time that had advanced humanity to the point when it asked itself, "Why can't things be invisible?"

For many, there were steps to take backward—to try to stop the world and look upon it as if for the first time. The summer would record the event while the planet lay in ignorance and great nebulae and vast vacuums of space would continue to shift and gnash and invert upon themselves in ageless energies of creation and destruction—attempting to overhaul a machine that once was thought to have been perfect.

BOOK 1

What Rough Beast

1

At least the summer offered a beginning—fresh on a hot day in late May. The president of the State University of New York at Old Ford had announced in a thicker-than-usual German élan that he concurred with the recommendations of the faculty and would confer our diplomas later on in the "*sporthalle*." Though we never met, I think we both knew why he simply found it impossible to say "gymnasium." The Nigerian next to me had laughed, "I say, Hawkes, what a bloody fop, eh? Such a marvelous bore." Walking away after the ceremony and turning for my last look at academia, I saw the big striped graduation tent begin to buckle and descend in a sad slow motion. Casually dressed undergraduates were already breaking it down for next year. I had expected more.

Afterwards at the curbside, I stared into my mother's bleary eyes, let her cup her hands and the mortarboard tassel against my cheek, and kiss me. She reminded me to fold my gown and to return it promptly so there would be no difficulties with the rental company. My father's hand appeared at the window and we shook hands without looking at each other—exactly as we had four years earlier. I decided at that moment that I would never forgive him for not showing me how to love him. In the back seat my Norwegian grandmother smiled. "Be a good boy for your mother, so she won't have to worry about you," she said and paused as though she forgot what she was saying, then blurted, ". . . like I do over a fifty-year-old no good!"—her son, my uncle.

The car shuddered to life and Mother added hastily, "Don't forget you've got a home," and to call often, especially in times of illness and low fortune. More words and the sedan eased away. There were waves and I knew I would not see any of them again for a long time. It all seemed a rather ironic adieu, and I remember having the distinct impression that the instant the car rounded the corner it was summer. It began at that very moment.

I had expected my family would want to leave early even though it was my graduation day. I knew how they felt more secure at home, among familiar surroundings. Home gave them a sense of safety and comfort; unknown things were on the outside and they liked what they knew best. In more alien environments like colleges, an extraordinary inwardness and paranoia took them over, and invariably, my mother, grandmother, and father would grow impatient and testy with each other and generate old personal arguments. The most illustrious was in a Washington D.C. hotel room when my grandmother told my mother she had refused to come to the hospital to see my mother's first born, my oldest brother, because he would look "too Italian" and "like a monkey"—from my father's sullied Sicilian lineage. Mother had cried, Father had become angry with Grandmother, and the whole scene ended when Father threatened to bludgeon Mother with a steam iron because she had yelled at him not to curse at her mother. He had to be restrained by my brother, the monkey.

I was relieved they were gone. Now I could concentrate my energies on more important things: I was running out of money and in the midst of trying to move out of my apartment as quickly and inconspicuously as possible. Being low on money was nothing new to me. I was accustomed to rationing and budgeting and had known the complex route expense money had trickled up to me at college—always with the same excruciating agony of near-adequacy that seemed malevolent because of the hopelessness of its struggle. Even when I was a boy, my mother had thought it necessary to detail the monthly mortgage payments, utility charges, food and gasoline outlays, commutation expenses—always ending very solemnly, "You know, Dalton, it's been over five years since your father's had a new winter coat and a new pair of shoes." Often she would cry, and if I were not reduced to tears, she would invoke her old standby about my father having to work as a waiter a few nights a week at the local beach club, serving condescending people half his age—a club we couldn't afford to join. He had a special pair of shiny black pants and old polished shoes he wore. Oh, yes, Mother made sure I knew well the feeling of always needing money, never desperately, but always with enough urgency to confine me and make me begin to hate my world by the time I was thirteen. Suddenly now, quite without fanfare, the haunt over money seemed petty. There were much more meaningful things in my life. Surely, the world was not going to let me die.

I stood and watched the broken cloud of dust raised by the car's back wheels and the way it was whisked away by the breeze and evaporated into thin air. I smiled and reached up and pulled at the collar of my graduation gown—until there was the ripping sound of a great tear and its jagged trail reaching to my waist. The only thing I knew for sure was that I was free and I had the whole summer ahead of me.

The next morning I got up early and worked until noon moving my belongings into the living room where everything sat in a big mound. There was the portable television that weighed nearly fifty pounds, had a broken antenna, and a sound control that fluctuated involuntarily between painful loudness and dead silence—when it worked. There was the narrow metal bed frame and mattress with the large hole that had served as a cache for an old roommate's drugs for a year. The rest were books, clothes, college memorabilia, pots, dishes, silverware, toiletries, and towels—all draping out of supermarket fruit cartons piled randomly like some strange dystopian city.

All morning I had the sinking feeling of hearing a knock on the door and the manager standing there—a tall Hungarian with grey wirehair cut short into no particular style or shape— discovering I was secretly moving out. I was convinced that Josef Stargallus was a communist. All communists wore their hair like that—the emphasis on the hair being cut, not fashioned. Stargallus also kept a loaded German luger on the front seat of his VW van and practiced shooting at soda bottles heaved into the air by his wife in the woods behind the apartment complex. She, too, was a foreign flavor—Polish it was rumored—built for endurance, not luxury. They argued constantly in guttural insults and took mysterious night drives out towards the mountain. I had always planned to follow them one night but never had. As far as being found out, I figured I had treated Stargallus with a strong enough blend of youthful arrogance and native aloofness that, if he did catch me, I could dismiss the entire affair to his ignorance of American custom and stoutly invoke the unwritten law of indigenous superiority—a kind of no-fault patriotism.

Checking the refrigerator out of habit, I realized I had defrosted it days before and there was no food. I could not remember when I had last eaten a proper meal. In truth, I had counted on my parents taking me out for a graduation dinner. Against my better judgment, I decided to grab something quick at the local Jack in the Box— though I sincerely believed the crass commercialism of the hamburger chain was inexcusable, not to mention newspaper accounts that the food was just a shade better than what zoo animals were fed. I felt ashamed when I had heard a new European installation was being considered in Paris—picturing the fatuous clown head, red logo, and the foul, greasy smells wafting past the Arc de Triomphe. Such a possible debacle compelled me to construct a telling joke about the hamburgers, and whenever conversation turned to fast food, I would calmly interject, "I could lube my car with one of those things."

It was important to me that I be funny and considered funny, though when people came to know me better, they discovered I was "serious with funny overtones." At times I found myself erecting the serious facade as carefully as I tried to be funny. The secret of appealing to a person's serious nature, I concluded, was merely the inverse of what made him laugh. Thus in that mystery, it was good to feel that no one truly knew who I was. Sometimes I think I even fooled myself.

If I had remembered Kaplan worked at the Jack in the Box, I would have gone to the diner. I had never trusted Kaplan. In college, he was the kind of friend who would tell everyone he never studied for exams but would go to the library late at night and study and inevitably get a good grade—then boast about his success to those who did poorly. He loved maneuvering people into awkward situations by saying embarrassing things and standing back and watching how they would respond under the pressure of being caught off-guard. All this happened often enough as not to be random. Kaplan was six foot four, had a dirty laugh, and was one of those clumsy, mediocre, second-string athletes who always had injuries and would sit on the bench, nursing an array of conspicuously positioned bandages that never got dirty.

The scratched plastic window pushed aside routinely. "Haaaaawkes!" Kaplan bellowed in his obnoxious sports cheer.

I nodded and stared at his feminine-looking mouth.

"Okay, let's see, two burgers with just ketchup. You'll have to wait—they're being made up special." He took a deep breath and smiled with his fleshy lips. "So, how's it hangin'? What's new and exciting in your life? . . . Oh, hey, that hotel job I told you about—it looks good. I went up there and spoke my best Yiddish for the old lady owner. Stayed very cool—threw in a *goyim* and *schvartze* every once in a while. She ate it up. She loves me! . . . Oh, you're Jewish, too, but I'll let you know."

"I'm moving."

"To Calypso, right?"

"Uh-huh."

"I heard."

The hamburgers came via a pimply runner.

"And a large coke," he snapped at the underling. "Yeah, Birdie was in yesterday. She told me." He raised his eyebrows suggestively. "That's right, you lucky dog— she'll be right downstairs from you now—nice, convenient. She said you, Fontana . . ."

"No, Fontana dropped out. It'll be Mason, Mauberley, Davenant, and me. Fontana's going to Colorado."

"Excellent! I heard they got good weed in Colorado. I should get out there, too."

"It's a free country."

"So, you'll be in the attic apartment across from Mauberley."

"Yeah. . . . Look, I'm not sure we have a phone yet or if we're even going to. I'm packing up my place now, so I'll be in and out. If you hear anything about the hotel thing, come by."

"Will do. . . . Okay, my man, that'll be a dollar eight," Kaplan said loudly and smiled his blubbery smile as he handed down the assembled package.

I stuck up a bent five-dollar bill but he narrowed his eyes and made a gesture that it was free.

"I only said that for them," he whispered. "It's cool, the manager's not here." He grinned and laughed through his nose. "He went out for lunch!" He stopped and wagged a finger. "Hey, since when have you descended to lowly hamburgers? No more *flambé pâté* washed down with an insouciant Bordeaux '56?"

"Oh, I'm not going to eat these. One is for the stray dog around my apartment building—a going away present—and the other I'm going to use to lube my car."

Kaplan's shiny head pulled back in laughter. The plastic snapped shut and he continued roaring in pantomime. I drove off, vowing to shun fast food places forever.

Kaplan was the kind of Jew who gave Jews a bad name.

2

When I returned home, Hugh Davenant was sleeping in my living room. He had pulled down the mattress and lay face down with his mouth open and a substantial saliva patch was spread beside his face. He was wearing his familiar long, dirty white caftan bunched up from sleeping and revealed raw red crisscross impressions up his calves. His legs looked horribly pale. A pair of sandals with thick leathers straps lay deflated in a jumble on the floor.

I first heard the name Hugh Davenant when he had hosted a poetry reading for Luther Greene at the university. Greene was the mildly known, unofficial "Poet-in-residence" at the college—occasionally writing flowery poems for college events—and Hugh was considered the "Bard of Old Ford." His was a very precise title Davenant explained in his opening statement introducing Greene: "Bards have a prophetic vision, whereas poets," he paused for flippancy, "merely finger-paint with words."

Whatever, I was never much impressed with either Davenant's or Greene's poetry. Others defended Hugh, arguing he was the protégé of a semi-acknowledged poet and that was something. To which I thought, big deal. What does that make him—some kind of secondhand rose?

These days Davenant could be found on the bench outside Gannon's, the oldest bar/pub in Old Ford, reciting from a bible and pontificating about how the world had yet to appreciate his immense talents. It was also the perfect location for his newest part-time job—working as the local bookie for Mikey Cigars and Bonesy, two low-level bookmaker/thugs from New Jersey.

"Want to go to India?" Hugh muffled face down.

"You awake?"

"No, I'm talking in my sleep."

"No."

"No, what?"

"No, I don't want to go to India."

"Why not?"

"Because India doesn't appeal to me."

"How do you know? You've never been there." Davenant propped himself up on an elbow.

"I haven't been to Auschwitz either. . . . Besides, I don't think the climate would agree with me.

"Give me a fucking break." It was Davenant's favorite expression. "What's the climate got to do with anything? It's peaceful, it's harmonic, it's contemplative . . ."

"How do you know? You've never been there either."

"There's none of that small-minded guilt crap about purpose in life and responsibility to the world. And I happen to know because Kendricks just came back. He put it a nice way. 'It's a matter of learning how to adjust living with the world, rather than the world having to adjust living with you.' Think about it." Davenant closed his eyes ethereally.

"That's funny. I saw Kendricks, too, and he told me he came back because he was getting sick of cleaning out filthy latrines for some fat teenage guru, not to mention his teeth were rotting away from too much ghee and god knows what else. . . . Could you hand me a piece of cord there, Padre?"

"It's the crucible, man. There's a solemnity there. All the other stuff is just chaff."

"What 'solemnity' is there if your teeth are decaying and everyone around you drinks his own urine?"

"I'm serious, man." Davenant tossed a ball of twine across the room. "I take my life seriously. Don't you wanna stop being washed around this jerkwater town?"

"I'm serious, too. . . . Listen, is it against your religion to help a friend pack up and move out of this hellhole before I get found out by the Nazi?"

"You're supposed to be intelligent, an enlightened guy. What does it matter *where* you live as long as you *do* live? This may be the only opportunity you ever have to go."

"Maybe, but I don't want to. It's that simple. Anyway, I don't have the money."

"Money. Who needs money? We'll depend on the kindness of strangers. If you don't want to go there, we could go somewhere else."

"Giving up on India so quickly? Go where you want. You don't need me. I'm not ready to travel vagabond chic right now."

"No, it's bad karma picking up and taking off alone. It spooks me. . . . I just keep thinking another opportunity like this won't come along for a while. You know—with the summer, no pressure, the right personnel, no war, no strife, no protests . . . only bliss."

"Where's the bliss in Kashmir? . . . Why don't you take Birdie and bliss out with her—her man's gone to California?"

"Gimme a fucking break. When are we going to do all the things we talked about? Let's stop talking and do it, man—follow your inner moonlight, don't hide the madness. . . . We only get one chance at all this. We have the rest of our lives to grow up. Our only job is to live our consciousness."

"Look, I'm just not into it right now. Is that such an impossible thing? Not everyone roams around the world and they're perfectly happy to stay in one place—maybe forever. You should understand that: 'To see the world in a grain of sand.'" I stopped and looked at his sad puppy face. "I just want things at my own pace for now. If I miss out on something, so what. It's my life. Why is it necessary to live every second for as much as I can squeeze out?"

"You just don't get it, man. And don't go quoting Blake on me. I think we both know why you've suddenly grown roots."

"What's that supposed to mean?"

"It means I've seen the yellow MG around town again, too."

"Fuck you."

His smug expression expected more of a challenge, and when it didn't come, he reached for his well-worn tobacco pouch—filled with pot, a pipe, roach clip, and a pack of rolling papers—and started constructing a joint.

Truth be told, I was endlessly fascinated and hopelessly in love with Maxine Cooke and had never made much of a secret of it to Davenant. Her star and yellow MG had first appeared in Old Ford five years earlier. The gen was she had grown up motherless in Panama—the daughter of the infamous Lieutenant Colonel Maximillian "Mad Max" Cooke—where she and her twin sister Phoebe (equally wild and equally beautiful) lived the privileged life of spoiled American army brats. Theirs was an upbringing filled with horses, servants, military protocol, lavish parties, midnight swims, endless cocktails, and a doting father who couldn't say "no" to his girls—not to mention legendary escapades with fawning cabana boys, beach attendants, canal workers, and any other thin, dark-skinned, pretty Panamanians who happened to cross their orbits. When the girls graduated high school, Mad Max promptly retired and relocated to the upper Midwest, where he reinvented himself into a wildly wealthy helicopter manufacturer—in no small measure aided by his longtime military contacts. Once there, Maxine enrolled for a brief semester at the University of Chicago, her mother's alma mater, but it soon became clear she was more suited to the exploration of fraternities than to the rigors of academia. Then heeding the siren call of New York City, she headed east and briefly became a model—easily meeting the height requirement but, in the end, proved much too curvy to compete with the Twiggy-obsessed couturiers. Soon, New York's pace and vibe rang coarse and uninspiring to Maxine's Central American sensibilities and was further aggravated by all the nightly, hippie hangers-on who kept crashing in her uptown apartment. One day reading the travel section of the New York Times, she came upon a real estate listing for an old colonial stone house on the outskirts of upstate Old Ford—that had once belonged to a renowned Hudson River School painter—and purchased it on a whim. Perched above the Valkill River, the property included a large, bright art studio—picture perfect for her latest, newfound passion, painting. Enrolling in several art classes at SUNY Old Ford, she soon discovered a newer passion, Maurice White, a married painting professor who took Maxine under his artistic wing and irretrievably stole her heart. On their first date, he told her of the local Indian legend that spoke of the Valkill flowing from south to north and those who ever lived along it would always return. As their affair progressed, Maxine saw this as proof positive that she and Maurice were destined for each other. Over the next four years, the legend was tested many times—with their tempestuous relationship playing in and out along the banks of the Valkill, the mountains beyond, as well as Maxine's far flung globetrotting exploits. Yet, somehow, she always found her way back to the little Hudson Valley aerie that had become her fortress of solitude—and into the loving arms of Maurice White.

It was during that early time I had met Maxine quite by accident, literally—when she had run into me with her Vespa outside the campus Art Building. Mesmerized by her dark blue eyes and heartfelt apology tinged with an almost imperceptible foreign accent, the collision spawned occasional meetings in the dining halls, in hallways between classes, and along the leafy quad. Finally, one glorious night it had blossomed into a prodigious one-night stand in her painter's studio—when in perfect synchronicity, the earth moved and the angels sang beneath a rare super blood wolf moon. Completely taken over and desperately wanting more, I quickly learned that Maxine's love life was dictated by two concerns: her nomadic thirst for travel and adventure, and the vagaries of her feelings for Maurice White—both contingent upon the present condition of his marriage and the fragile state of their happiness. As a college freshman, the prospect of making love to an older woman— no questions asked, no demands made or given—conjured images of glorious possibilities. But as time went on and my yearning for her grew, Maxine made it clear it could never be. While she understood my feelings and loved me "in my own way," she professed her heart would always belong to Maurice, and I mustn't let myself fall in love with her. Sadder still, over the intervening years—seeing and following the MG along the streets of Old Ford; hoping to hear the snarl of her Vespa on campus; or helplessly watching her from afar with other men—it became painfully apparent I was not the only one chosen to make her forget her heavy heart and bouts of melancholy. The queue was long. . . .

"Hey, man, why don't you join me on planet Earth," Davenant said with a smile, holding out a smoking joint.

After taking a hit and passing it back, I said, "Look, this can wait. Let's go to Gannon's, play some chess, relax and figure out the world over some drinks."

"Now you're talking." Davenant sat up and began to sort out his sandals.

We walked the half-block to Gannon's. My idea was to spend an hour or so, get him drunk, and then go back and finish packing. I wanted to be out by the weekend, and it was already Thursday.

We each had two shots of Wild Turkey at the bar, then ordered a pair of beers to take back to one of the wooden booths whose scarred tabletops were inlaid with a chessboard and chess pieces already set in place. After a few moves, Davenant knocked over his king.

"I don't feel like playing."

I could tell he had lost his buzz of enthusiasm and was feeling the Turkeys and sorry for himself at the same time.

"This beer is warm!" he blared. ". . . Do you realize we've lived almost a quarter of a century? Twice that and we'll be almost fifty years old."

"Pithy."

"Imagine when you're forty, forty-five and you're almost a half century? Shit, is that the saddest time of your life or what? Your body starts betraying you and you wither away a little bit each day—right in front of your eyes and you can't do a goddamn thing about it! You'll be just like your father."

"How inspiring. But maybe that's not so bad. Maybe he's happy," I said. I gestured to Fungo, the bartender, for another round of Turkeys.

"Bullshit happy. Happy working for the telephone company for thirty years? Happy that he's been mugged in the subway—twice? Happy he's got a gold pen and a gold watch? It's all dénouement the rest of the way, man. . . . Picture it—the 'Presentation of the Company Watch'—otherwise known as the tick-tock transfer. 'To S.S. Hawkes, 30 years.' All pretty, engraved letters. 'For all your obsequiousness and servitude' . . . Then he goes home, shows the wife, and she says, 'Let's go get pizza and celebrate.' He agrees because her food tastes like cardboard. They get to bed at nine o'clock, he works out on her, and she lies there with her eyes closed and her fists clenched, bleating, 'Hurry up, S.S., do it—just do it!'"

I marveled at Davenant's threnody and his thoughts going in five different directions—becoming full-fledged drunk. For some reason, his complaining reminded of my old summer job before college—working in Manhattan for the telephone company (arranged by my father)—sitting in the back of a utility truck every day, picking up broken equipment and bringing it back to the warehouse. One day at lunchtime, I had been looking at guitars in a shop window in midtown, and I was approached by an older man who announced himself as, "Leon Skir, the writer!" After my initial wariness—I was fairly certain he was a homosexual—we exchanged addresses and started sending letters to each other about writing, art, music, the war, politics. . . .

One time I sent him a long poem entitled "Hypocrisy," complaining about the same things Hugh was, and I still kept his response after all these years:

"Just stop it! You bitching about the guy who is going to work complaining about 'hippies'! It's you who spens all yr time complaining, not he. He works works works gets up in morn, puts on those clean clean clotes (gotten clean at some cost and care) to get nice respectable job, uses subway instead of cab to save money for his kids and wife (for whom he works works works). He has done all this for LOVE (Really, love for wife, society, kids who he wants to think well of him. He may spend a moment looking at some kid who hasn't taken pains with his appearance (at lest the pains he has taken) and feel mad/bad but only for a moment. Then he is worrying about his wife's kidneys, his children's school problems the job, his income tax. Yr outfit for him, with the hat is as dates as a WPA drama fat-capitalist. Now all the younger Linsay-type execs do not wear hats. As for yr longing for an IRT catastrophe, when you are older you will only patiently hope the journey not with too many stallings."

"You know what bothers the shit out of me?" Davenant continued. "College seems like epochs ago. . . . I like that—'epochs'—from the imperfect: *Eram, eras, erat, eramus, eratis, errant . . . epochs!* You know, I can't even remember what I did in college. Everything's a blank and a blur. It was there and, bang, now it's gone. Puff the magic dragon, man," he said and began humming the song.

"You were the Bard of Old Ford, remember?"

He wasn't listening.

"You know, sometimes I see a girl in town I used to go out with and she doesn't even say hello, or she might be courteous but *very* cool. I can't help thinking maybe I tried to bang her on our last date or I stood her up or did *something!* . . . Circumstances. I've forgotten all my circumstances. . . . Ah, this place stinks! We should have gone to the Cacique—at least it has some atmosphere." He was talking loudly. A few people at the bar were looking in our direction. "Let's face it— everyone in this burgh is ignorant, provincial, and clueless. They don't stand a chance. . . . We know better, man."

"Then leave. Stay away for a while and see what happens."

"That's what I've been saying for two hours!"

One of the regulars at the bar leaned over to Fungo and he nodded, staring at us.

"I mean, what's the big news here: Red Carpet Week; a cat got stuck up a tree; they closed down a bar for serving a minor? . . . You can't even sit on the corner bench for ten minutes without some redneck cop locking you up for loitering. Even the town justice—what's his name Tex something, I mean, how apropos is that?—said, 'The longer your hair, the longer your sentence.' Do you believe it?" He burped loudly. "It's bad, man, bad. Bad cheese." He swept aside some chess pieces. "Take Fungo," he whispered, indicating the bar with his eyebrows. "He's the perfect example. Been painting for how long now? Hell, he must be sixty at least. His stuff sucks and he's been a bartender forever. He should've left a long time ago. He's stuck, man, just stuck and he can't fuckin' move."

Davenant sat back and raised his glass, as though what he had said pleased him.

"Fungo played in the Yankees' farm system. Supposed to be a helluva hitter—before the accident."

"Big fuckin' deal. What's he now? A one-eyed wonder staggering home every night with a pint bottle in a paper bag."

I couldn't let him go on. Fungo was a friend of mine and right now I wasn't going to convince Davenant one way or the other about anything. He was a sad sight sitting there—wilted-looking, beads of beer foam glistening on his upper lip, feeling lost—thinking I was deserting him.

"Listen, I have to go. The new people are moving in on Saturday."

"Want another beer?"

"Okay, one more. Then come back with me while I pack. Keep me company."

He saluted with a forlorn face.

Leaving Gannon's, I realized I was a bit drunk, too, as everything seemed to be part of a grand undulation set into motion from the exit blast of air-conditioning shooing us out the door. Outside, the sun was intensely bright and contained the sounds of things I could hear but not identify.

As soon as we reached my apartment, Davenant fell onto the mattress. He kept moaning that the room was spinning and he might get sick. I put a pot on the floor next to him and told him to go to sleep. Looking around, I realized I had too many possessions; half the stuff I never used anyway. It was time to get rid of the "chaff," as Davenant would say. One truckload should make the entire move. That is, if the Arco station in town would loan me their pickup again. I had cracked it up last time, but that was over a year ago. Maybe they wouldn't remember.

Two hours later, everything I wanted to take was disassembled, tied up, and packed away as well as I cared to make it, and I sat in the corner watching an ant lug a crumb twice its size across the floor. It was a lesson in determination—nothing else seemed to be on the ant's brain other than "food" and "bring back to nest." It was fascinating the way it only knew about living or dying and nothing else. It took each moment as it came—working continually and not knowing or caring whether it could be killed in an instant. No matter, there were millions to take its place. Time was not as important as contribution.

I stood up and brushed off my dungarees, listening to Davenant snore intermittently. I walked over and hovered my foot over the ant as it continued to drag the giant crumb. I lowered my foot slowly almost to the floor and invented dramatic music as an accompaniment. Silently, I issued a proclamation that this ant shall live. Hell, it wasn't my apartment anymore.

"Hugh," I said, shaking his foot. "Get up. It's almost six o'clock."

He sucked in a last snore and swiveled his head back and forth very deliberately, blinking himself awake. He knuckled his eyes. "What time is it?"

"Time to eat."

"That last shot must have done something."

"That's what drinking is for—puts off the long swim for another day."

"Huh?" He was sitting up, rubbing the back of his neck. "Where do you want to go?"

"I don't care. How about the diner? I've been chatting up one of the waitresses—she's been giving me anything I want and charging me for just coffee and a doughnut."

"She'll give us *anything?*" he yawned and smacked his mouth like a toothless hobo.

We looked at each other and laughed.

On the way to the diner, we spoke about how—in Old Ford at least—the urgent noise about the war and all the associated turmoil had died down. Maybe it was the warm weather. Maybe people were tired of marching and protesting and crying out for some new weekly hero—heroes in a country that deep down never really wanted heroes. Davenant's sentiment was, "What can you do? The word is out—now it's up to them. We've done all the hard work, all the heavy lifting. It's time we watched out for ourselves." To him, the upcoming Apollo 11 launch was emblematic of everything wrong with the world, as man was about to violate the cathedral of the moon. We had abandoned reason and were hell bent on mucking around with the natural order of things. It was a reckoning he was memorializing in a new sonnet called "The Lonely Planet." Pulling into the diner's parking lot, he made me wait in the car as he recited a first draft:

You may turn around now, my chaste moon,
And gaze last upon this mean emerald ball
Of blue-scrimmed horror and white-toxic fume.
Enshroud me with a newly refracted pall,
For I've divorced myself from reason
And taken with the ways of the hereafter.
I stand accused of sidereal treason;
Whisper farewell, there can be no more laughter.

So long ago we had planned to conjoin.
Whoever dreamed that fate would have us drawn
into such a forsaken universe?
I, a lonely planet in foreign void,
Beside my dead lover and forever borne
Of thoughts of suicide I often rehearse.

"I know it needs work. What do you think?"
"Why don't we just pour gasoline on our heads and set ourselves on fire?"
The diner's air-conditioning was a relief. The dinner crowd had already funneled in and it was busy. After waiting on line a few minutes, we were ushered to a booth in the section where my friend was serving. A hostess perfunctorily placed paper placemats in front of us with a sketchy, undecipherable map showing how to get to the diner from the surrounding towns, then plopped down two small glasses of water with ice chips and slid

menus in protective plastic jackets onto the middle of the table.

"Enjoy."

The waitress, Rachel—I knew her only by her first name—came to take our orders. She was plump in a seductive way; had long, nondescript, sandy-colored hair; and was well proportioned with a body carriage that made men stare. She wore a black uniform that was conspicuous because all the other waitresses wore white.

"Hello, Dalton . . . coffee and doughnuts again?"

"Rachel, you hurt me," I chided. "Must my low funds be a continuing source of ridicule to you?" I was feeling good. It was cool and the busyness of the diner made me seem unnoticed. I could say and do things and remain anonymous. There was a power in that I liked.

"Try the hot turkey sandwich. It's fresh." She pointed it out with her pencil. And in the same tone, "You never called last week. What happened? Low funds again?"

Instantly the whole arrangement came back to me—dinner, perhaps a drive, and then a movie at the Athenaeum I had wanted to see. Simply, in the welter of leaving my apartment I had completely forgotten. "I'm sorry, Rachel, I really am. You know I'm moving out of my apartment and . . ."

"Excuse me, but I could not help overhearing," Davenant interrupted, smiling enough for both of us. "Would you care to consider a pinch hitter who is widely known for his punctuality *and* also happens to be one of the new lions in the current pride of contemporary poets?"

She looked at Davenant blankly and turned away.

"Oh, sorry. Rachel, this is Hugh Davenant, my new roommate. . . . Look, let me make it up to you. When do you get off tonight?"

"In about two hours. But they asked me to work overtime."

"Do you have to?"

"Not if I'm busy."

"Good, you're busy. I'll meet you at the Cacique. The wine cellar is open again. And I think there's supposed to be something going on in the mountains later on."

She smiled, and for her, in a rather sophisticated manner, I thought.

"Should I bring a bathing suit?"

"It's more fun to improvise, I've found," Davenant chimed in again.

"Okay, two hot turkey sandwiches," she spoke at her pad as if Davenant did not exist. She had learned early on how to quash leering hecklers who thought waitresses were always in heat. She scooped up the menus and walked behind the counter to a small microphone. "Two hot turkey sands, one mash, one French, B-beans and string B's." Her voice was tinny over the speaker inside the kitchen.

"Charming," Davenant said. He reached into his pocket for his cigarettes. He lit one and blew out a yard of smoke. "And unless I'm mistaken, and I don't think I am, she ain't American. Better check her papers before you do the beast with two backs—you could be hauled in for harboring an illegal alien."

"What are you talking about? And what's with the 'pinch hitter' and "young lion' shit?"

"I was helping you out, man. If I come on like a dragoon, she flees into the arms of her new lothario. Basic wooing 101."

"Well, I don't need your help. And what would Tracy say?"

"Why bring her up?"

"Face it, big fella, you're kept. You can't have *all* the privileges."

"Who says?"

When the food came, we ate in hungry silence. Afterwards, Rachel brought the check for two coffees and two crullers—80 cents. I noticed she had brushed her hair and put on lipstick. We left a dollar tip, paid the bill, and returned to the heat outside.

Hugh said he had to meet some people, and we parted company outside the Cacique. He might meet me in the mountains later on and wished me good luck.

3

A cool breeze had assembled since dinner—making its way down the mountain and asserting itself against the stagnant heat that had settled into the valley during the day. The streetlights and neon signs had come on, and the local bank sign blinked the time and temperature. The main intersection—whose four corners were occupied by the Cacique, an ice cream parlor, an abandoned Victorian house, and a reputed Mafia-owned pizza joint—was made more orderly by Old Ford's lone traffic signal. At this hour the sidewalks were cluttered with summer semester college kids out for a stroll and a good time, trying to avoid the hard-drinking locals who sat in front of the bars and stores, watching everything go by and itching for a fight. They were joined by hippie motorcyclists and high-heeled, counter-culture tourists from Long Island and New Jersey, who invariably made their way up the Hudson Valley and invaded towns like Old Ford—finding them quaint with corn fields, farmers' markets, antique Sundays, European history, and Indian lore. . . . Everyone relished the breeze.

The Cacique was one of the stone houses built by the French Huguenots in the 1700's. It was on the route of the Old Post Road that had run mail from New York up to Albany, then a blossoming mercantile wilderness. Standing across the street, I imagined a sweating rider pulling up to the tavern, horse blowing, saddle creaking, and calling for a drink while a fresh mount was readied. Then it was off again along the woodsy trail.

I walked around to the backside of the Cacique— to the basement accessed by a psychedelic door with "Wine Cellar" painted freehand in purple letters and held open by an empty beer keg. The yellow light inside was inviting, as music spilled onto the sidewalk. Fish netting hung in billows off the low-beamed ceiling above old wine casks that served as tables, each one with a checkered tablecloth and a lighted candle atop a wine bottle. Off to one side, a clappy-looking upright sat in a dark corner that served as a makeshift stage. Four large speakers, one in each corner, were attached to the original stonewalls and piped out a bluesy jazz that provided good background. This early, only a few of the tables were occupied—men in beards and long hair, talking in whispers to braless ladies in peasant blouses and airy floor-length dresses. I waved to a few regulars and they nodded back.

The bartender was wiping the bar counter with a damp rag and looked up without stopping, "What can I do for you, my friend?"

"Hey, Dutch. A pitcher of Sangria," I said, measuring a large vessel with my hands.

I sat down at a table next to one of the small basement windows and watched couples strolling by hand-in-hand, passing the night in town, waiting for something to happen.

A cute waitress came with the wine and a glass. I smiled as she poured. "Will you join me?"

"Can't, not on working time. But thanks."

"Good girl. I'll remember your loyalty when I speak to Sam."

Sam was the owner of the Cacique. He had run for Town Council the year before and had lost convincingly. Most of the townspeople were conservative and didn't like the longhairs or the Cacique, which was considered their Alamo. They also didn't like that SUNY Old Ford was notorious for its drug use and consistently voted one of the top five party schools on the East Coast. I remembered what Sam had said at one of the Town Hall meetings: "I do business with an element in this town that everyone else wants to forget exists—except when they spend their money in your shops and restaurants."

A good-looking woman with shoulder-length, straight blonde hair and a loose fitting tee shirt passed by quickly. I tapped on the window. She turned and our eyes met in an expression of *Alas, two ships passing in the night*, and she continued happily around the corner.

Across the street, Rachel walked into view. She didn't see me as she stood waiting for the light to change. She looked more whorey now that she was out of the diner and in a practiced gesture clasped a long-sleeved sweater across her chest, despite the heat. Her face looked concerned with all the traffic and activity. An unusually large handbag rested over one shoulder. The whole outfit—the tight black waitress uniform, black stockings and black ripple-soled shoes were wrong for her, wrong for the Cacique . . . probably wrong for me. As she crossed the street, the breeze caught her hair prettily— drawing attention away from her heavy thighs that muscled with each step. I wished she had changed before coming. Through the window, I waved my glass in happy comradery, pretending to be excited she had come.

"Welcome. Sit down," I said, pushing out the chair opposite me with my foot. "Aren't you hot in that sweater?"

"A little, but I hate walking around with the uniform and all," she said, setting the huge pocketbook on the table and leaning it against the wall. She looked around, "Nice in here."

I stared at the bag that must have weighed thirty pounds. "Yes, it is. I'm glad they finally opened it again. You haven't been here before?"

"No."

"Oh, good, let's celebrate your initiation. Sangria?"

"I'd love some. I could use it." She paused, presumably waiting for me to take up the *Everyone needs a drink after work* cliché, but I didn't. Nervously, she pushed her hair away from one eye, and for the first time I noticed how beautiful her green eyes were—literally sparkling in the candlelight. "It got really busy after you left."

"Is that right?" I caught the waitress's attention, held up my glass, and mouthed, *Another, please.*

Dutch took all this in with his bartender's efficiency and already had a fresh glass waiting. The waitress brought it over and stood looking at Rachel.

"That's all, sweetheart, thank you—the tip comes *after* we leave."

She widened her eyes and one side of her mouth smiled. "You're welcome, Sir," and sauntered away.

"What a pretty girl," Rachel said and coughed into the back of her hand.

"Your eyes are prettier," I said and poured the wine.

She took a noisy guzzle and leaned back more assuredly. "Thank you, but I know what men see in me, and it's *not* my eyes."

"Maybe so, but . . . 'one's eyes are what one is, one's mouth what one becomes.'"

"Poetry will get you everywhere. . . . Sorry, do you mind the uniform and all?"

"Oh, no, it's perfect for the mountains."

"Okay, wise guy, I'll change." She looked around. "Is there a bathroom down here?"

"Upstairs. But what are you going to change into?"

"I've got a spare outfit in my bag. Be right back."

She shouldered the huge tote-style pocketbook and walked away lopsided. Probably has a spare set of wrenches in there, too, I sighed. I refilled my glass and resigned myself that it was going to be a long night. And on top of it, tomorrow was a busy day. I was not in the mood for either, but one had to suffer for one's pleasures. Rachel might prove interesting.

She returned in a tumescent, lime-colored blouse stretched precariously by a line of hard working buttons and translucent enough to detect a black brassiere underneath. The black skirt was replaced by tight bellbottom dungarees and white low-heeled sandals, exposing large bunioned feet. An improvement, I thought, but not a spectacular one.

"You look exquisite, my dear," I said smiling and kept my eyes on the buttons.

"Cut the crap, Dalton," she said, looking directly into my eyes and buttoned another button. "How'd you get that name?"

"A gift from Mommy. . . . As the story goes, there was a famous crooner back in the 30's whose real name was Dalton something or other, but he had an Italian stage name. Apparently, my mother was crazy about him—I can't believe my mother was a groupie—a real pretty boy and a rival of Frank Sinatra. She was heartbroken when he was shot under suspicious circumstances. Only 26."

"How sad. . . . Maybe Sinatra had him bumped off?"

"Maybe. Hungry?"

"Not right now. Served too many French fries today."

Suddenly, there was a big commotion, and a diagonal shaft of light illuminated a portion of the stairwell. We could hear the jukebox upstairs, loud voices, and the scuffling of footsteps.

"Shut the door!" Dutch yelled. "Either you stay up there or come down, but close the damn door!" He turned to the waitress. "See what's going on."

After a minute, the footfalls revealed a half-dozen laughing revelers. "Patience. We are descending, innkeeper," one of them bellowed. "Don't stand there, wench. Flagons of wine and tankards of ale for my crew. . . . Off with you, harlot."

"Fuck you," the waitress said and walked back to Dutch.

"Saucy bitch, I'll have you flogged for your impudence."

As they came into view, I recognized the loud one as Kincaid, one of Hugh Davenant's literary friends—yet another poet who adored Luther Greene's *oeuvre.* I grimaced and turned away. Kincaid was an obnoxious braggart—a lot like Kaplan—especially when he was drunk. I wasn't in the mood.

"Friends of yours?" Rachel asked.

"I know the big mouth."

Kincaid turned with a massive sweep of his arm and caught my stare. "Hawkes! Hawkes, what a surprise!" He put his arm around a woman in the entourage and spilled his drink on another in the process. "I spy a compatriot at yon table. Let us avail ourselves of his hospitality."

"Shit, does anyone have a napkin?" asked the woman whose blouse had been sullied.

Dutch gave me a hard look. I shrugged and rolled my eyes in displeasure.

"Hello, Kincaid," I said, raising my glass. We shook with our left hands.

"Hawkes, this is my court. A motley crew at best, but they're loyal and, more important, they have drinking money. . . . No formalities. Names are not important." There was more handshaking and "How's it going?" all around.

Kincaid took in Rachel. "And who might this fetching tart be? . . . My god! Fellows, you know who this is—it's Mary Mammatus! It could be none other than she, *yavol?*. . . Quick, call the State Department—I think we've found the last two undetonated torpedoes from the Bismarck."

"Don't be an ass, Kincaid," I said.

"*Calme toi, mon vieux,* I pose no existential threat."

Everyone laughed and started scraping chairs around our table.

"Is he making fun of me?" Rachel whispered.

"Kincaid, since you asked, this is my sister, Betty Lou. She visiting from the Mayo Clinic. She has terminal leukemia."

Kincaid stopped laughing as he held a chair aloft. "Oh, but I didn't . . ." Then he looked hard at me and started laughing again. "You bastard, you almost had me going."

"Go ahead, Betty Lou, show Kincaid your leukocytes."

He waved me away and ordered fresh drinks.

Kincaid's woman, Sioux, was big-boned and wore a brown leather vest over a thin tee shirt. Her dungarees were patched and tucked into cowboy boots. She snapped her fingers to the music—sucking in her bottom lip, tapping her boot, and moving her head up and down with her eyes closed—as if entranced. They were all drunk.

"Hey, Hawkes. We're all going up to Fallen Rock. Interested?"

"I heard there might be something going on," I said dourly and looked over at Rachel who was biting a corner of her fingernail. She nodded yes. "Sure, why not? You can drive." Let Kincaid and his big boat of a Pontiac eat up all the gas.

Kincaid whispered something to Sioux and turned to Rachel. "So, tell me, Betty Lou . . ."

"My name is Rachel. Rachel Levy."

"Oh, well, Miss Levy (he pronounced her name as a spondee), have you been following the Defense Department's reports that there are now over a half-million GI's in Vietnam—our greatest involvement to date?"

"I don't know anything about that."

I felt the need to defend her, but as I looked over, Rachel's face was sweat-shiny and smiling almost admirably at Kincaid—as though she were happy to be included in the group. Suddenly, it felt unbearably stuffy and I excused myself to the bathroom and walked upstairs. I needed fresh air. I had trouble getting past all the people standing and drinking around the bar, but I managed to push through politely and went outside.

The slight breeze was warm but its movement felt good against my face. I remembered Leon Skir taking a picture of me looking into the wind: "a good author shot," he'd said and showed me similar pictures of him as a young man. A crowd had already filled the outside bistro tables set into the gravel area leading into the Cacique. I stood by the wall. Above me, a neon sign buzzed and hypnotized moths fluttered around it—soon to join their dead brethren below.

Most everyone was smoking and talking above the music pulsing out the front door. A few held drinks they had taken from the bar, even though it was against a town ordinance to drink outdoors. Some had bottles in small brown paper bags that fit neatly into their back pockets—the cowboy look. I wondered how it felt to walk around with a liquor bottle bulging out against your ass. It represented a different kind of superiority than Kincaid's—more dangerous perhaps. There was the strong smell of pot in the air.

I looked down the street at the fraternity bar from earlier college days—The Hole—that had died out and had evolved into a quieter place to get good hamburgers with grilled onions. On the walls inside there were still composite pictures of old pledge classes that served as conversation pieces for an older drinking crowd who remembered those years. Without warning, a yellow MG noisily passed by the bank and screeched to a sloppy, diagonal halt in front of The Hole. It was Maxine Cooke's car. There was no other like it in Old Ford.

A handsome man was driving and two other men squeezed into the passenger seat had Maxine perched on their laps. When they all got out, the two men pulled her in opposite directions and her deep-throated laughter echoed off the storefronts. Her dark hair was wet and dangled in strings halfway down her back, shining dully in the streetlights. They rushed through The Hole's front door with a quick blast of noise. A stray dog barked in protest across the street.

I looked at Maxine's car—bright lemon-colored (for some reason it had to be yellow) with running boards and wire wheels with spinners. The black convertible top lay flattened and lashed down haphazardly behind the seats. I remembered walking up to it one day and smelling the interior—leather mixed with a woman's smell—and the way the dashboard was with all the knobs and a tiny furry animal wrapped around the gearshift.

As quickly as they had entered, Maxine and her three suitors emerged, still laughing and carousing. "I must have another drink!" she announced and pointed to Skag Harbor, a biker bar a few doors down. As though giggling at an inside joke, they all weaved down the sidewalk and pushed through the rough-looking crowd that loosely clogged the entrance.

I ordered a beer and sat down, waiting. Ten minutes later they burst out of the bar and stormed towards the yellow MG. "I'm driving," Maxine commanded and happily skipped around to the driver's side door. Her hair had partially dried and the top layer was a fuzzy aureole above the ropes of strands that were still damp.

The car started, lurched forward, and made an illegal U-turn against the red light and headed off in the opposite direction towards the mountain. I watched as the taillights reached the edge of town, dropped down the hill, and disappeared on their way to the little bridge over the Valkill River and the cornfields beyond.

Above everything, a branch of lightning snapped on without a sound.

4

It had rained drearily for more than an hour. It wasn't a full-fledged storm—just rain that started and stopped, and then started again. You could tell it was a pattern that was not going to let up, and everyone agreed it would be too messy to go to the mountain.

Waiting the rain out in the Cacique's basement, a number of us discussed the Mylai Massacre investigation and the certainty that indictments would be handed down. Similarly, the Chicago Eight had been formally charged a few months earlier and a trial was scheduled for the fall. Overarching everything was the growing call for a general strike if the Vietnam War wasn't over by October. If not, there would be another Moratorium March on Washington and, to keep the pressure on, an even bigger March Against Death. Despite all the heady activity, it all seemed so far away.

Waiting and talk of politics had sobered those who were drunk, and in silent musings with the soft background music, we fell to thinking and staring nowhere. Every once in a while a roll of thunder pounded in the distance and the sounds of hissing cars passing by on the wet streets resumed. Kincaid and his court were all slumped down in their chairs like tired jesters.

Inwardly, everyone had called it a night.

I looked at Rachel leaning on her elbow, looking glumly out the window. She seemed softer in a way. She was the kind of woman who could look attractive when her guard was down—when she was engrossed in something—the child's pose.

"Want to go?" I asked.

"Yes."

"Where to?"

"We could go to my place."

We left the Cacique and walked slowly in the rain up the hill towards Gannon's. For the first time that day, I felt right. I liked walking in the rain. It had always intrigued me the way horses would stand very still in the rain with their behinds pointed into the direction of the storm. It was as though they did not want to see where the weather was coming from—behold the face of Gorgon and ye shall turn to stone!

As we walked, to my surprise, Rachel was making interesting conversation. I shouldn't have second-guessed her. She seemed more feminine now—no longer the gruff diner waitress—and it suggested a complexity and, therefore, a mystery.

She stopped at a door along the stores on Main Street and rooted around for a key inside her handbag.

"I didn't know you lived here."

"Just for a few weeks."

"Do you know Melanie?"

"She's my roommate."

"She's a friend of a friend."

She found the key, dropped it, and we bumped heads bending down to retrieve it. We couldn't help laughing—such a cliché. We climbed the stairs to the second floor.

"Oh, I forgot the mail," she said. "Could you?"

I bounded down the stairs two at a time. There were only a couple of damp circulars. For some reason, I looked in both directions along the sidewalk and then sprang up the stairs to Rachel's open door.

The living room also served as a bedroom—divided by a low chest cluttered with paperbacks and magazines, a milk glass vase with pretty weeds, and a wind-up alarm clock. Rachel was standing in front of an old bricked-in fireplace, drying her hair with a towel taken from a pile of folded laundry in a wicker basket on a nearby rocking chair. The mantel supported a confusion of knickknacks and below was an arrangement of logs artfully stacked in front of the hearth.

"So this is the apartment with the painted windows," I said, happily solving a minor mystery I had always noticed from the street. Someone had painted delicate tarot card figures on the large glass panes of each old-fashioned, arched window. I walked over and inspected them—perhaps longer than my curiosity should have dictated. I was a bit anxious in anticipation of the evening.

"'The woman behind the tarot card windows,'" I said, tracing an imaginary headline.

Rachel threw me the towel. "Would you like something? Coffee or tea?"

"Sure."

"Which? It really doesn't matter, just as easy."

"I think I'd like some tea," I said, following her, drying my hair—through some paisley curtains, into a bedroom née dining room, and then into the kitchen—a world of pale yellow, even the refrigerator.

I sat down on a squeaky bentwood chair. On the wall there was a shelf supporting a line of hand thrown spice jars. Two thriving Wandering Jews hung from the ceiling in planters on either side. Like the other rooms, this one had a homey, controlled confusion with everyday objects placed randomly—with an obvious, sensitive female hand behind everything.

Rachel was working between the counter and the stove.

"Did you throw these?" I asked, inspecting one of the spice jars.

"Oh, those, yeah. They're from my ceramics class. I'm taking a course this summer. I'm seeing if they work. 'Functional pottery must work!'" she proclaimed in a contrived, deep voice. "As Professor Trenholme says a thousand times a day."

"You like it?"

"Yes, but it would be fantastic if he'd just stop lecturing and let us work more. Every day—slide shows, lectures, discussions, 'What is art?' I think he just likes to hear himself talk."

I examined the piece and thought it of good quality: not too heavy, thin walls, nice foot, good choice of earthy-colored glaze, simple cap that fit well. "Levy" was written neatly on the bottom.

"Don't they all?" I said, replacing the jar. "It's very nice,"

"Thanks. You into ceramics?"

"Not really. My old roommate was a working potter. Still is, I think—kiln, studio, helpers from the college, does all the craft fairs—the whole shebang. I guess I appreciate it by osmosis."

"I'd like to meet him—talk shop."

"I'll ask. His name is Aldo. He could show you the commercial side of the business. Doesn't seem too glamorous though."

"We all have to suffer for our art," she said pouring my tea.

"By the way, do you know a professor in the art department—Maurice White? A painter, I think."

"Who doesn't?" she frowned. "The 'pretty boy' they call him. He hits on everything that moves. Even tried to give me a tumble once; he actually drooled on my hand. Yeech! Creee-py! The word is he's seriously involved with a former student. Why do you ask?"

"No reason. Just one of the Old Ford legends."

Drinking our tea, we walked back to her room. She wanted to show me some "automatic writing" she had been doing.

"Rachel, I didn't know you were so complex?"

"Yeah, I'm very deep," she laughed. "I'm going to change. Why don't you get the notebook? It's next to the bed somewhere under all the mess. I'll be right back." She grabbed the basket of clothes and hurried happily from the room.

The "bed" was a thin mattress on the floor with an arrangement of fluffy comforters and bright bedclothes with cute animal pillowcases and a flowered coversheet in matching pastel shades. I was surprised at how comfortable it was. I did not know too many women who essentially slept on the floor. From this vantage point, I could see the roof of the building across the street and "1888" carved into its old-fashioned façade. I wondered what Old Ford was like back in those days. I pictured hazy/lazy scenes of horses and buggies, dusty roads, long skirts, and weathered farmhands in town for a Saturday drink.

"Find it?" Rachel asked, returning in her bare feet, her toes cracking in my direction.

"No."

She had changed into faded dungarees and an oversized tee shirt that had "Property of the Athletic Dept." stenciled across the front. The black brassiere was obviously gone. She dropped down next to me and rummaged through the stack of things beside the bed.

"Ta-ta!" she proclaimed, extracting an old black and white-spotted composition book. She opened it and on the first page "20, May, 1968" was written and underlined. Below it was a wavy line resembling a chain of mountain peaks. "In the beginning I just got this kind of pattern," she said flipping through the next few pages that had similar variations of the first page.

"Then I started to get letters. Here's the first on the 28th—my initials R.L."

"That's R.L.?" All I saw were unintelligible scrawls.

"It's Hebrew," she said matter-of-factly. "It's strange—I can only automatic write in Hebrew."

"You know Hebrew?"

"I should—I was born in Israel."

"Well, a true Sabra."

"Yes, I am."

"What was that like?"

She paused and looked at one of the Tarot characters. "As a kid, it was wonderful—we were changing the world. Here we were—everyone uprooted from their pasts, full of doubts and horrors and hardships and tragedies, but we were determined to make new lives for ourselves. We were explorers leaving our old home— anxious to create a new world, a new future, and new traditions in a strange land—never to return. And to survive, we had to discover what God required of us to go on living as Jews."

"Heady stuff. So, why did you leave?

"After the army, I fell in love with a guy—a gentile—and Sabra's aren't supposed to fall in love with gentiles. It doesn't perpetuate the Jewish state. The Rabbis have a lot of power."

"What happened?"

"In the end, he wasn't the person I thought he was. I was young. I got hurt."

"Enough to leave the Promised Land?"

"I guess I had always wanted to run away—to find my own compass, to live *my* dream. . . . I felt the pull and promise and adventure of America. I'm American, too—

my mother was born here when her parents were on vacation in San Francisco."

"And a California girl to boot! Rachel, you're an evolving wonder."

We looked at each other for a long, intimate beat.

"So, you were in the Israeli army, then."

"Yep."

"And if you wanted to, you could kick my ass, right?"

"Pretty much," she said and laughed.

"So, which is it—Israel or America?"

"It's funny—sometimes I feel like an exile in both places. When I'm here, I feel detached from Israel, but at the same time, I admire it from afar. To me, Israel is an ideal in so many ways, but I'm not sure if it's the best place for me to live. A woman can get lost there—almost as if she's more a part of some antiquated, feminine archetype—rather than an independent woman with an individual spirit and aspirations and ideas how to fulfill herself. There are times there if you try to defend yourself and your values and stake your place, you can feel like you're living on an island. . . . I don't know if I'm making sense."

"No, I see what you mean. . . . I think a lot of Americans our age feel the same way—like exiles. We stand apart—refusing to be a rubberstamp for the last generation. Socially, politically, morally, we're polar opposites from them. That's the real struggle—we can't endure the hypocrisies anymore. We want to set the record straight and make it right. . . . Yeah, it's a good time to be young, but it's a helluva responsibility. I mean, look around: Vietnam and My Lai; the Cuban Missile Crisis; Martin Luther King, Malcolm X, John Kennedy, Robert Kennedy—all gunned down; Watts; the Chicago Convention; Weather Underground, Black Panthers, Ban-The-Bomb, Campus takeovers, the Zodiac killer, Richard

Nixon—nothing works, the center isn't holding. What do all those things *really* mean? How do we articulate the rage?"

Rachel had a sympathetic look on her face. "Boy, when you get going. . . . Yes, that's all true, Dalton, but we *are* going to the moon."

"For what—to open a Jack in the Box . . . to play golf?"

"But that's the wonder of America—we're playing among the stars," she said and ran a tender hand along my cheek.

We just stared and were quiet with the moment.

I kissed her hand. "What does Tarot Man say?"

"He says don't be frightened—be as wise as the lilies of the field."

"The wonder continues."

She looked back at her book. "Oh, look here. . . . For a while, it was mostly letters, then here on June 1st, I started asking questions to the 'force'—that's what I call it—and all I kept getting was the same design I got in the beginning. I took that to mean that it didn't want me to question it about itself. So I started asking things about my family, testing it, and it came up with all the right answers."

"But isn't that just you talking to yourself? You *know* all the answers," I theorized, still surprised that she was from a foreign country. Davenant had been right.

"That's what I thought, too. But I was writing down things that I hadn't thought of in years—the kind of stuff I never would have come up with if I tried."

I smiled and lay down on my side, looking up at her.

"After a while I realized I was *learning* from this. Look at it now," she said, fanning through swaths of pages filled on both sides with her small, neat Hebrew characters. "Some of it is really incredible stuff—

elaborate fantasies, wild ideas, even philosophical things. . . . You wouldn't happen to have any philosophy books?"

"Sure, some Sartre, Heidegger, Husserl . . . oh, and a big anthology and two translations of Merleau-Ponty. Heavy stuff. I'll bring them over after I unpack."

"You're moving?"

"Just to Calypso Street."

"Thank you," she said, looking back at the composition book. ". . . Of course, there were a few bad things, too—like when it said my uncle back in Israel was dead. I wrote to my parents, and they said he's still with us but having serious issues. Now I can't help worrying."

"Spooky."

It started to rain harder and we talked about the rain, how we had marched in a few of the same protests, and the growing excitement of a big rock festival being planned nearby in August.

"Be honest. Do you think I look whorey enough for the diner?"

"What do you mean?"

"You know—the boobs, the uniform, the tousled hair— playing the bored-sexy-waitress-always-ready-for-a-roll-in-the-hay bit. Sometimes I feel like I'm on a one-woman crusade to bring back burlesque. You know, *real* Americana—sleazy truck stops, 'The Postman Always Rings Twice' roadside stands?"

We laughed.

"I don't know. It seems to work. I get more tips than the other girls. But it's a hassle sometimes. Some guys take it seriously. One of them followed me home once."

"Really."

"The only money I have this summer is what I earn on my own. A lass has to keep her wits about her. . . . My family's been on a big Horatio Alger kick—pick yourself up by the bootstraps an' all."

"Tell me about it," I said. "It's funny though—I never noticed you looked like that at the diner."

"Liar. . . . You must be one of my failures."

The rain was still asserting itself when the needle scraped methodically into the middle of a record, the last in a stack of Miles Davis.

"I really like him," Rachel said after a pause. "It's like he *becomes* the music." She scooted off the bed and went over to the stereo.

"I know what you mean. He really puts you in the mood," I said, stretching. I felt like a dog wanting to shake itself awake. "Do you know what time it is?"

"I'll check."

When she walked, she perched on the balls of her feet—in such a way, that I would have bet she had studied ballet. Invariably, girls who danced from a young age had that distinctive walk. No doubt, her breasts were her downfall—not exactly the textbook body type for "Swan Lake."

"Ten after eleven," her voice came from the kitchen.

I remembered the alarm clock on the credenza. Why did she have to go into the kitchen?

"I better be going," I said loudly. "I have a lot to do tomorrow." I stood up and kicked my pants down over my boots.

Rachel stuck her head through the curtains and pulled them around her face. "Won't you get wet?" Her face looked pretty between the two crushed waves of hair. I could see she had applied fresh lipstick.

"No big deal. I don't mind."

There was a close crack of thunder above us that sounded like a tree limb breaking.

"Don't be ridiculous. Didn't your mother teach you to stay out of the rain?"

"No, we never spoke. She spent all her time dusting and vacuuming. . . . I'll wait a few minutes and see if it lets up."

"Suit yourself," she said, walking through the curtains. Gone was the loose athletic tee shirt—replaced by a tighter, purplish V-neck top that left little to the imagination. She started sorting the records into their jackets. "I don't know about you, but I'm beat," she said and breezed back through the curtains, saying over her shoulder, "You can always stay here."

The moment of truth had finally arrived, but for some reason my immediate thoughts weren't about possible lovemaking, but rather the cleanliness of my underwear, that I didn't have a toothbrush, did my socks smell?—things my mother would have considered. I hated myself for thinking like her.

Suddenly the lights flickered once, tried to come back on, and then went dead.

"Ah, there goes the juice again," her voice came in the blackness. "God, a little rainstorm and it's like I'm back on the kibbutz. . . . Just a sec, I'll light a candle."

She came back in walking stiffly behind a skittery flame whose life she was shielding with a cupped hand. Now she was wearing only the tee shirt, revealing a V of polka-dotted panties stretched tightly between two sturdy thighs. I tried to act as if I didn't notice, or even if I had, to me, it would be nothing out of the ordinary.

"Come spring and September, this place is like a strobe light," she laughed.

She put the candle in a holder and set it down on the chest next to the alarm clock. Turning her back to me, she reached up and pulled the tee shirt over her head. The back of one formidable breast slung out to the side and settled. She threw the shirt onto the bedclothes and slipped down quickly between the sheets.

For several minutes, there was nothing but the pelting rain and the occasional crackle of the frayed candlewick eating into the wax.

Still standing, my boots made a grinding sound on the hardwood floor. More thunder.

"Dalton Hawkes, come to bed! Mommy's orders."

I smiled and laughed. "Yes, Sir. . . . Yes, Sergeant. . . . Yes, mommy."

Noisily, I shed my clothes—boots thudding, coins rolling along the floor, and finally my belt buckle clanging dully dead. I walked past the tarot card figures, crouched next to the bed, and arched down to get under the sheets. Rachel put her arm around me and gathered me in beside her.

"You know, any money I find in the apartment belongs to me. House rules. It's in the lease."

"You run a tight ship"

I kissed her and felt her warmth against me. We moved so our bodies were touching in as many places as possible. She ran her hand along my back and stopped when it found my underwear. She stuck her thumb underneath the waistband and snapped the elastic.

"And what are these, little boy?"

Catching me off-guard, I felt as though I had to make a complementary statement, so I snapped her panties in retaliation. "The same as these, little girl."

Without hesitation, she slid her hand inside and around to the front. "And this fella?"

"Oh, that's Harry." I tried not to fidget—her manner was ticklish.

"Nice to meet you, Harry," she said, contriving a handshake.

I tugged at her panties. "Why don't you join the party?"

We laughed and made love and said tender things—it all seeming as natural as brook water smoothing over a stone. Afterwards, we smoked a joint, watched the stars through the tarot card figures, and looked at each other in the light of the moon. After we made love again, she cried.

"Is something wrong?"

"No, I'm sorry. . . . It just that it feels so good . . . so right."

No one had ever said that to me. We hugged and fell asleep, making vague plans as the rain started up again.

In the morning, a truck's horn blared below on the street, and I squinted into the brightness behind the tarot man. Rachel was gone. I looked at the place where she had slept, at the flattened sheets, and around the room. A pale blue sheet of writing paper was propped against the alarm clock.

> Dear Dalton (Tom, Dick, and Harry),
> Had to go to ceramics class. There's
> coffee on the stove.
> Thanks for last night. . . .
> Love,
> Rachel (Naomi, Esther, and Bathsheba)

I found a pen and wrote below her note.

> Dear Sarge,
> The boys and I had a good time, too.
> Say hello to the girls.
> Talk soon.
> DTDH

5

It was difficult to make 42 Calypso Street disappear, although some of the townspeople wished it were possible. It had a reputation—drugs, loud music, hippies, sex—all the unsavory things ushered into the world by the Baby Boomers in the year 1965. Since its sale to an absentee owner, the police had raided the house a half-dozen times. Each time they never found or even said what they were looking for but warned that the house was on their radar. On the last occasion, they had made an arrest for public intoxication, though the man in question had been sleeping it off in his own bed. Officially, the "search and arrest" was still under investigation because it had "drug overtones"—inciting the townspeople to gossip and rail against the offending house in restaurants, in church, and at raucous town meetings.

Forty-two Calypso itself was a big two-storey affair perched on a narrow strip of infertile land squeezed between two other homes with impeccably maintained exteriors and garden club landscaping—making the "hippie house" stand out like a rat-infested tenement. At one time, a long sturdy porch had stretched across the front, but now it sagged—rotted to the point that it was unusable on one side. Similarly, most of the house's white paint had been weathered away by ancient storms and what remained was curled and buckled like dead birch tree bark.

The house sat very close to the street where a conspicuously new sidewalk had been installed. Having formally complained to the highway department that 42 broke up the "sidewalk stroll," neighbors had argued that the treacherous gully of refuse and wild vegetation was virtually impassable, and one day cement trucks and whining police cars had appeared and laid a fresh walkway. In the aftermath, the only buffer that remained between the house and civilization was a front lawn that measured a few scant feet—in truth, more of a jungle swatch of tenacious weeds and twisty swirls of unknown growths that had been digging in for years and refused to die. At some point, a barren thorny hedge had been planted to line the new sidewalk and remained scratchy and grotesque all year round, a perennial. The only usable space was on the right side of the house, where a thousand cars had beaten down two tire grooves that served as a driveway to the small blue-pebbled parking lot cum picnic area out back.

Moving in had been a lot of work. I had rented the van from the Arco station—after much discussion and promises of driver safety—but after a few miles it had stalled whenever it was put into first gear, and I had to limp back to the gas station for repairs. An hour later, I unloaded only those belongings I deemed indispensable, and the rest I tossed out at the town dump—where a man in a small bulldozer pushed everything into a pile to the great delight of a maze of gulls that swooped down to pick at the treasures.

Our apartment was on the second floor and a narrow staircase had to be negotiated. Unfortunately, just scaling the stairs was not the end of it, as that level contained only a dirty bathroom, kitchen, and the living room, which my roommate Ray Mason had converted into his bedroom. The two attic bedrooms were accessed by walking through Mason's room and ascending yet another treacherous staircase. Since Mauberley had already been living in one of the bedrooms, Davenant and

I had the privilege of renting the second vacant attic room.

The "garret" as we preferred to call it (more romance and sacrifice), remained as stark and splintery as the day it had been built and was made inhabitable by nailing blankets and old sheets down from the roof studs—instantly creating two rooms separated by the stairwell. The areas behind the hanging sheets and blankets were used for storage. There were no storm windows or screens and there was only one outlet in each room. Next to my bed a chimney burst through the floor and out again through the roof. Rent was $23.75 per month, per man.

I had not seen Rachel for almost a week and the phone was ringing. I was sleeping and those two facts came to me as I forced myself to sit up. Even from the downstairs kitchen, the strident trilling was loud with the sound of raw metal. Twice. . . . It was dark. The alarm clock was on the floor, but all I could see were a cluster of phosphorescent green dots. Three . . . four. Since I moved in, it seemed all I had done was take messages. I stubbed my toe badly hurrying out of bed. Five . . . six. . . .

"Hawkes?" someone bellowed inside the receiver.

"Yeah."

"Davenant. Listen. Wait, hold on a sec. . . ." The phone was jostled. I looked around for a place to sit and chose the floor. From this vantage point, the glaring floodlights on the corner of the garage next door were pointing off in oblique directions—illuminating the neighbor's precious domain against any possible interlopers, especially from 42 Calypso.

Davenant was talking to someone. "Okay, I know, I know. . . . Hawkes, guess who's here?" More jostling. "Let her speak to Hawkes—just to say hello. Give her the phone. . . . Jesus! Hawkes, you still there?"

"Yeah, yeah."

"Listen, where the hell are you?"

"You called me, remember?"

"Didn't Mauberley call you?"

"No, why?"

"Goddamnit." Then to someone else, "He said you never called, schmuck! . . . Mauberley said he forgot to call. Anyway, we're having a little post, post commencement gangbang down at the Cacique. Everybody's here. Come on over. I think it's going to get good."

My first thought was that my hair was dirty and I needed a shave. "I don't know. I'm all grubby."

"So what? It's not the inaugural ball, man. C'mon."

Though I didn't particularly want to muster the energy to make myself presentable, the idea of a few drinks was inviting,

"Well, is you is, or is you ain't?"

"All right, I'll be there as soon as I can."

"Beautiful," and in a lower voice, "Hey, you never know? Luck is a fickle mistress, my man."

Knowing Davenant, he meant sex, and I was faintly up for that, too.

"Hold on a second, someone wants to talk to you."

The phone banged and scraped, presumably into new hands, as I heard louder background music.

"Stop it! I don't *need* . . . to speak with him," a distant woman said and the line went dead. I couldn't identify the voice amid all the noise. Judging from Davenant's tone and level of drunken chatter, things were heating up. Maybe Davenant was right—it could be interesting and I might get lucky—without even trying.

I stood up gingerly and hung up the phone. I could see the light inside the old man's trailer behind our parking lot. Other lights up the hill indicated there was something going on at the sorority house—hazy shadows moved behind drawn drapes—and a stereo tinkled lightly somewhere inside.

I thought of the matter at hand and felt my face. I hadn't shaved for days and my beard was at its ugliest stage—that stubbly juncture between needing a shave and starting a beard. Whatever, I knew exactly how I looked, and glumly ran a hand through my hair—dislodging dandruff flakes in front of my face. My hair was matted, and I pictured a silent race of loathsome scalp oils rushing out along each dirty shaft. I felt ugly.

Someone knocked at the other upstairs apartment, and there was a quick tunnel of voices until a door slammed and the hum of silence returned. I showered and shaved as though I were late for reveille and minutes later pounded down the stairs onto Calypso Street.

I saw Davenant in the back—standing in the alcove formed by the angle of the staircase and the bar jutting out beyond the two wine casks set into the wall. Dutch was his usual busy overlord.

"Hawkes!" Davenant's voice arched over everything.

Threading the crowd and seeing expectant faces, I had the sinking feeling I was expected to be gay and funny and say all the right things as the engaging latecomer. I realized in order to do that, I would have to feed everyone back to himself—so they all would love me and think me swell. I didn't know if I could muster the effort required.

My first impression was that not everyone was having the wonderful time Davenant had implied over the phone. The smiles were there but forced and lackluster, and there was the unspoken assumption that "*la grande fête de remise des diplômes,*" as Davenant continually characterized our ongoing summer graduation celebration, was a forgotten ghost. The gathered cask-tables were wet and flecked with broken pieces of peanuts, potato chips, and pretzels. A small mound of cigarette butts lay in among the orange rinds of a spent pitcher of sangria.

"Here he is, ladies—Rip Van Winklehawkes!" Davenant said, trying to be clever and perk up the atmosphere. "Let's see, by rank and serial number: Lia, our token widow and Norwegian, MFA ceramics. . . . You know him. You know these two sexy creatures. That is my new protégé Hank Reese. You know Kaplan and Lucy K. . . ."

"Take a load off, roomie," Steve Mauberley interrupted, as he pushed a chair out with a battered construction boot and it fell over backwards with a crash that caught Dutch's attention.

Everyone "Ahhhhed."

"Very classy, Mauberley, extreme class," Kaplan laughed. "Hey, say that five times fast: very classy, Mauberley; very classy, Mauberley. . . . Now like a Chinese: Velly classy, Mobelly; velly classy, Mobelly. . . . Ha, ha."

Everyone tried and laughed.

"As I was saying," Davenant continued. "Of course, you already know Jane—the sexy creature soon to be Mrs. Raymond Mason. Or is it just fiancée for now, mademoiselle?"

"Hello, Dalton" she said.

"Hello," I said and noticed that Ray had a mild scowl on his face.

Kaplan stood up and tapped his glass with his college ring. "Friends, I bear news."

Everyone waited, as Kaplan turned to Jane with his dirty smile, and she glowered up at him. She turned to Ray for help. He just shrugged and shook his head.

"Let me be the first to formally congratulate the expectant couple. . . . Everyone, Jane just found out she's pregnant!"

We all clapped.

Under the noise, I took her hand and said tenderly, "Congratulations."

Jane looked at me clear-eyed and sober—almost as if to say, *funny how things turn out.*

"C'mon, Hawkes, doesn't the mother-to-be get a little *mazel tov* kiss?" Kaplan continued with an unctuous smile. He just couldn't resist. He knew Jane and I had a history, and he was probably hoping we would betray some still-smoldering hidden affection.

Seizing Kaplan's moment, Jane bounced up jarring the table, threw her arms around my neck, and smacked a loud kiss on my lips. It was just the right thing to do and instantly disarmed the awkwardness of Kaplan making the premature announcement without Jane's and Ray's permission.

"Jesus, now look at what you've done," Mauberley complained, scraping his chair away from the sudden dripping from an overturned glass of beer. He pounded his boots against the floor. "You owe me for the beer, pregnant lady."

Laughing, Davenant raised his hands for silence, as a pair of female legs came down the stairs. "And, Dalton Hawkes, last but not least, your date for tonight—flown here from directly from Latvia for this special occasion—your long lost cousin-*cousine, Magda Svinsh!*"

Hearing Davenant's introduction, Rachel danced down the remaining steps and struck a pose as though she had just ended a gymnastic routine. More clapping and laughing.

"Yes, after more than twenty years, the improbable reunion continues," Davenant said and began to sing, "*Oh there she is—Miss Latvia. . . . There she is—your ideal. . . . With so many beauties she took the town by storm—with her all-Latvian face and form. . . .*"

Amidst the laughing, Rachel executed an expert pirouette and plopped down on my lap.

"Hello, cousin," I said.

"Hello" she said in a foreign-sounding accent and kissed me.

Maintaining his stride, Davenant went on, "As you all know, Magda is the daughter of Ludvig Svinsh, an obscure violinmaker from the Black Sea. And from such humble beginnings, who would have imagined that young Magda would break all existing tumbling records at this year's European Championships!"

Kaplan, Mason, and a few others were now laughing and almost crying at the same time.

"Remember me?" Rachel said softly.

"How could I forget a world tumbling champion? Like a drink?"

"I'd love one."

A short while later things perked up even more—courtesy of two bottles of Wild Turkey from an unknown benefactor and someone's request for Brazilian music. To everyone's delight—and as I had suspected—Rachel was an accomplished dancer and eager to show it. Her natural sense of rhythm and innate musicality allowed her to create subtle steps, gestures, and lines of movement that made her one with the music—never missing a beat and seamlessly allowing her body to go wherever the music took her. She surprised everyone even further by displaying an equally lovely singing voice—in fluent Spanish!—to the catcalls of all the men and women, many of whom took turns dancing with her. While they tried futilely to match her talent, it was clear Rachel was the star, relished the attention, and her newfound happy acceptance into our group.

No stranger to demanding attention and impervious to making a fool of himself, Davenant was in a world of his own. When he wasn't cutting in on

Rachel's partners, he gyrated around her like a whirling dervish in a caftan—making choppy swirls, jerky twists, and awkward lunges that bore scant resemblance to dance and more to mindless supplications to an atavistic deity. Rachel smiled and laughed at his cavorting, giving him space to unleash his demons.

As the dancing reached its crescendo, Dutch the bartender had had enough, and he cut the music and scowled, "This ain't a dancehall. You wanna jump around like a buncha Indians, take it upstairs—*now!*"

Laughing drunkenly and almost without missing a beat, Rachel, Mauberley, Davenant, Kaplan, and the others formed a loose conga line and began stuttering up the stairs. Putting Mauberley's hands onto her hips, Rachel looked back and gestured for me to join her. I raised my glass as if to say, *go have fun, I'll be there in a minute.*

With the revelers gone and peace restored, Dutch turned the music back on—now an appropriate muted jazz. I looked over at the bar to thank him and was surprised to see Maxine Cooke standing there as if she had been there all along—leaning backwards facing the room, her forearms resting on the bar—staring at me. Dutch brought her a drink and she tossed a bill into the air, then walked over, sat down, and looked into my eyes.

"Oh, Dalton, I'm at the end of my rope," she said and started crying.

6

The yellow sports car sped across the old iron bridge leading out of town and whined along the flats bisecting two large cornfields. Even after the recent hot weather, the fields still had remnants of the previous weeks' torrential rains that had flooded the road for days—forcing eastward traffic to detour ten miles north or south and circle back around to get into Old Ford. It was rumored that one of the fields was being rented by the Jehovah's Witnesses, who planned to grow corn to feed the livestock on their large nearby farm—providing a continuing supply of slaughtered meat for the faithful at their world headquarters in Brooklyn. Away from the rigors of farming, they spent weekends canvasing Old Ford to discuss God and make converts.

Impossible to talk above the tinny clacking of the engine, I watched Maxine drive—switching gears smoothly making the MG respond with one continuous acceleration—as though a predator cat digging its claws into the roadway with every stride. With no lights along the road, there were only the car's headlamps bouncing atop the asphalt in a jittery whiteness. Maxine's eyes were still wet with tracks of tears caught in the reflective glow from the dashboard.

Drawn to the mountain, now beyond the bridge in the open darkness, its presence was strong. We were in that sacred space that surrounds large natural wonders—where it was suddenly cooler, more oxygenated, and somehow more foreboding. At one point, Maxine downshifted sharply and came to a swerving stop. She asked me to pick some dried reeds along the side of the road, saying they would look good hanging above her sink in her kitchen. She even had a strip of leather in her glove compartment for me to tie the bundle together.

Breaking away from the pull of Old Ford's artificial illumination, the sky was brushed with a swath of stars and the top ridgeline of the mountain was clearly visible in the ancient light. Atop its sheer rock escarpment a small beacon in an old stone tower shined weakly against the firmament. Past the flats, the woods suddenly closed in upon the road, and travelling at 60 mph through the dark tunnel created inside the trees was exhilarating. More than once a pair of yellowish eyes stared transfixed at the headlights as we sped by. Near the base of the cliffs, the road became a switchback that led up to a small lookout point that, in the daytime, afforded a panoramic view of this portion of the Hudson Valley. Veering off the rod into the small parking area, Maxine shut down the car and we faced the blackness below us and listened to the wind blowing high in the trees. From this distance, the lights of Old Ford were a diffused, glowing patch at the far end of the snaking road we had just followed up to the ridge.

Maxine got out and ran to the guardrail that protected onlookers from the cliff's steep drop off. Startled, I hurried to her side and held her in my arms. She was shaking like a distraught child.

"Kiss me," she said and thrust her lips up to mine—a kiss of desperation.

I let her sink into me and tried to invoke something more passionate, but she pulled away.

"Please don't."

"Please don't what?"

"Please don't make things more difficult."

"I didn't know kissing me was problematic."

"Kissing you *is* problematic."

"Why?"

"Because if I start kissing you, I won't want to *stop* kissing you."

"Is that so bad?

"It is if your life is totally off the rails."

I took her hand and led her away from the guardrail to a huge flat rock where people sat while gazing at the valley. We sat silently as the lights of several cars swept past behind us and wound their way further up the mountain.

"They say these rocks were formed 420 million years ago," I said, gesturing with both arms. "This whole valley was carved out by glaciers. Imagine."

She reached into her shirt pocket for a pack of cigarettes and lit one. She blew a nervous cloud of smoke at the valley.

"I just got back from Texas. . . . My sister's pregnant."

"Congratulations—you're going to be an aunt."

"I don't want to be an aunt."

"Why not?"

"Because I'd rather be a mother."

I paused. "That can be arranged."

"Tell that to Maurice."

"Oh, him. . . . I think I'll pass if you don't mind."

"Don't be small. You know how it is."

"Yeah, I know how it is."

"I can't believe it. . . . Phoebe told me she was walking down a street in Austin, saw a good-looking guy in a restaurant window, went inside and said, 'I think we'd make beautiful babies.' Just like that—like she was buying a cake."

"I've always heard the Cooke girls were a bit impetuous."

"I've given Maurice four years of my life—four of my *best* years! . . . And he has the nerve to show me pictures of *his* kids!"

"Love doesn't ask for rewards. . . . Maybe you should start looking in restaurant windows."

"Don't be mean." She kissed me quickly. "Hug me, it's cold."

I took her in my arms, kissed her several times, and closed my eyes inside her hair.

"I love your smell. I've loved it since the day I first met you."

"Why couldn't it have been you?"

"What am I—the road not taken?"

"It should have been you."

"It still can be."

"Oh, Dalton . . . you know I love you—in my own way."

"Oh, yes, those same encouraging words. . . . Which way is that?"

"Please don't make me cry."

"The sad truth is I love you better."

"I know, I know. If only . . ."

"Now you're going to make *me* cry."

She turned and looked at me straight on and caressed my cheek gently.

"I told you not to fall in love with me."

"Too late."

Maxine turned away and looked up into the moonlight. I could see fresh tears. Somehow I felt there was more.

"Max, what's really going on?"

She took another deep drag on the cigarette. "When I was in Austin, Phoebe got a phone call from my father's company. . . ." She paused to fight back new emotion. "They found him in his office. . . . Suicide. . . . I still can't believe it. It's even hard to say the word. . . .

We flew back to Chicago, made all the arrangements, sat through the funeral, played the game. . . . It was horrible. . . . There was a note. . . ." She couldn't go on.

"Oh, Max, I'm so sorry. What can I say?"

"He said he loved us—that we were the only things that had kept him going after Mother's death. She was the love of his life. . . . But he said something had gone out of him—he was broken. He'd had enough. . . . He was sorry. We should try to understand."

"Did you ever know her?"

She shook her head. "He told us stories and showed us pictures—but there are no memories, nothing to hold on to. . . ."

"It's the oldest story there is, Max. We all have to face it. . . . Whoever our parents are, however they raised us, regardless of the way they treated us, whether we knew them or not—they are our most seminal connections to the world. They gave us life and took care of us when we were helpless. . . . We owe them a consideration."

She paused in thought.

"I think he would have liked to have been a grandfather."

"Of course."

For a while we listened to the strong breeze playing above us in the trees.

"I was supposed to be a boy, you know—Max, Jr. He had everything planned out: follow him into the military, live the life, serve with honor. . . . But Mother gave him twin girls instead. I became Maxine, after him, and Phoebe was named after her. . . . There were complications. She never made it out of the hospital. Hung on for a week or so and that was it. . . ." More tears. "In his will . . . he wanted me to have the gun. . . . Can you believe it?"

"Jesus Christ."

"A pearl-handled .45 that he always wore on his hip in a fancy leather holster—like the Lone Ranger or General Patton or some kind of gunslinger. . . . Taught me how to shoot it, clean it, take care of it. I loved that gun. . . . How can I—now?"

Before I could answer, there were horns and the lights of cars barreling up the incline towards the lookout. Abruptly, the lead car braked with a screech—causing those behind to splay across the road, cursing and protesting as they skidded to a halt. It was Mauberley and the gang. He had seen Maxine's MG.

"Hail voyagers!" he bellowed, a silhouette outlined inside the headlights.

Fallen Rock was a part of the mountain's immense water complex—along with Upper and Lower Falls, Splinter Rock, and Dallas Hole—all beautiful and all good places to go skinny-dipping in hot weather. At some point in the Silurian, a great shelf of sedimentary rock had dislodged from its mother lode and fallen into a strongly fed stream. After millennia of provident winds, aggressive vegetation and advancing wildlife—filling in and reconfiguring the huge cracks and fissures—the result was a long, gently sloping incline, where water sheeted down and collected in a basin large enough to accommodate twenty people and then seeped off slowly, emptying into a series of terraced levels for the entire length of rock. To see the whole confluence each time was as fresh and breathtaking as the first time.

Maxine parked onto the dirt shoulder now cluttered with several vehicles and shut down the MG.

"Are you up for this?" I asked.

"Yes. . . . But stay with me."

"As long as you like. . . . Wherever you like. . . . Whenever you like."

Holding her hand, we walked the quarter-mile path through the woods in silence. At the halfway point, we began hearing dull-thuds of voices and laughter that grew louder and louder as we approached—until the trees opened up dramatically and announced the wonders of Fallen Rock.

In and out of the clean, cold freshness of the swimming hole was a small tribe of naked bodies in motley arrangements of sizes and shapes, whose nudity gave their familiar faces an almost disembodied appearance. Adjacent to the water Davenant, Jane, Kaplan, and Rachel squatted around a thin fire seemingly doomed on the next puff of wind. I watched Jane with her breasts between her knees, her womb becoming more alive and complex with each passing second—laughing and barking orders to Kaplan, who cheered and sighed on the rise and fall of the flames. Rachel looked up at my arrival—a quick, sad, sober, knowing glance. Seeing Maxine, she unconsciously straightened her back and thrust out her breasts—throwing down a silent gauntlet.

Most eyes were on Mauberley who had climbed to the top of the massive sloping slab and was gauging the scary descent into the pool. Raising his arm like a saluting gladiator, he cupped his genitals and bellowed, "We who are about to die salute you!" and conquering his nerve, stepped into the flow of rock water and immediately slid down with gathering speed until he slammed into the pool with a giant splash. Thrusting back to the surface with a raised fist, he acknowledged the drunken cheers—"Fuck, yeah!"

"They look like aborigines," Maxine whispered.

"Nudity has a way of levelling the playing field," I said. "In the end, we're all savages."

Despite her troubles, Maxine smiled weakly. "I've always loved the way you say things and how you can make me laugh with your words. Say more words." Her phrasing sounded foreign.

"Observe," I said loudly, sweeping my arm along the shiny flesh of my friends. "The Owaneezee are one of the last remaining tribes in the region. . . . Pay particular attention to how they stay in the water for up to twenty hours a day—leaving only to forage, prepare their meals, and defecate."

A few by the pool heard me and made chimp sounds.

Mauberley climbed out of the water, more drunk than the rest. "Hey don't you two feel funny with your clothes on?"

". . . Because the Owaneezee spend so much time in water, they've developed into deadly, seasoned hunters—as they want to do things in a hurry on land. When they capture game, they kill it by shaking it to death. Notice their highly developed, powerful forearms—which has prompted rival tribes to refer to them as 'Popeye-zees.'"

Maxine couldn't help laughing.

"Hey, why don't you and Olive Oil join the party?" Mauberley called, gesturing mischievously to Kaplan.

". . . Lately, with the exposure to the outside world, the Owaneezee have become scavengers—gathering debris left over from the growing number of hikers and bikers on their ancestral mountain trails. Sadly, for the first time in countless Yernies, their equivalent of our year, the Owaneezee are experiencing crime—fighting among themselves for the white man's worthless bottles, cans, and assorted garbage."

Kaplan and Mauberley ran over, howling like Banshees, and grabbed me by the arms—dragging me towards the water. We fought and twisted in confusion—until suddenly the world seemed to stop—as everyone watched Maxine step out of her sandals and begin unbuttoning her blouse. Removing her clothes in such an innocent yet seductive manner, it was obvious Maxine had no problem displaying her body in public. Probably from her Panamanian days, I frowned. As she tiptoed down to the pool, her hips, legs, arms, breasts and rear-end all moved in a perfect wondrous symmetry of motion and beauty. She knew the effect her body had on people, and watching the moonlight shimmer off her olive skin, she almost appeared Polynesian.

"Illiki of the West Wind!" I cheered inwardly but despaired that I had to share her gifts with everyone else.

Perhaps to divert attention away from Maxine, Jane jumped up and exclaimed, "Just call me Queen of the Fires!" and thrust her fingers at the growing flames like a pregnant Pele.

To celebrate, Kaplan stood over her with a wineskin and squirted a stream of wine into her mouth. The red liquid leaked over her chin and glistened down her neck and chest. Helplessly, she scrunched her shoulders and held her palms up as though she were caught in the rain.

The sweet scent of marijuana carried on the air, and in the pool, the burning glow of several joints moved haphazardly back and forth like fireflies.

As I quickly undressed and went over to join Maxine in the water, Mauberley slid down Fallen Rock again in a flurry of noise—only this time crouched on his feet like a surfboarder. Maxine glided over below me and looked up at me between my legs and at the stars behind my head.

"My Adonis," she smiled.

"How is it?"

"Cold but fantastically refreshing," she said, thrusting backwards—the length of her body accepting the motion then settling gently back to the surface.

I tested the water and deemed that "cold" was too euphemistic a term to justify the number of degree-days it would take to make it bearable. Throwing caution to the wind, I dove in, not wanting to become conspicuous. The rush of icy water along my body was a shock, but I prided myself on how long I could hold my breath underwater and surfaced grandly with an ostentatious twist of my hair on the opposite side of the pool. No one was watching.

Rather, Mauberley was lighting two cigarettes and offering one to Maxine. They glided to the lower end of the rocks where the water exited to the next level. The wineskin was being circulated and marijuana smoke hung over the water as though the Earth were still cooling.

Davenant and Rachel were talking intimately by the fire.

Lia, the token Norwegian widow, had run back to Mauberley's car and returned with a transistor radio, now tuned to Hawaiian ukulele music, perfect for the occasion. I wondered if she had felt exhilarated running naked along the path—a lithe Pavlo Nurmi muscling through the woods to the cheesy plinking of pacific overtures.

"We're out of wine," someone complained, having been passed an empty wineskin.

"There's some deer bown dy . . ." Kaplan began and smacked his hands together. "Whoa, slow down world! God am I wrecked! . . . Man, is this place beautiful or what? Look at us! Mucho beautificano. Ha-ha. . . . Oh, shit, what was I saying?"

"What you were *trying* to say is that there's some beer cooling down by the runoff," Davenant said, attempting to move his stringy, sexless body to the music like a hula dancer.

I'm not sure how it began, but a short while later everyone was taunting me to accept Mauberley's challenge to slide down the rock—on one foot! A few of the women warned that it was too dangerous, not to mention we were all too stoned and drunk for such macho posturing. It was a stupid thing to do, but having always considered myself a natural athlete, I sincerely thought I could pull it off. I remembered vividly that I never had to learn how to ride a bicycle. One day my father had simply put me on the seat, told me what to do, and I rode away down the sidewalk as if I had been doing it all my life.

Soon I found myself gingerly climbing barefoot through the snarls of undergrowth—acknowledging all the catcalls as I ascended. Every now and then, I looked out on the expanse of Fallen Rock and dismayed that, in places, it was covered with patches of slick green moss. The only sensible navigable route was down the middle, where the flow was strongest but had clean rock underneath. Why hadn't Mauberley warned me about steering clear of the algae?

Once at the top, the pool and naked bodies below were merely a part of the mountain's confluence. More prominent were the loud insects and chirpings from deeper inside the trees: double beats of an invisible squeaking rocking chair, trilling sounds and sharp whistles that droned continually . . . all backdrops to the ever-present gurgle of water.

To get in the proper position, I had to step into a narrow trough of water whose current was strong enough to make me aware of it. I decided the worst thing to do would be to linger, so I thrust out my arm Nazi-style—a member of the SS sacrificing life and limb for the Fuhrer—charted a hasty course, and planted my foot firmly onto the mountain rock that dinosaurs had once trod.

Perched there momentarily, a wave swept through my head that was out of sync from the rest of the world and the whole glide down Fallen Rock was a convoluted fantasy: skidding uncontrollably off course . . . screams in the night . . . flames on the surface of the water . . . head banging hard on rock like a coconut slammed against concrete . . . skidding on my side, one leg forward . . . jamming my foot into Jane's stomach as she moved to help me. . . .

It all came to a stop as suddenly as it had started, but with the cracking echo still in my brain, I knew I had fallen very hard, yet I felt nothing. A growing lump came away with no blood on my fingers.

I had hurt Jane. She was holding her stomach and breathing in spurts. Her pained face called out to her unborn child. As people attended to her, others were pulling me from the water and transferring me to a blanket by the fire. Voices everywhere.

"Did you hear the sound his head made?"

"I never heard anything like it."

"It was sooooo eerie!"

"I can't believe it."

"Is there blood?"

"Get Jane out of the water!"

"Dalton, are you all right?"

"Oh, shit."

"I talked to Jane. She seems okay," Kaplan's voice from somewhere.

"How's Hawkes?" Mauberley's voice.

I lay by the fire, my arms pressed against my sides inside the blanket like a papoose. Blinking widely, I tried to recall more clearly what I had attempted to do and what the disastrous results had been.

"I must really have a hard head," I said, trying to sound bright. "I really banged the shit out of it. Did you hear it?"

"God, yes!" Maxine was looking down at me. She seemed genuinely worried, and I thought of the moments before the accident when I was jealous she was spending too much time with Mauberley.

"How's Jane?" I asked. "Do you think anything happened to the baby?"

"She's fine, she's fine," off in the night. "Don't worry. You're both okay."

"And the great slab abides," Davenant said with poetic finality.

Among the faces, Mauberley was tugging loudly on a joint and handing it down to me. For some reason, the sight of a dozen naked bodies hovering over Jane and me—still drinking and getting high—seemed extraordinarily funny and I burst out laughing. My smiles caught Jane's glance and she smiled back. Warily, the others joined in—relieving the edge that something very serious could have happened—figuring, if they're laughing, it can't be that bad.

But long moments later everything began to have the bad aftertaste that imprudent things had been chanced. There was the unspoken consensus that we should clothe ourselves, make our separate peace with the mountain, and depart quietly. Before driving home, Maxine and I snapped on the convertible roof—perhaps an act of shutting behind the recklessness and creating an atmosphere of healing. We all left in a somber caravan back down the mountain, leaving things behind to sort themselves out—on a hidden breach of dead rock where hippies once swam naked.

I was conscious of the sound of a pebbly driveway. A house loomed up beside us. We stopped by a weeping willow.

"I have some medicine and things," Maxine said, pulling up the emergency broke. "I think we should take a good look at your head—see if we should call a doctor."

"I'm fine. It only hurts when I shake it. My brains must be loose."

"Don't you ever stop joking? And don't shake your head yes or no!"

It was Maxine's house. Another of the stone houses that Old Ford was famous for.

In town, an historic plaque announced that Water Street was the oldest, continuously occupied street in America. In accordance, high holy days were set aside each year to commemorate the glory of the stone houses and their 1677 French Huguenot heritage. On such days women dressed in long skirts, aprons, and bonnets of the period, and the town charged a hefty fee to look inside the seven extant structures: a former fort (now a very mediocre restaurant); several prominent houses of original Huguenot families, one boasting "an interesting sub-cellar"; a reconstructed church; the original Old Ford burial ground; an archeological site; even a replica Munsee wigwam.

Maxine's house was outside the National Historic Landmark District and therefore accorded little scrutiny in the publicized portion of Old Ford's antiquity. A printed program listed it under "Other Stone Houses of Interest." It was beautiful. Slice upon slice of stones and rock painstakingly set and cemented to form walls of great height cut out with square windows of wavy glass trimmed in white shutters. A heavy wooden Dutch door painted a robin's egg blue contrasted with two wide chimneys rising straight and white on each side of the house. Out back in the moonlight overlooking the Valkill River was the small red barn that had been converted into an artist's studio by the previous owner—and had hosted our glorious one-night stand years before. Walking to the house, we passed a small overhanging shelter where a long pole once lowered a bucket into a hand dug stone well.

Maxine's living room contained one of two the large fireplaces and perfectly bisected a full wall of hewn bookshelves and was the focal point of the room. Through one doorway a homey kitchen lay dark and waiting. Another doorway separated by a curtain of beads led to Maxine's bedroom. I followed her into the kitchen where she sat me down on a stool with the admonition, "Stay here and don't move!"

I waited and stared at the old farm implements, baskets, brass fish molds, clean-rusty tools, and hanging pots and pans that populated the walls and ceiling. By the window was a small alcove with a desk and a portable typewriter sitting on top. There was a word-filled paper in the machine. Hearing Maxine opening cabinets and collecting medicaments in the bathroom, I carefully stepped down and tiptoed over to the typewriter, just close enough until the words came into focus.

Here I am, damn near thirty-five, banging (mostly) my typewriter, writing the words and painting the pictures that will never change the world. And if they ever were sold, any jerk could throw them back in my face and scream, "You wrote that! You painted that!"

God is dead and all is open. We are all sons of a Nietzsche. Panama never existed, the past is over, and who knows if another year will ever begin. . . .

Sleepless nights. The last days of some generation. The good ones are dead. Our time is up . . . . Oh, fuck. As I write to myself, I can't help thinking—can one talk to oneself without being insulted?

The King is dead and all is permitted. I'll never go home again. One learns at least that.

"I told you not to move," Maxine said, walking through the beads with clacking sounds. She smiled that sexy-friendly expression that one wears when confronting another's embarrassment.

I walked back to the stool sheepishly. "I never could resist the printed word. You know, McLuhan and all that. . . . I like it," I said, gesturing to the typewriter.

"Please, it's junk and you know it."

"No, there's wit there," I said and assumed an exaggerated orator's stance. "'Wit is not only the luck and labor, but also the dexterity of thought, rounding the world, like the sun, with unimaginable motion, and bringing swiftly home to the memory, universal surveys.'"

"That's very good. But *that* is still junk."

We laughed and I felt my brains slosh against the sides of my skull. Maxine went over to a kitchen island and plunked down all the items she had brought in from the bathroom. She yanked the paper out of the typewriter in a whir of gears, balled it up, and tossed it in a wicker wastebasket. She had changed her clothes—now a navy blue body top that I knew snapped in the crotch inside beltless jeans. She was barefoot and her hair was unbound in one thick dark brushstroke—with just the proper touch of dishevelment that attractive women naturally had and mediocre women tried to emulate with brushes, creams, beauty parlor treatments, and hair devices—to no avail. She looked young and artsy, and was all woman.

"I'm writing, too, now," I said, bending my head down as instructed—letting her tend to my wounds at close quarters under proper light. If I appealed to her as a fellow artist, perhaps she might forget that I was snooping around her house and take pity on my condition, which could possibly lead to more amorous pursuits.

"What are you writing?"

"Some fiction, a few political articles, couple published. Still in the 4H stage."

She had discovered a hidden abrasion and daubed antiseptic on it with a Q-tip. I felt no sensation from her poking. My head was touching her stomach.

"Ticklish?" I said, impishly reaching up and fluttering my fingers at her sides.

"Yes," she squealed and shook her hips to chase my hands away. "Stop, please. . . . Keep doing that and you'll have hydrogen peroxide in all the wrong places."

"And you know how painful it can be to have hydrogen peroxide in all the wrong places, eh, little girl."

"Um-hmm."

I loved her. I loved the way her life seemed to be. And when she wanted, I loved the way she could draw me into her world and make me feel as if I were on a calm ocean with the sun shimmering off the water like Golden Fleece. But I also knew another side—the side that watched her have to fight for her happiness, always protecting a special place she had set aside for someone worthy of her unconditional love. It was a place that no one—maybe not even Maurice—had been right enough to reach completely.

As she worked, Maxine spoke as though she were alone, looking at herself in the mirror.

"I was thinking it would be good to have you more in my life right now."

"Really. Are you saying you need me?"

"Yes, . . . in my own way."

"There's that phrase again. . . . Another scalp in your wickiup?'

"Would that be so bad?"

"I thought that's what Puerto Rico is for?"

"I don't have to go to Puerto Rico for that. Besides, what's wrong with making you a nice breakfast once in a while?"

I turned and looked up at her. "You always know what I want to hear."

"And I'm prepared to say it."

"I suppose I should jump at the chance."

"That's up to you. . . . No have-to's, no demands—just fun, good times, companionship, and that you make love to me whenever it moves us."

"Would Maurice know?

"Of course. I tell him everything I do, especially when I do it with other men."

"Sounds like a soft revenge."

"I don't need to get revenge."

"Ah, yes—the luxury of the beautiful."

"There," she said, kissing me on the cheek. "Good as new."

"Let's celebrate," I said and coaxed her body to mine.

She pushed eagerly into me and smiled as I traced a finger down her neck, over her breast, and left it there. She knew I wanted to touch her and it was good to do it. I kissed her more urgently.

"Whoa, take your time, cowboy. I'm here. You don't want to bust a stitch—especially since I'm going to France tomorrow. I won't be around to patch you up again."

"Up, up, and away . . . again," I frowned.

Later on in her lightless bedroom, we lay on the polished brass bed and did what each desired. Those were the only words. Sleep came sometime late in the afterglow and there was the silent pleasure that I was making love to a beautiful woman, that she wanted me, and that there would be nights of love to come.

In another part of Old Ford, Jane was sleeping, not knowing the life that had begun within her was dead.

BOOK II

Towards Bethlehem

7

It was the kind of late June-early July that had long rainy spells when you thought the sun would never shine again, and when it did, a devastating heat would take over and linger until you wished it would rain again. In either climatic condition the garret of 42 Calypso Street was not the ideal spot to live or even spend a great deal of one's time. But soon I came to respect the heat as a fascinating energy source—and through it I established links with nomadic tribes of the Sahara or some coarse-looking warrior who banged his teeth out with a rock to mourn a great man's death. All things considered, I fared well enough—preferring to live coequally with the elements—and let those who were compulsively paranoid try to control the planet. With the aid of a tiny desk fan and occasional anointed winds, I made my separate peace.

Of course, the slow but steady stream of lady callers were totally unprepared for Calypso's conditions, and in a matter of minutes, all but the breeziest would wilt and sweat down into shiny-faced schoolgirls. After a while it became commonplace, as part of the courting ritual. Mauberley termed it, "Diathetic foreplay! Man, they get steamy just sittin' here," he said and punctuated it with the laugh that automatically engaged after everything he said—a perfect mutation between a giggle and a slow snicker. But Mauberley was right—our women were responsive.

When it rained, the screens remained in the lower half of the two opposing garret windows—compromising wetness, disease, ghosts . . . everything for airflow. Davenant and I had fashioned the screens from layers of old chicken wire nailed to four two-by-fours, which let oxygen in well enough but also assured passage to virtually every phylum of flying and crawling creatures. During the day, insects could be coped with, but at night one grew anxious that perhaps inches away a plotting tribe of hateful spiders or some mindless bedbug was inching its way towards your eyes and mouth. Then, too, Mauberley reported in his blasé manner that a pair of amorous bats had begun "spooning" there the year before—laughing his villain laugh at our queasy reactions.

What wind there was had to negotiate the north/south passage between the window in Mauberley's room and the window in Davenant's and mine. This precious air tunnel was partially blocked by the chimney and further complicated by 42 Calypso squeezed in by houses in both directions. Fortunately, Old Ford's weather came from the west, and sometimes sitting on top of the porch roof, I would watch a fresh storm rumble down from the mountain: first, forming mist on the cliffs; then visibly spreading and gaining strength—until it rushed across its face, blowing trees on the upper slopes and sent buffeting winds and rain slamming directly into town. That was my favorite time—when the leaves were blown back and their silvery-purple bottoms fluttered—the way things were lighted during an eclipse. I was convinced it was the secret to Van Gogh's landscapes. Contrast: sunlight is brighter for shadow; music is made between the spaces.

Though airless, pest-ridden, barren, and crude, the garret was a decent place to live, and I didn't have to worry about spoiling anything. The apartment was already dirty, and all I needed in the kitchen was my own clean, properly lighted place to eat my spaghetti and can of tomato soup (as sauce). I managed to stay alive on 27 cents a day—17 cents for the pasta and 10 cents for the soup. Supplemental food was also provided by various lady friends who took pity on us.

Downstairs, when we went to her place to escape the heat, Birdie always had good thirst-quenching iced-tea she kept in a big green plastic pitcher. She was alone for the summer, and she was the sort of direct, earthy woman you could talk to on an everyday basis without feeling awkward. Mauberley and I would go down there to drink and cool off, smoke grass, and listen to her records. She had all the newest albums of any group we could name, as well as a fantastic collection of 45s we were planning to play one day in a marathon commemoration I had dubbed "Le Sacre du Quarante-cinq."

At about this time I decided I was smoking too much. I had started back heavily on cigarettes and using more weed than I had since a freshman in college. The funny thing was I had quit cigarettes over two and a half years before, but now there was that old craving mindset and guilt all over again. Gradually compelled to buy cigarettes—sufficient to make it the sole purpose of a walk into town and a necessity after meals or in social situations—I kept telling myself that it was a temporary vice, and daily I would set dates and times when I was absolutely going to quit forever. Until that day, I endured the smelly clothes, headaches, bad breath, and the green phlegm I coughed up. Luckily, marijuana could easily straighten out and rationalize away any chinks in the world such as one's weakness to cigarettes. I romanticized the smoking. I was the famous expatriate who enviously wasted and abused my body and talents like a brief meteorite's stretch across a shallow sky. What was important was the act—the becoming not the being. I had never forgotten what Leon Skir had written to me: ". . . yr art which is supreme all-consuming egoism blow-up of the self, Must be so. Having personal life controls the explosion."

My art was a ninety-six page first draft of a dog-eared manuscript whose rickety plot told of an established Old World family that ran a musical conservatory—whose artistic vision was complicated by duplicity, natural shocks, unexpected love, and flashbacks to an old friend who was involved in the political upheaval in 1956 Hungary. I thought it contained what reviewers might deem "flashes of brilliance."

I was always in the process of rereading it aloud, which helped me sense its flow and pace better. Movement in a story was what gave fiction the amount of life it possessed, a writing professor had once declared—the same man who had tried vainly for forty years to match the success of his acclaimed novelist father. "It's like fishing, Dalton. You cast your line out and reel it back slowly. Things have their pace. Corn does not hurry (his father's line). Slow, man, slow. You've got to give the reader the bait—just like the fish. . . . Can you dig it?"

Another time he had called me before eight one morning, imploring me to come immediately to his office at the college. It turned out he was trying to learn how to smoke cigarettes—"So my characters will appear authentic. . . . Teach me how to smoke, man," and I had sat there bored and tired, listening and answering his questions, commiserating politely with his mediocrity.

To get the full effect of reading my manuscript out loud, I would climb through the window at the bottom of the garret staircase, go out onto the roof of the porch, settle on the small mattress in the shade of an eave, and listen to my words carom off the neighbors' houses like a soft kill shot in handball. Afterwards, I would clamber back inside and invariably glance at the TITS ARE SILLY graffiti someone had painted in red above the attic door. To me, it was profoundly true and summed up the

essence of breasts—silly, wonderful, crazy things—
something Mauberley could have written.

Living at 42 was crowded but knowing each other
in a friendly, undergraduate way made it easier to get
along—in stark contrast to other living situations, where I
had wanted to kill the people I lived with in cruel and
medieval ways. We had our separate lives. During the day
we attended to our own responsibilities and on any given
night, at least one or two of us would not be sleeping at
home. Thus, there was the perception that there was
plenty of room. Even the domestic chores blended into
each other in such a way that the kitchen and bathroom
always seemed to be somewhat clean and available. And
having to pass through Mason's room enroute to the attic
was not the awkward situation I had anticipated. Simply,
Mason was rarely there, and almost spiritually, the same
forces that drove us apart so naturally brought us into the
kitchen at the beginning of each month to pay the rent.

I had met our landlord, Lorenzo Nostromo, a stout
Calabrian, back in early June. A crusty, old-world Italian
widower, he had lived on Calypso Street for thirty years
until a professor from the college had opened the Third
Word Bookstore at the end of the block and began selling
pro-revolutionary pamphlets and Leftist books and
newspapers. Weather permitting, the inflammatory
materials were placed on stands in front of the
bookstore—many offered free to any passerby who took
the trouble to pick them off the racks. For months
Nostromo protested, claiming he had fled the horrors of
Fascism and knew firsthand what such a depraved
ideology was capable of.

Despite meagre backing from a small cabal of
local rednecks, the scandal grew and seethed through the
body politic of Old Ford. Things came to a head when
another glib professor (and communist sympathizer)
presented a compelling first amendment defense of the

bookstore at a town meeting—spawning a general ordinance allowing the sale and distribution of the controversial materials—and avoiding a thinly-threatened boycott of other Old Ford commercial establishments by college staff and personnel. Without college monies the town was dead.

Shamed and dishonored by this ominous turn of events, Nostromo had abruptly pulled up stakes and moved across the Hudson River—but not before chopping up the interior of his house into four apartments and becoming the first homeowner on Calypso Street to rent rooms to hippies, college students, and other undesirables. Everyone cried that Nostromo was exacting revenge against the town, and they were right. Not long after, even more troubling was the mysterious early morning firebombing of the Third World Bookstore—according to the fire department, under "suspicious circumstances." Rumors flew that Nostromo had enlisted the services of a trio of Italian arsonists from Brooklyn—until a Nigerian exchange student confessed that the bookstore bombing was to have been just the first in a series of proposed fire bombings in support of the oppressed peoples of Vietnam, Laos, and Cambodia. Through it all, 42 Calypso remained steadfast and the bookstore professor was eventually fired and left for the Midwest to devote his life to chess—never to be heard from again.

Since the fire, on those days Lorenzo Nostromo came to Old Ford to collect the rents, he always took a moment to stop in front of the once boarded-up bookstore. Then later on, when it had been transformed into a plant shop—his was the stoic pride of a peasant villager sneering at the grave of a hard-hearted overseer, silently celebrating a revenge now turned deliciously cold.

His routine was the same: He would burst into the apartment without knocking, plant himself in the middle of the kitchen, and stand with arms akimbo and bellow in jagged English, "You gotta da rent?" his black Picasso eyes glaring out from his unshaven face like shiny aggies.

From the start, Mauberley insisted on dealing with Nostromo exclusively, as, for some reason, the old man feared him.

"Hey, Mr. Nostromo, how's it going?" Mauberley would say and clap him forcefully on the back.

"Yeah, hi-ya, kid," Nostromo would reply hesitantly, not knowing what was going to happen next inside the head of this *animale.*

Of course, Mauberley exploited this fear and took delight in watching Nostromo flinch and feint in defense every time Mauberley coughed, jerked, or scratched his head suddenly.

"Hooooo!" Nostromo had howled a few days earlier when Mauberley had stamped his foot unexpectedly.

"A leetle jumpy, eh, *signore,*" Mauberley smiled and invoked his sinister laugh.

"Yeah, you funny. You a funny crazy kid."

"I beg your pardon," Mauberley rose up on his toes, imitating Frankenstein.

Nostromo shrank back but tried to remain composed. He was determined to sound truculent and generate pushback against this thin, disrespectful hippie.

"Youse quit makin' afun with me," he scowled and looked around at the rest of us. "An' I donta wanta chippies ora drugs ina dis house. You hear?" He pointed at Mauberley. "You getta me, Buster?"

Mauberley smirked and nodded his head as though davening.

"Animale! All you do isa laugh."

"Dear, fellows," Mauberley intoned. "Hark, the *immigrante* doth speak. Go, Ramapithicus, go! . . . Please, there must be quiet. Quiet for the *brutta faccia* that looks like ten miles of bad Roman causeway. . . ."

Mason and Davenant tried to stifle laughs.

"What you say?"

"Lorenzo, you hurt me. Perhaps I have offended you by our unusual customs. After all, you've only spent fifty years in our strange land—things in the New World must still be peculiar to you. . . . I must greet you to our country with dignity and on equal terms, in the proper way." He paused and went to the refrigerator. "Allow me this small courtesy, Lorenzo, please. I offer you cheese from my home. It is our way. . . ." He waited for the landlord's fear to gather and take root. "Have a piece of mozzarella that I bought last winter for special occasions like this. . . . Lorenzo Nostromo, I invite you in front of my friends and my god to break cheese in my home. I wish to make peace in the American peasant fashion."

Mauberley gently seated the old man and gestured everyone to surround him, as he unwrapped the yellowed protective plastic wrap that fell open like a fetid pop tart.

Nostromo stopped, sniffing the air, uncertain of the cheese's freshness.

"I ain'ta hungry," he brayed and waved the cheese away, a petulant Mussolini.

"Preposterous, Lorenzo! This is a matter of honor. I must insist! *Mange.* You cannot insult the hospitality of my ancestors. Eat! *Mange! Mange!"*

Nostromo's hairy hand reached and paused at the mozzarella like Adam receiving the spark of life, then broke off an imperceptible crumb and placed it gingerly into his mouth.

"Hurrah! Bravo! You alike, Lorenzo?"

The old man nodded feebly.

"*Danza! Danza! Musica!* Lorenzo Nostromo approves of the cheese! Our hearths shall have wood this winter. Our women shall make fresh bread for the breaking," Mauberley mock-cheered and rolled his eyes, as if to say, I don't believe I have to go through this shit every month. "The tribute!" he shouted.

Everything became silent again as Mauberley counted out the rent money to Nostromo's satisfaction but did not give it to the old man when he reached for it. Instead, he insisted on recounting it again and finally placed it into a little paper bag.

"This is a lot of money, Lorenzo. You mustn't lose it," he said, folding the bag over and over into the smallest package possible and jammed it into the landlord's shirt pocket. "There! Ciao, Lorenzo Nostromo. Ciao, my friend. Depart and be fruitful—bring many more Guineas into the New World."

Davenant and Mason waved as Mauberley gestured us all to extend an American goodbye—bidding the landlord adieu for another month—and watched him close the door with a soft click.

Mauberley leaned back and shook his head in disbelief.

"Dumb schmuck," he smiled and produced a five-dollar bill he had palmed from the rent money.

We all laughed and were happy—we had drinking money that night.

8

The next day, as soon as Mauberley stuck his head inside the door and said he wanted to speak with me out in the hall, I knew something was wrong.

Rachel and Birdie, who recently had become fast friends, were plunking away on guitars, offering background to my improvised blues lyrics and fulfilling my part in a bargain to sing for my supper—"a chicken dinner with all the trimmings," their treat. A representative phrase was in progress:

"I got the jackoff blues, mama. . . . I get them ev'ry day an' ev'ry night," I sang.

"Ev'ry day and ev'ry night," they harmonized.

"Yeah, I've got the rabbit-ass blues, mama. . . . But don't pay me no rabbit-ass mind."

Mauberley was insistent, waving his arms against the confluence of instruments, singing, and hissing pots—bringing everything to a halt.

"Stop! Stop!"

"C'mon, let Dalton sing," Birdie complained.

Despite my apprehension, there were speculations: Mauberley had figured out a way for us to make workless money to pay next month's rent? No, he wouldn't have called me out into the hall. He could have something lined up for tonight—in the way of "silk panties" (an old black friend's contribution to Calypso's lexicon)—and didn't want Rachel and Birdie to be offended? No, his face spoke of something troubling, and besides, this was

Mauberley, who didn't give a rabbit-ass mind about offending anyone. What else—someone got busted?

I stepped out onto the hallway landing, and it was one of the few times I had ever seen Mauberley's face truly serious. I kept waiting for his expression to crack and give trace of his signature laugh, but it never came.

"I have bad news," he said and stopped, emotion welling his eyes.

I waited. . . . "Well, say it, for crissakes! What are you waiting for?"

"Jane committed suicide last night," Stephen Cornelius Mauberley said evenly and soberly, then leaned back against the wall to watch another reaction to the news he had been bearing for an hour. The words lay dead in the hallway.

"What . . .?" I tried to grasp it, to accept it as real. Something inside told me I should dispute it like a man. At the same time, something told me I must also feel it like a man.

Mauberley and I stood staring at each other and then looked away, both thinking of Jane in death. . . . For me, the kaleidoscope of Fallen Rock twisted into geometric clarity: bits and beads refracting the length of my fall, my leg inexorably downward, the look on Jane's face before I hit her—the end to what had been.

The thought that Jane had killed herself because she had lost her baby was no great mystery: it was simply more than she could bear. Around that monolith, others would reconstruct her depression after her divorce, money problems, and the long, unsuccessful artistic plunge— how everything she did had just seemed to go against her.

Then there was the baby itself. It had been the longest of long shots, against the whole damn system and all the odds, and the white-hot euphoria that the sun had finally shined on her at last. It had been wonderful but overheated, unnatural, a desperation born of yearning for the nearly impossible—almost daring the world to withhold her birthright.

Maybe I should have done something then, I thought—brought her back down to a less manic view of everything, a more manageable happiness. I had noticed, but God how she could be such an arrogant, difficult woman at times. Spring and fall she was up, over the moon—there was no telling her about anyone or anything. She knew it all, so damn smug that she was right and overdue to be happy. The rest of the time, depression—howling on the floor ennui. The baby was simply the last thing she could not let go unpunished—she'd get even with the world by killing herself. Poor Jane. And to think what I had to look forward to now—to know that I was the last thing that had pushed her beyond what she could endure from life and still consider herself competent, honorable, and worthy of happiness . . . better among the living.

"What would you do if you just found out a friend of yours, an old lover, had just killed herself because of something you did?"

"C'mon, man. . . . I knew you were going to say that. How is it your fault? It was an accident. . . . You know how she was. And Ray said the cops found some speed. They're not even sure yet. Who really knows? . . . And don't give me some kind of last link in the chain bullshit."

"I can't believe it. I just can't believe it. I'm never going to see Jane again. That's it. She's gone. Right back into the dirt, man, recycled. . . . Shit."

Mauberley was silent. But in a way, I could see what he was driving at. If there were anyone who I thought could ever commit suicide, it would have been Jane. But at the same time, I know I would never understand what it meant to have a life inside you, a potentiality, and then have it taken so unfairly. . . . God, she must have been so bitter.

"Do you feel like I do?" I asked. There was a skittishness assembling in the bottom of my stomach. "Like something heavy sinking down in your gut but never reaching the bottom . . . just the fall."

"Yeah."

"How'd you find out?"

Mauberley gathered himself, as though he was about to say something he had said before. "I got a call from her roommate. Apparently, she had had some kind of fight with Ray, and they had to stop in the middle of it—nothing resolved—because Ray had to go to work. . . . After work, he went to the Cacique. Jane was supposed to pick him up there and then drive back to her place for the night. When Jane never showed, Ray waited around, got pissed, and hitchhiked out to her house. When he got there, she wasn't home, so he had something to eat, watched television 'til about one-thirty, then decided, fuck it, he'd sleep there and went to bed. Before he fell asleep, he thought he heard a noise downstairs. . . . He checked the basement and found Jane."

"Ray found her?"

"Yeah."

"Oh, Jesus." I tried to envision everything as Mauberley described it. "So, she was there the whole time?"

"I guess so."

"How'd she do it?"

"Stabbed herself."

"Stabbed herself! Are you're shitting me? How could she stab herself to death?" I was thinking of other ways I'd rather die. Then the thought came to me. "Where?"

The question caused Mauberley to hesitate. I had caught him in that moment of ineffable silence, which often precedes a lie, but in this case, a euphemism for the terrible truth.

"The lower stomach area," he said with no emotion.

I felt like moaning. "Oh, fuck. . . . How goddamned symbolic could she get? Who would do such a thing?" It was all still too much on the fantastical level. "Oh, man. Please tell me you're putting me on, and that this is all some kind of freaky . . ."

"Believe me, I wish I were. This is the real thing, man. It's happening right now, and I'm straight, and I'm sober, and . . . I don't know."

I sighed heavily trying to get a new bearing, to see everything freshly—the way life gives you answers when you see it early in the morning. Goddamn crazy Jane—unbelievable.

"The strange thing," Mauberley went on . . . "was that she killed Bhagvita, too."

"What? Oh, my god. Jesus, that's sick. I don't care what the hell you say, that's sick. Why would she want to kill her dog, too?" I barely screamed the last words.

"I know, I know, I know. . . . They think that maybe she wanted to remove all traces of her life, you know, so she wouldn't be a burden to anyone else."

"Bullshit. There's a thousand reminders everywhere."

"I know . . . but she really loved Bhagvita. Maybe she wanted to take him with her."

"What, like the pharaohs? To some kind of fucking dog heaven?"

"I don't know. I just . . ."

"I can't believe it. . . . I'm afraid to ask. How'd she kill Bhagvita?"

"Stabbed it, too."

"What the hell! It's like some kind of Bergman movie."

Downstairs someone came in and started knocking on Birdie's door. I focused my attention to where I knew she was and could still hear her singing with Rachel.

"You know, it's funny," I mused. "Just a couple of days ago, I ran into her and, I don't know, I just couldn't help noticing that she was very nervous. It was a little scary. I even mentioned it to Maxine." Again, for some reason, I remembered Maxine and Mauberley being so cozy at Fallen Rock. He gave no reaction. "I was telling her that it seemed like a lull before a storm and that something was going to blow. If only I had done something."

"Sure, if any of us had done something. That's the shitty thing about it. It's too late. It's done, man."

"Where's Ray?"

"He went to the airport to meet Jane's mother. She's flying in from Georgia. Ray's mother and an uncle of Jane's are at the house now."

"What's his mother doing there? She didn't even know Jane."

"Who knows? Ray must have asked her. What could she do, say no? . . . Anyway, he said that it really wasn't necessary for any of us to be there just yet. A lot of arrangements have to be made and they're taking care of all that. . . .What's there to do?"

"I want to go."

"For what? We can help later on—clean up in the basement. There's supposed a fair amount of . . . blood."

"Fuck! Are you kidding me? What's the matter with you? I'm going to wash my old girlfriend's blood off the fucking floor. Are you crazy? That was my woman, man. That's Jane's blood!"

"I know whose blood it is. . . . It has to be done. Do you expect Ray to do it?"

"I can't stay here. There's too much going on." I thought a moment and the decision came to me that I had to see everything for myself—to see what Mauberley had described. "I'm going over anyway. You can come if you want."

Mauberley saw that I was determined and would not be persuaded otherwise. "Okay," he said and started down the stairs ahead of me.

I opened the door to the apartment. "Hey, something important came up . . ." I waved my arms to get Rachel's attention. "I have to go. I can't explain. See you later. Eat without me. Sorry," I said and made a helpless face.

Rachel nodded and pointed the guitar at me like some cubist phallus and sang, "Well, if you're gonna ball me, Daddy . . . then you better do it all night long. . . . 'Cause I'm gonna do things to ya', baby, that are gonna fuckin' blow your mind. . . ."

I raised my eyebrows meekly and hurried to follow Mauberley.

He stopped on the way to the car. "You know, this is the one time I really do need a drink."

"Yeah, me, too. Let's stop on the way. But just one."

The kitchen window opened and Rachel stuck herself through it like a willowy nymph on the prow of a ship. "Are you coming back soon?"

"I don't know. I'll try," I called and waved goodbye.

In the car I could not stop thinking of Jane. The times when she could be the most wonderful lady you would ever want to meet. The times when she was unbearable and vindictive. The times we went horseback riding and made love in the fields. The times . . . the times . . . the times.

"Got a cigarette?" Mauberley asked, his tall lean body looking cramped behind the steering wheel.

I handed over the pack. "Keep 'em—I don't want to smoke anymore. . . . Was there a note or anything?"

'No."

"Somehow I would have expected Jane to leave a note."

"Me, too, but this whole thing is so fucked up to begin with." It would have been the expected moment for his distinctive laugh but it did not come.

"It's crazy, but I can't help thinking I know Jane is dead and she killed herself with a knife and she killed Bhagvita—but all that doesn't seem to surprise me now."

"I know what you're saying," Mauberley paused for a deep drag on his cigarette. "The craziest thing is Ray actually saw Jane and the dog . . ."

". . . and the knife and the gore," I imitated his same tenor. "Let's not get into it."

In town, we passed the heavyset retarded man who lived with his parents across the street from us. He was thirty-five years old with the mentality of a first grader—who shoveled snow, swept sidewalks, and cut lawns around some of the commercial buildings in Old Ford. The rest of the time he would wander and stumble his way around town looking like he was drunk. One day his mother had confessed to me he was her cross to bear in life, but he was truly happy in his own world. She worried what would happen when she and her husband were no longer around to take care of him.

"How about Gannon's?" I said, watching Mauberley put the big car in a lower gear going down the hill and felt it accept the diminished ratio with a straining descent.

"Nah, that place is shit now."

"Well, that's how we feel."

"I don't want to," he said, sounding irritated that I had challenged his decision. "Forget the drink."

He slipped back into the higher gear and accelerated past Gannon's towards the bridge.

Today, the day of Jane's death, it was not raining but the skies threatened with a solid bank of overcast clouds that muted even more what remained of the waning light. Despite this, the mountain remained striking and wild looking, as though Indians still inhabited its trails and hollows. Within its deep secrets, it was peaceful and perfect—still asserting its beauty on a sad day.

The radio was whining down a melancholy ballad whose lost love I transferred to Jane. In many ways, she was just too beautiful for this world. If only she hadn't been so fragile. She had been broken in one too many places, and in that final reality she decided she would be the one who made the decision when she would leave this life. Like Hemingway, she wanted to control her death—give the world the finger one last time. I knew I would never be able to look at her in a coffin.

When we got to Jane's house, Ray's mother was pacing around the living room, acting out needless domestications, keeping busy so she would not have to think. Listening to her, it became apparent she really didn't care or know much about Jane, never had. Her tears were for Ray. She cried because she knew, like so many young people she observed these days, he was so unhappy and this might be too much for him to handle. She knew her Raymond.

Jane's uncle sat on the couch and spoke in a low voice about suicide-related things that sounded serious at their inception but were one-dimensional and meaningless after they were said. He wore an ill-fitting, generic-looking suit bought more with the idea of utility than purpose. He had spent thirty years in the Navy, and after he retired, had married an unattractive woman in her forties who smoked affectedly and had grown up in Finland. He had built her a house in a nondescript, hardscrabble area of rural Rhode Island—that had taken five years and all his Navy money. Now he was a broken man who spent most days cursing and drinking at the unfairness of the world and nights as a lone watchman in a paper mill. His only attempts to take control of his life were the drunken arguments and occasional beatings he gave his Finnish wife. Stoically, steeped in her nihilistic Scandinavian mindset, she accepted her marriage as it was—allowing his inadequacies to bubble to the surface, secretly relishing that he would see them firsthand and ultimately grow to hate himself even more.

"Helluva thing," he said. "Same thing happened to my buddy's sister in Providence—two, three years ago. A boy. Was thinkin' about the naval academy, too. . . ." He shook his head.

"That's terrible," Mrs. Mason said, walking back from the kitchen, bearing an ashtray for everyone's cigarettes. "I think suicide is such a terribly personal thing. These young people with everything to live for. Dalton, how old was Jane?"

"Twenty-eight," I said.

"Twenty-eight. Imagine that. Such a shame—she was just getting started in life. I mean, *they* were just beginning. . . . Twenty-eight. God, to be forty again!" she joked and the uncle laughed. I looked at Mauberley. His expression did not change.

Variations of this conversation filled the next hour—all of us waiting for Ray to return with Jane's mother. Notably, Mauberley spoke about the practical elements: insurance, power of attorney, health care proxy, the funeral, schedules of people to spend time with Ray so he would not be alone. "Or do something stupid," the uncle interjected. It all sounded so pathetic and empty.

Mrs. Mason reported having seen signs of odd behavior when Jane had visited her two months earlier to celebrate Ray's father's birthday. "Jane just seemed so . . . *detached* I guess you could say. She was obviously preoccupied with things. She spoke to me and was very pleasant and good company, but there was a distance between us. It was very strong. I thought it odd but I didn't say anything because I knew Raymond was happy—for once. . . . But, of course, there was the baby and all the concern."

I watched her talk and gesture with her thin-veined, smooth-tanned hands that were accustomed to the finer things in life. Suddenly, her eyes welled up and she began a series of sorrowful smiles—trying not to break up.

"I can only guess what Ray's feeling," Mauberley said.

It was more than Mrs. Mason could bear and she simply cried. "I don't know what Raymond will do now," she said between sobs, trying to control herself. "He's certainly welcome to come back home and live with us. . . . But I want him to make that decision. . . . It's his decision. I shouldn't interfere."

"Yeah, he's a big boy now," the uncle agreed. "Let him stand on his own two feet."

"Of course, should he decide to stay here, that would be fine, too. . . . I'm not even sure if he knows about our trip to Capri." She looked at us all self-consciously, then picked up the uncle's half-empty coffee mug. "Let me warm that up for you, Bill."

"Great, hon, I'd love some," the uncle said instinctively, in a Navy manner he had used with hard-faced women in shipyard bars along waterfronts around the world.

"It was nice of your boss to let you take time off," she added walking back to the kitchen.

"Yessirree, and with pay, too!" he added as though he were getting away with murder.

"Well, let's hope that everything turns out for the best and that everyone will help each other and things will get back to normal as soon as possible," she said returning.

William Guilbault, modern-day nautical man, cocked a smile and half-stood as Mrs. Mason handed him his freshened coffee. The legs of his trousers hiked up as he sat back down, exposing thin navy blue socks and thick, nondescript black work shoes—plainly wrong with the celery green suit he had bought in Warwick two years earlier when his niece had married.

9

The horses were jumpy from just having cantered the two hundred yard tier of grazing pasture below the mountain's rock escarpment. They were anxious to run again. Jane sat straight-backed on the pinto that jerked and twisted his head as though something was bothering his mouth. My mare was blowing and throbbing up and down, stretching down to nudge the grass instinctively, then walking off the exertion some more.

"Is his bit too tight?" I asked.

"I don't think so?" Jane replied, trying to control the pinto. . . . Watching her, just so beautifully healthy and alive, looking into the slight wind blowing back the extremities of her hair framing an oval around her face.

I dismounted. I could see the corners of the pinto's mouth stretched uncomfortably by the bit. I renotched the bridle to the next lowest hole and watched the horse adjust the loosened bit inside its mouth with the sound of metal against teeth.

"You've got a lot of whiskers there," David Crazy horse." I nuzzled the pinto's velvety nose and shook his jaw with the spikey line of coarse hairs that ran underneath.

"Dalton, smell the clover! Isn't it incredible? It's absolutely sweet!" Jane cried, thrusting herself backwards on the saddle and reclining on the pinto's rump— submitting her body to the sunshine.

"No wonder these guys love it."

On this uppermost pasture, we saw what the mountain saw every day: the jagged teeth of Old Ford, squares of farm fields, winding roads through clumps of woods, miles of lush quiet green—not seeing the struggle in relation to everything else.

Jane turned to me. "You know, I've been to a lot of places, drove across country two years ago, the Caribbean, all over. . . . But I have to say we're really lucky—there's some beautiful land on the east coast. Look at it! My God! And when you think New York is less than two hours away. . . . Look at *that!*" she gasped, gesturing with both arms, blessing the entire valley. "Less than a hundred miles from the Empire State Building!"

"I know. And it's our backyard."

"Oh, I'm really happy, Dalton. Are you?"

"Yes, I'm happy."

"No, I mean really *happy* happy?"

"Yes, really really happy happy. I'm happy to the nth power of happiness. I feel exultation. I sing paeans to happiness. I'm as happy as a snake in a wagon rut."

She laughed. "I love it when you're happy."

"*I'm happy. I'm so happy. I'm so happy . . . and gay,*" I sang in a high-pitched soprano.

"You're crazy."

"*I'm* crazy?"

Still laughing, she pulled herself up. "C'mon," she said, tsch-tsching the pinto into motion, "last one to the aqueduct cooks *and* does dishes," and galloped off.

My mare skittered sideways and jerked her head up, her ears pointing straight back, making starting-car noises in her powerful neck. I caught my foot in the stirrup, pulled into the saddle, and kicked into her sides.

Before the hay was cut, it was wonderful riding through the fields: The horses' legs swishing through the tall grass making melodies of reed sounds. . . . A wobbly bee airborne—there and away in a second. . . . Jane's hair buckling like folding copper as it absorbed the pinto's strides. . . . Purple clover flowers and the round flat petals of alfalfa that grew in patches inside the hay cut like channels through it—luxuriant cays fleeing by as though watching from a low-flying aircraft. . . .

My mare methodically pumped her neck up and down propelling her bulk forward—following the fresh hoof prints and whizzing paths the pinto had just pioneered. I veered slightly, making new channels, and looked back to see the patterns. Up ahead the pinto straightened as it slowed to a stiff-legged gait—in order to navigate a drainage easement that bisected the field. To catch up, I saw I could chance taking the trench in a jump, and began looking for the skinniest and shallowest section—so my mare wouldn't refuse. Jane was down and up the gully, cantering sideways towards the tractor path, halfway to the aqueduct. My mare saw the trench and there was a moment of hesitation before gauging her speed and adjusting her takeoff—then lunging headlong into the air, powering down massively and grunting on impact. "Good girl!" For a split second, I realized I did not know what was under the partridge pea—knowing there were always holes—but the croissants of blue flowers inside the green somehow gave me comfort. Catching up to the pinto, my mare encouraged and frightened it, and Jane's expressive face grew more determined as she screamed at my progress. A wonderful ride inside a wonderful day—two lovers on spirited horses running a carpeted field, saddles creaking, deadened hoof sounds against the earth—thrilling, swirling progress. Such a tiny freedom. At the aqueduct, I pulled steadily on the reins and leaned back, "whoaing" my excited, reckless, thousand-pound bay mare—finally slowing its choppy descent—I won.

"You cheated!" Jane cried, drawing up seconds later.

"No, I beat you fair and square."

"No, no, you did not! You weren't allowed to jump over the ditch."

"Who said? Get the rulebook. Where are the officials?"

"I'm not kidding, Dalton, you cheated," Jane laughed and tried to sound serious.

"Look who's talking—you started without counting to three." I dismounted. "C'mon, let's give these plugs a rest."

"Oh, that was wonderful!" Jane dragged a hand through her hair.

We walked with the horses alongside the aqueduct, where at that very moment the water bound for New York City was rushing through, ultimately to swirl around some toilet in the Bronx and gurgle into oblivion back out to sea. We tied off the horses on slender maples, leaving enough lead to allow each animal a small, peaceful grazing patch.

"It's so beautiful here," Jane said happily. "Who's your friend? You know the obnoxious one—the tall, jerky . . . Kincaid! Is this him or what? 'Let's go over to yon knotty countryman and avail ourselves of his luscious shade,'" she said in a deep baritone and laughed some more. "'Verily, forsooth, anon, my deareth, Dalton.'"

"Milady," I paused, holding her hand aloft and bowing. "I trust the thousand minor intrusions of the day have not fatigued thee beyond thy comfort?"

"Fear not, noble knight, this maiden's got her shit together," she said and tried to maintain a blasé mien of British nobility.

"What is this strange term thou speakest? 'Shit together,' you say?"

"Oh, look," she burst out and ran ahead to the base of a tree. "How beautiful!" She sat down, inspecting a cluster of orange-coral flowers, and delicately traced the perimeter of one of the petals. "I wonder what they're called."

"Jack-in-the-pulpit," I said, following her to the newest wonder of interest that had been picked up by her little girl radar.

"Jack-in-the-pulpit," she repeated, intrigued. "What an interesting name. I wonder how it got it."

"Here," I knelt down and positioned the flower forward, to demonstrate the upright spadix and the way the spathe arched over. "It's like an old-fashioned pulpit. You know, all those fire and brimstone boys berating their white-knuckled flock. You see the way it's like a sounding board to project the voice? . . . Let's hear it for the dear old reverend."

"Ladies and gentlemen, boys and girls, people of all ages, I give you The Right Reverend T. Lawrence Hawkes,' Jane announced.

Later on there were faint horse odors in parts of the moving air that curled around the tree and gently ruffled the Jacks-in-the-pulpit. The afternoon sun had descended until it sat on the cliff and was blocked by Jane's face above me—an aura of stray hairs like burgeoning prominences exploding off the sun—offering up her sexuality. We had talked, gossiped, laughed, and cajoled, and only one possibility remained. We both realized this, each watching the other in the shaded, charged contact of Jane's eclipse.

"Well, partner," she began, clearing her throat and tying her hair back. "Do we ride off into the sunset or do we mess up the prairie a little?"

Beyond her in the shade, I focused on the pinto's mouth, happily drooling a grass-colored lather as it chewed.

"Come here, you," I whispered. "Let's discuss the longest, outstanding crime in the history of the human race—the Case of the Lost Rib."

She smiled sexily and bent down, maintaining our shaded contact. "Okay, but remember, Adam was just a rough draft."

I laughed and pulled her onto me. We embraced and our eyes never wavered. Her hand moved along my thigh, fingers kneading the trail, as I caressed her breasts, and in that moment, we accepted what was at work beyond us and allowed ourselves to be caught in its swell—celebrating the dying of the sun and awaiting the stars. . . .

"Should I pick him up?" Kaplan's voice intruded my reverie and the fragile world with Jane receded.

I mumbled something, concentrating more on trying to reclaim the fading images of the horses and of Jane and me in the waning sunlight—to make it all come back—but they refused.

"Oh, shit," I groaned.

I felt the car decelerate and angle towards the shoulder of the road where an older man stood in low-slung, baggy trousers, weathered tee shirt and knapsack—and as we came to a stop, a big nose. A horseshoe of close-cropped chestnut hair attached to a very pale head thrust itself through the open window.

"Where ya' goin'?" Kaplan asked.

"Pelhamville."

"You're in luck. We're headed up to the Echo Acres Hotel," Kaplan said genially and motioned to the back seat. The man clambered inside and Kaplan resumed operation of his unwieldy station wagon. "I can drop you off right in town. How's that?"

"Fine. Thank you. That's very neighborly of you," the man said politely, settling back with a smile.

The next miles, from the flats to Lake Jenny, were crossed in silence. As the lake slid by, there was a pull on the front seat, and the bald man thrust himself forward.

"You know," he began, folding his arms and placing his chin on his hands, "Pelhamville is noted for three great contributions to modern American society. Do you know what those three things are?" He did not wait for an answer. "One, it's in Hamilton Fish Sr.'s old congressional district, and he called FDR a 'warmonger.' Ha-ha. . . . Fish said, 'Roosevelt did more to harm this country than any man who ever lived!' Well, it wasn't long after that that all the Washington newsmen called old man Fish 'the least useful member of the House.'" He paused and wheezed off a gaggle of happy screeches. . . . "The second thing is that Pelhamville is frequented by more Jews than any other ethnic group in upstate New York—you know, because of all the hotels and resorts." He stopped to laugh again, thoroughly enjoying himself. "And the last reason is because *I* live there," he said and smiled like a kid. He brought a hand to his mouth, tilted his head back, and tooted a fanfare of trumpets. . . .

As we approached the stop sign, which marked the beginning of the ascent over the mountain, Kaplan and I looked at each other—Christ, a real live one.

"Yessirree, Pelhamville is home to Nathan Paulding, member *oraculum* of the Socialist Labor Party. That means I'm the champeen letter writer in the SLP. Last year, in 1968 alone, I published 443 letters in newspapers up and down the state. One in Japan, too!"

"Mr. Paulding . . ." Kaplan began in a heavy Jewish accent that sounded like he had a bad cold and flashed me an evil grin, as if to say, we had struck gold this time—*he's that fucking Communist!* In that moment, I suddenly realized the man sitting between us smiling like a chipmunk was the local legend whose radio interviews and whacky, revolutionary Letters-to-the-

Editor we had read and laughed over for years. Yessirree, we had us a real live homespun hero—and a commie at that.

"I was going to say, Mr. Paulding . . ."

"Call me Nathan."

"Okay, Nathan . . . isn't it hard living in a small town like Pelhamville and openly admitting you're a member of the Socialist Labor Party?"

"No, not at all. . . . What's your name, son?"

"Kaplan."

"And yours."

"Dalton."

"No, fellas, not at all. No, I believe people respect me for my integrity, and they know me to be a man of convictions. I say what I have to say and whoever knows me, they know that I speak for my beliefs, whether they agree or do not agree. It's a known fact that people do associate my name with the Socialist Labor Party and I'm proud of it. It's a personal thing rather than a family thing. . . . My wife and children kind of think that I have a tendency to, how should I put it, to praise myself . . . but one kid told my boy in school that I'm a communist. . . . No, no, I must say that my children have not been discriminated against in any way just because their father happens to be Nathan Paulding."

With that, Kaplan nonchalantly reached into the pocket of his denim shirt and drew out a fat joint rolled in paper imprinted with the American flag. "Care for a smoke, Nathan?" he asked, holding up Old Glory.

"Oh, marijuana!" Paulding cheered. "We used to use that back in the Thirties. Ha-ha. Sure, why not, fire her up!"

The joint was passed around in silence, the only sounds being the sharp intakes of air and the occasional crackling of marijuana seeds. It was good grass, that is, if everyone was getting as high as I was. . . . After the roach could not be handled—even in Kaplan's deer antler roach clip—it was tossed out the window, and we all sat back and enjoyed our heads. I stared out the windshield, not watching the scenery so much as enjoying the sensation of staring—or as Kaplan remarked, I was "grooving." He snapped on the radio and started moving his head to the music. Paulding sat back quietly examining his hands. . . .

"You get off, man?" Kaplan asked.

I stared at his large teeth. They could have become gruesome if I stared at them long enough. "Yeah, you?"

"Yeah."

"What an intelligent conversation: yeah . . . yeah, you . . . yeah," I grunted.

"Our brain cells are disintegrating as we speak."

"We are the living proof of the evils of marijuana," I said and stretched my fingers to transfer the curse to the world, emphasizing it with a guttural clap of thunder. "Reefer madness!"

"Think he's off?"

"I don't know."

"Nathan," Kaplan called out, as though playing outside and it was time for lunch. "Are you high?"

The bald man was not listening.

"Herr Paulding, calling Herr Paulding. . . . So, Herr Paulding, your family suffered while you continued to pursue your dangerous political thinking, yavol?" Kaplan shot me glance for approval and concocted a veneery smile.

"Oh . . . yes . . ." Paulding began and then stopped as if he were trying to remember what he was thinking. "There were others who would . . . were very, very malicious. They offered to buy me a one-way ticket back to Russia. I'm un-American. . . . Are you familiar with the name of Smedley D. Butler?"

Kaplan and I shook our heads in counterpoint, then broke up laughing. "Smedley?" we chimed in unison.

"Yes, General Smedley Butler—used to be commandant of the United States Marines. And I quoted what Butler said after he retired—about the true role of marines. He was a muscle man for Wall Street. I quoted him on Armistice Day or what we now celebrate as Armistice Day. I said, 'It's about time we stop using our young people as cannon fodder to preserve the capitalist system!' A woman called the next day and said she hoped I dropped dead. There were other malicious calls."

Kaplan took the hairpin turn leading up the mountain at 30 mph even though the signs cautioned 5 mph well in advance. The heavy ass of the station wagon swung too far for the approach to the upper straightaway and we skidded along the gravel shoulder almost hitting a rock outcropping. . . . Counterturning, Kaplan brought the swaying rear-end back into line. No one said anything.

On this section of the road, at the base of the cliffs, there were the usual cars and vans of mountain climbers who were here every day during the summer, regardless of the weather. Among the cognoscenti, the eastern cliff facade of Mount Lenape was the premier mountain climbing region on the east coast—offering varying degrees of challenging ascents to scrape and hang off rocks until you stood on top of them. Some of the vans were open and exposed their disheveled interiors—smelly mélanges of sturdy-looking camping gear, sleeping bags, old towels, boots, bedclothes, flannel shirts—hidden from the outside world by burlap curtains on the windows. The valley overlook Maxine and I had visited that fateful night at Fallen Rock glided by—glimpsing neat verdant patterns of rural farmland below.

Paulding coughed as he lit a cigarette and jettisoned a plume of smoke between Kaplan and me. I had to admit, he was certainly a welcome diversion from having to make the hour-long drive with Kaplan alone. But he seemed a sad man, like a city peddler I had once seen in the city, who sold things from a little demonstration table rigged on the back of a bicycle.

"Nathan, what does being a socialist mean?" I asked, recalling some of the more outrageous letters he had written and that had always ended with: "Member of the Socialist Labor Party . . . and proud of it!"

"When a man says he's a socialist," he sat back contentedly, "it means that his aim is to abolish capitalism and institute a socialist society. By a socialist society, we of the Socialist Labor Party mean a system of society wherein the means of life and the industries of the country will belong collectively to all the people and wherein we shall have production for use. The way present-day society is instituted, the means of life are owned by a tiny minority."

"Would there be any profit then?"

"Under socialism we'll have production for use."

"So, there wouldn't be any profit?"

"No."

"Then how would a man better himself or his family?"

"We'll all be part owners of industry, classes will be abolished. By virtue of the fact that we will have an industrial democracy, no man will be compelled to be a slave for another man. What is the incentive today? If a man works in a factory and he has a wife and kids to support, his very life, the very welfare of that family depends on his having a job. All of a sudden, he comes into the plant one day and he's told his job's been abolished. They have a machine to take his place. Today, under capitalism, we do not have economic security. Under socialism, when the new machine is introduced, instead of taking the bread out of a workingman's mouth, we'll reduce the hours of labor. . . ."

Kaplan interrupted like an annoyed Nazi. "Yavol, but vat vould be dee *incentive* for und man to vork under dis socialism?"

"By virtue of the fact that we will all be part owners of industry and nobody will be exploited."

"You mean to tell me," I said, somehow wanting to prove him wrong, "that the incentive under socialism would be to own one/nineteenth of a tractor or an eighth of a breeding bull?"

"It's estimated today that out of every dollar's worth of wealth a workingman produces, he gets back twenty, twenty-five cents. And here's another thing: according to a survey conducted by the University of Michigan, listen to this, only five percent of the American population when they get to be sixty-five are well off. Only five percent! People that have slaved and worked a lifetime to survive, to keep the family going. And what the heck do they got to show at the end of the long road?"

"And that wouldn't happen under socialism?"

"No, absolutely not. The younger generation would take care of the next generation—each generation will take care of the older generation. You won't have such a thing as poverty in the midst of plenty. How can any rational person defend the present system of society? We're living in the richest country in the world and what do we see—poverty in the midst of plenty!"

Now the mountain road was lined strikingly with white birch trees and straight pines whose branches all sagged down like Chinamen's hats. The dirt path that led to Fallen Rock came into view. Nondescript in the daytime—potholed and ill kempt—it was nothing like the tunneled mystery at night. Once more, the montage of recent events came tumbling back—my hair-trigger memory operating like a thermostat, automatically replaying the past. I tried to shut out the images and concentrate from memory how the road and trees would look up ahead.

Kaplan screwed on the radio and there was an audible click in the rear speaker behind Paulding's head. I figured him somewhere around sixty, somehow getting hooked on socialism and spending his youth (and life) arguing with people—a good-natured, local pest whose name brought laughter to those who knew it. A safe and harmless fool, he was content to bellow at the world in political clichés and worn-out union slogans. I wondered if he truly thought he would ever see the world he carried around in his head.

"Do you think you'll ever see the change, Nathan?" I asked.

The bald man cleared his throat, as though he had encountered this question many times before. "Yes, I expect to see socialism."

"Really?"

"Oh, yes. I believe that we're gonna see a tremendous change in this country in the not too far distant future—because things aren't getting any better."

"Pithy, I say, old man," Kaplan lauded, this time a foghorn Englishman.

"And we believe it can be accomplished peacefully. It's gotta be two-fold, political and economic, see. On the political field, we have the Socialist Labor Party. We have the right to cast our ballot in this country. On the other hand, the ballot without the economic might of the working class is worthless. The working class has got to be organized on the economic field into revolutionary industrial unions for the purpose of taking, holding, and operating the industries of the country. To back up the ballot. And then when that's done, we won't need any politicians, we won't need any bureaucrats, we won't need any political parties, including the Socialist

Labor Party. We'll have the Socialist Commonwealth. . . .
And we have a plan."

"Who's gonna do the planning?" Kaplan asked
and gestured across the road. "Great waterfall, hah."

A small two-tiered ledge of water cascaded very
close to the side of the road.

"The Socialist Brotherhood Union."

"Jesus, it's hard to keep all these socialist outfits
straight," Kaplan laughed.

"So, won't that be a ruling body?" I asked.

"Right, and the rank and file will be the actual
rulers, because if a man is elected to the Socialist
Congress, it will be considered a high honor. And if he
thinks that, you know, it goes to his head . . . he'll be
recalled, see?"

"Nathan Paulding, you are being recalled!" said
the Nazi steering the car.

"See, in the old days there wasn't any way of
accomplishing the revolution peacefully. It had to be done
forcefully, through violence. But Karl Marx . . ."

"Ah, yes, Karl Marx," Kaplan boomed like a
happy Fascist. "Of course, my friends and I always called
him Skip. Yessirree, Skip Marx. Helluva dancer."

". . . Karl Marx did come out with a statement to
the effect that in countries that are well-developed . . ."

I pictured a globe with each country sporting
different sized breasts—the degree of buxomness
dependent upon each nation's GNP.

". . . industrially such as the United States, Great
Britain, France, the revolution can be accomplished in a
peaceful manner."

I could tell Kaplan was thinking. He had been a
clever history student and had the facility to gather and
remember historical information he always liked to
regurgitate in class. "What about things like welfare,

public housing, the model cities program? Those are socialist oriented, aren't they?"

"No!" Paulding said emphatically and punched the back of the front seat.

I laughed and looked over at Kaplan. He looked betrayed. Some tweedy, elbow-patched professor probably had said that one day, and it obviously had made an impression on Kaplan.

"Under capitalism . . . you can't have socialism under capitalism. Public housing isn't socialism. Socialized medicine isn't socialism."

"Why?" Kaplan had once told me that whenever in a quandary in college classes always invoke one of the five W's or the H. "How?"

"It's all reforms designed to placate the people—to try to keep them content with their lot under this outrageous system of society. What we are aiming at is the fundamental and internal change—a complete brand new system of society."

"So, what country *does* have socialism?" Kaplan banged the steering wheel on "does."

"There isn't any country in the world today that has real socialism—that has socialism as advocated by the Socialist Labor Party. And we mean the real thing."

"Then how do you tell the difference between reform and socialism?"

"You can't build socialism through piecemeal methods. When a woman gives birth to a baby, one leg doesn't come out today, an arm tomorrow, and a head the following day, and so on and so forth. It comes out as a brand new organism, right. There's a new human being. The same thing with a different system of society. In a country wherein you have industry, you don't go about building socialism through piecemeal methods. This is it . . . and the whole thing where we differ fundamentally with other so-called outfits that claim to be socialist is in the fact that all these parties are out to gain political power and stay in power. And you know what that breeds: it breeds a new ruling class. They have classes in Russia. So, what the heck. We are aiming at the real thing. We don't want to have any regimentation."

He went on: The concept of private property would not be abolished, and one's private property was determined by the amount of labor completed. Hence, a man's buying power was directly proportional to his work output. Money would not be used, and workers would be paid in labor vouchers. Products would be better under socialism because each person would be a part owner of industry. Who would be paid more for their labor—a research scientist or a garbage collector? It seemed that people who worked harder mentally and had trained a longer time would be paid the same but work fewer hours. According to Nathan Paulding, present-day society was not conducive to bringing out the best in man. But socialism would create more leisure time, and a man could earn the equivalent of $50,000/year by working four hours a day, four days a week. . . .

We were all very stoned.

Why socialism in Pelhamville, New York, the end of the world?

"A meningitis epidemic took the life of my father, and we moved up here to get away. As far as I'm concerned, it's the best part of the country to live in. I like to live in a climate wherein you have a change of seasons. Under capitalism my ambition is, when it comes to the bad winter months, to be able to stay home." Laughter. "Devote more time to the cause. Although my wife raises hell with me. Says I devote too much time to the party. Then there's the problem, you know, of a growing family. You have to have communication. Yesterday my boy wanted to get a learner's permit. So I took the day off and I drove over to Kingsbridge. So, you know, you have to keep the lines open. They see more of the mother than they do of the father. How can that be?" Laughter. "You know, I'll tell ya', it's the hardest thing in the world, you'll find out. Are you married? You have children?"

"No."

"No."

"Wait." Laughter. "The hardest thing in the world is to be a successful parent—'cause you never know what's going through their minds. You never know. As I say, they see more of the mother than they do of the father. When I get up, they're still sleeping, see. So they see more of the mother than of the father—then who's going to influence them. Then the fact that the father sleeps with the mother. You know, until they understand, there's resentment. I remember my own experience. I resented the fact that my father was sleeping with my mother." Laughter.

Kaplan turned to me and whispered, "The father fucks the mother and the kids are fucked for good."

". . . But the idea is to keep the lines of communication because when I grew up there was no thing as—who the hell heard of the atomic bomb? This generation, you know, don't think it doesn't bother them. It certainly does. There's much more, way ahead of my generation as far as they have TV. You know, everything happens they're right with it. I was raised on a farm— went to a one-room schoolhouse."

Sliding down off the mountain early in the morning, we passed spindly, bleak towns, fields, and farms between long stretches of scrub scenery. As we approached Pelhamville, the tasteless patches became pockmarked with factories, small corporate satellites, an electric plant, a Jack in the Box, country gas stations, even a gothic-looking prison—all of it peopled with migrant apple pickers, clandestine pockets of Ku Klux Klan, and everyday, rotting, gap-toothed, prejudiced, god-fearing, vengeful, low-horizoned, dirty Republicans. . . . This side of the mountain was another world.

"You can let me off at the next right there by the light. You see, by the bank?" Paulding pulled himself up between us again. "I want to thank you, fellas. It's been nice talking to you. Hell, I'll probably see you around Old Ford. I'm there a lot distributing leaflets. Lots of Lefties at the college, you know, not to mention budding, impressionable students—tomorrow's socialists! Ha-ha. Yessirree. And thanks for the turn-on, too."

"Our pleasure, Nate," Kaplan said.

"Nice to meet you," I said and meant it.

We all shook hands formally.

"And, Nathan," I said.

He turned and adjusted his backpack on his thin shoulders.

"Good luck to you."

"Thanks, friend. You, too."

"Maybe you should run for president someday," Kaplan joked and nudged my ribs.

"I already have. . . . Last year I got 52,588 votes in thirteen states. My slogan was: 'unless we abolish the capitalist system, it's going to abolish the human race!'"

"An endearing sentiment," I said.

"Yessirree! How do you kids say it, 'I tell it like it is.'"

We all looked at each other, understanding, and the old socialist winked and sauntered away, whistling.

Twenty-four years later, I would read of Nathan Paulding's death. His obituary spoke of his lifelong political activism, his prolific letter writing, his brief jailing for draft resistance during World War II, his run for president, five subsequent runs for mayor of Pelhamville, and finally being expelled from the Socialist Labor Party in 1984.

10

The Echo Acres Hotel loomed up like a maroon candy land—seemingly made out of the same sugar-frosted marzipan as cheap Easter bunnies. Once off the main drag and onto the hotel grounds, the roadway metamorphosed into a graveled tree that branched off in different directions, one bough semi-circling up to the main entrance and others webbing into tributaries that led to parking lots and various outbuildings beyond.

"We'll go around to the kitchen," Kaplan said, as he nodded agreeably to the hotel attendant directing Saturday arrivals. They seemed to know each other. "We're supposed to meet Arnie. He was going to speak to the owners, the Shindlers, about us again."

"You mean this whole thing isn't set up yet?" I hated the feeling of crashing a place unexpectedly. This half-baked, awkward pushiness always seemed to happen with Kaplan.

"Don't worry. It's set, it's set. . . . He's just confirming things. Relax."

We angled sloppily into the delivery bay behind the kitchen, which immediately brought the stench of rotting food. The cement loading dock was stained from years of spills. A big metal garbage container was patrolled by a mistral of flies. Out from behind all the cans, pails, mops, and stacked boxes came Arnie.

Arnie was a bullet-shaped, 36-year-old mound of suet that strained at all the stays, ties, and ports of enclosure in his clothes. His hair was a greasy divot parted low on one side, a broken rag of which slinked down over an eye and rested on the bridge of his nose. Our ambassador, I thought dismally.

Kaplan remained cheerful. "Arnie, my man, good to see you. Lost some weight?" he laughed and patted the jiggly fat barely constrained by a stretched Echo Acres Hotel polo shirt. "Arnie, this is my friend Dalton Hawkes I told you about."

"Shit," Arnie tossed his head to knock back the hank of hair from his face and clicked his tongue. "Jesus, his hair's too long. I told you, no hippies. The Shindlers don't like hippies. Jesus—leave it to you," he whined.

"Whaddiya mean, 'hippie?'" Kaplan said, irritated momentarily. Then resuming his bonhomie, "What's a hippie anyway, Arnie? Hippies wished they looked as good as Hawkes."

"Fuck this," I said flatly. "I'm out of here."

"Wait, wait! . . . Arnie, stop with this hippie bullshit. Don't worry. Everything's gonna be fine."

"Ah," Arnie wheezed and waddled towards the kitchen's shiny double metal doors. "I don't care anymore. Who gives a fuck? . . . But don't blame me if ole lady Shindler don't like 'im."

"She'll love him."

Arnie's shifting bulk stopped suddenly and swung around. I pictured an invisible fleet of tugboats struggling to keep him from bursting and becoming a puddle of guts on the dirty cement.

"You're in the bimmie shacks," he said and snickered.

"The bimmie shacks! Ah, c'mon, man. You gotta be kidding."

"That's all there is right now." He shouldered against the doors. "After dinner I'll see about getting you into the old main house."

"Now you're talking. Thanks, Arnie." Kaplan jerked his head towards the car. "Man, if we get to stay in the main house, we got it made," he whispered. "Fantastic. We're going to have some fun tonight."

"Why's that?"

"Because that's where all the chicks stay, man—fresh, nubile, steamin' an' creamin'—jus' waitin' for the night games to begin."

"And what's with all that hippie crap? He pisses me off—fat piece of shit."

"Oh, that's just Arnie. Don't worry."

"And will you stop saying 'don't worry.' What the hell is a bimmie shack?"

"Shit, don't you know?" Kaplan laughed, rubbing his hands together as though this were an adventure. "That's where all the jungle bunnies stay, man! God, we'll probably get stabbed or something."

"Great."

"It's fun. You'll love it." Another cackle.

Out beyond the parking lots was a pair of weather-beaten white clapboard cottages that made 42 Calypso look like Tara in comparison. The stoop of our bimmie shack was a half-flattened oil drum lying on its side, wedged in among cement chunks that once were the steps.

"Charming," I remarked, catapulting from the ground to the oil drum and pushing in a rickety door rattling with a broken glass pane. Pieces of the window lay in shards on the floor of the entryway—and ground and pulverized beneath our feet.

I pictured an angry black man slamming the door in a drunken rage—smirking and smiling with large, yellow horse teeth—happy to hear the shattering glass and stalking off drunk into the night.

Immediately we were confronted by a crooked set of stairs worn in the middle like old piano keys. At the top of the stairwell, a window with a water stained roller shade levitated out and slapped back lazily against the sill. The house seemed deserted. I trailed Kaplan up the stairs and into an empty room with two surprisingly serviceable beds.

"Home sweet home," he smiled, trying to make the best of the situation. He seemed at ease in this place—as if he had been here before.

I mumbled assent and started laying out my black chinos, thin black tie, and a narrow-collared white shirt—my hotel uniform—and fell backwards across the bed.

"Let's get dressed and go down and meet the Shindlers," Kaplan said.

"Meet the enemy head on, is that it?" I said rubbing my eyes in frustration. "The best hippie defense is a good hippie offense, is that it."

"You bet your ass."

There were voices downstairs. Men speaking in that unmistakable lilt, which at a distance sounded like lazy patterns of long vowel sounds—a's, e's, i's, o's, and u's undulating along the stairs. Their feet scraped through the glass and a door slammed.

We dressed in our shiny, worn, out-of-date pants and frayed dress shirts that miraculously would appear fresh and presentable in the muted lights and hubbub of the dining room. Clomping back down the stairs, there was the acrid smell of liquor in the air.

Mrs. Shindler loved me.

"You and I both know you're not Jewish," she said imperiously, "but you're cute. Long hair on you looks good. I don't usually let my boys wear it, but on you, it's fine." She was a meaty woman with conspicuously displayed breasts and a sensuous face that read of experience and a let's-cut-the-shit-and-get-down-to-business mentality. She turned me on in a curious way.

As she talked and gave direction to the afternoon hours, my eyes sank and watched her breasts wobble slightly on top of her full fold of stomach. When I returned to her eyes, I saw her watching me. Acknowledging my interest with a smile, she continued with her instructions and an unspoken—*the answer ain't down there, boychick, but you'd be interesting just the same.*

Wheeling abruptly as though she had lost interest, we followed her towards the maître d's station. In the eddy of his wife's wide wake, Mr. Shindler trailed hesitantly and, despite his great height, remained a nonentity. His job was to appear a few steps behind her and offer meek entreaties—"Yes, Elaine. No, Elaine"—delivered in a watery voice born of respiratory kvetches and years of belittling and put-downs.

The maître d'hôtel turned out to be the maître sot—revealed by a pitted, spidery-veined, bulbous red nose. His domain was that ambiguous terrain just inside the orange foam dining room where he manned a narrow stand complete with phone and reading light. Quickly, Mrs. Shindler imparted her demands and, looking directly at me, swung her breasts and rear-end away—direct signals for her husband to pad after her.

"Ah, *oui, certainement, Madame,*" the maître d' said with a crisp flourish and beckoned to Kaplan. They talked softly. I was pointed out. Dismissing us with a flick of his hand, he put on a pair of reading glasses and busied himself with a guest list—making quick directives and gestures to waiters clanging silverware at nearby tables.

"Look, they only need one for lunch," Kaplan reported. He did not seem particularly upset. "We'll have our own station tonight. They want you to park cars and carry bags for the arrivals."

I assented, relieved—frankly a bit wary of the dining room and its myriad responsibilities—eager to get outside in the fresh air, away from all the cartoon characters.

My interim duties were simple: stand by the greeting attendant as the cars pulled up, wait until he nodded, trot over enthusiastically, park the car, then carry the luggage to the guests' rooms before the guests arrived. It was important that guests never have to wait for their bags. There could be no wasted time. Time was money. *Hurry! Faster!*

There were two of us and together we worked out a system of humping bags and parking cars—so there was always one of us to receive the nod. I was told it was more crowded than usual, and we spent the next two and a half hours bearing other men's burdens for a price. In the process, I earned a dollar for every car parked, a dollar for lugging suitcases, and a dollar for delivering messages. Everything was a dollar. To my surprise, several women came on to me in very direct ways, and I was lip pursed, ass-patted, tit-shaken, and liddy-eyed for most of the afternoon. By three-thirty, a big clump of singles bulged embarrassingly in my front pants pocket—$97. I moved a handful of the bills to a back pocket and kept checking that it was buttoned. Afterwards, I met Kaplan in the lobby and showed him the bulges, amazed at how easy it was to make money—a true sinecure.

Kaplan's reaction was avuncular, "Stick with me, kid."

Dinner was packs of carnivores—eight, ten, twelve to a table—with bad attitudes and pointy incisors anxious to devour anything put in front of them. Secret flatulence floated through the air mixing with expensive perfumes, after shave colognes, and light dinner music. Under the subdued recessed lighting, the burnt orange carpeting blotched with old coffee spills and ancient food accidents appeared fresh and new. Overweight Jewish women sashayed about in rustles of crepe and satin. Their suited escorts grinned and smoked fat Havanas or unfiltered cigarettes—telling off-color jokes and discussing windfall business deals. Everyone tried to act important by demanding his or her slightest whim be acted upon immediately and each wanting his meal prepared in a specific manner. Thus, under the strength of imperious expectations, they all seemed satisfied when everything was served relatively the same.

Kaplan used me shamelessly—to retrieve extra forks, return spotted glasses, steal other waiter's orders. On several occasions I was forced to deal with the cranky immigrant chef whose dictates for speed and accuracy had to be adhered to instantaneously or you would be gestured away scornfully to the back of the line of waiters—until you were dead sure what you wanted and did not waste his time. Eating and serving in a hotel dining room was a delicate balance whose inertia could not be reversed or diverted. Once the machinery was set into motion, it became a doomsday device that had to run its course— through coffee, dessert, and clean up.

Then, too, the job was fraught with dangers: Inadvertently a dollop of pickled beets had slid off one of the plates on my serving tray and sullied a Long Island woman's silver fox cape. Praise be to Allah the merciful, it went undetected. A matronly woman asked me to adjust a rear, half-mast zipper, and I jerked it off its track on the first pull. In the ensuing horror, the maître d' was called over to mediate and in seconds had do-si-doed the entire matter away by assuring Madame that a couturière-in-residence would revitalize the garment without a trace. There were beautiful daughters back in Great Neck and New Hyde Park, "who would love to meet a college graduate like yourself;" pointy elbows to the groin accompanied by a wink; poorly capped teeth with succotash caught in the crevasses; promises to buy me drinks at the night club; nebulous golf arrangements; eyes that spoke of trysts . . . icy glances . . . ripped stockings . . . fallen spouses hoisted to vertical. . . .

Then the dining room was empty, waiting to be cleaned and reassembled for the next meal. It was a dull, repetitive time, whose tedium spoke for itself—until the last smoke ascended and two waitresses emerged from the children's tables hidden in the room's hinterland. One was tall, lithe, oriental; the other short, fleshy, built for pleasure, and both abundantly mascaraed to conceal the dark eye rings of lost nights in similar hotels.

"Some of the local talent," Kaplan chuckled. "Monica's the zipperhead. Could be nice if she grew a decent pair of tits and lost some of the backwater edge. . . . Beeze, the one with the zeppelins, very nice," he said flicking his tongue out lasciviously. "The kind of girl you'd bring home to mother, if only she'd pick out the pubies from her teeth first. . . . We can do better."

The nightclub was an extension of the same tackiness as the rest of the hotel—only done more formally in gold-flecked lapis lazuli foam. The audience sat in ascending tiers from the stage to the bar in the rear, which ran the entire arc of the audience and overlooked everything. Kaplan and I had decided to catch the last show at one o'clock when the stripper came on. We had been offered to work the lobby but had refused politely. This was cocktail waitress country.

We went to the bar, ordered daiquiris, sought out barstools along the narrow ledge overlook, and began pointing out couples we had served at dinner. Interestingly, now a new game was required from that of dinner, and heretofore nondescript bald men and their lumpy spouses suddenly had found their element and their middle-class sophistication rose to the surface like tiles in a fortune-telling eight ball—teasing, joking, gesturing, smoking, drinking in open-mouthed laughter and over-the-top comradery—seemingly, all newfound movement and complexity in their lives. It was an after hour's febrile jungle. Ladies and gentlemen only . . . please.

Finally, the MC walked out on stage to disinterested applause. "Now's the time you've all been waiting for. The time that'll get you thinking about how it's going to be back in the room tonight." He brought his mouth close to the microphone so his voice sounded deep and husky. "It's Saturday night. You're in a strange hotel room, the kids're back home having pot parties, and you're about to see someone who can perhaps give you ladies some ideas in case Milton starts nodding off too soon. . . ." He paused for laughter, which came feebly.

"C'mon, bring her out already," two men called from the front tier.

"Oh, listen to these two—can't wait. No wonder you don't have dates. What, you got so worked up, you left the wives back in the room?"

Everyone laughed, including the two men.

The MC paused for drama. "And, now, ladies and gentlemen, children of *all* ages—it's Showtime! . . . Straight from the Playboy Room in Monticello, New York, ten gallons of pure heaven! A lady with the eighth and ninth wonders of the world, and someone, believe me, you will never forget—Miss Cyclone Stevens!"

A rap of a snare drum and all of Echo Acres shook. Outside thunderous rain exploded, its rap of thunder detonating exactly in harmony with the drum. The lights dimmed and a red spotlight followed a small woman with an unbelievably proportioned body stealthily advancing onto center stage—writhing, dancing, shaking her shoulders, positioning her hips, and thrusting her ass in perfect time to the piano, bass, and drum trio that filled a second spotlight, this one blue, at the rear of the stage. Instantly, it became abundantly clear why the introduction, "ten gallons of pure heaven" applied, as Miss Cyclone Stevens was wearing a huge ten-gallon hat, the only variation being that it was attached to her breasts—sideways. It was amazing. And the way it bounced and slashed and wheeled to her movements, just like a real saddle bronc's—it was a minor miracle it stayed on at all. With this came the second consideration in everyone's mind—what wonders could possibly be keeping a dented oblong spheroid on a concavo-convex disc in place on such a slip of a thing.

Kaplan nudged me and raised his eyebrows. His lips were glistening from trying to coax the last of a daiquiri from the ice in his glass. "Either she's got elephantiasis or that hat's suctioned on, man. . . . Want another drink?"

"Sure."

"Good. You buy. Spend some of that bulge money, so it doesn't look like you have a permanent hard-on."

"I do have a hard-on."

Kaplan roared in laughter and summoned a cocktail waitress.

Meanwhile, Cyclone Stevens was making grand sweeps and turns, getting the feel of the stage, mentally noting those places where she would perform the more critical parts of her act. She felt the warmth of the room and how it pulsated back to the stage. It was a good feeling to have the space to dance—compared to some of the places she had played recently: a garish amusement center crammed with pinball machines, bowling contraptions, and rude college kids; the Playboy Room, which was owned by a bookie and done completely in Naugahyde. In both places she had danced on a tiny island behind the bartender, where people sat close around her—ogling, drinking, and muttering obscene suggestions. . . . At least this was a legitimate stage. People had dressed up to see her. She wound the good feeling around her, as she changed tempo, arched her back, and swayed her backside rhythmically—about to set it free as she paused coquettishly in a deliberate silent film gesture and prepared to unzip her tight capris.

She had built-in timing—drawing out each movement until it was saturated perfectly with anticipation, forcing everyone to wait eagerly for what would happen next. A few of the men in the audience were leaning out of their chair as though they were ready to bound up on stage at the slightest grind or pucker of invitation. In her enthusiasm, Cyclone kicked off one of her spiked pumps into the darkness. A one-hand stab by a plumpish man caught the shoe just as it was about to impale the face of an elderly woman behind him. He held the shoe up triumphantly and smiled at the applause. He sat down and after his few seconds in the sun, he brought the high heel up to his nose.

"Did you see that guy just smell the shoe?" I said.

"No, where?"

"There."

"Jesus Christ. Probably'll whack off in it back in the room."

"It doesn't take long to revert back to mongrels."

"So what would you have done if you'd caught it? Contemplated it?"

"Are you kidding? I'm gunning for the cowboy hat."

We laughed and slapped fives.

The Cyclone wound around the entire coast of the audience, wreaking havoc and winning friends wherever she went. . . . When the ten-gallon hat was finally set free with much tease and panoply, there was an audible gasp from the audience and the incredible blockages were revealed in all their glory. "As Mauberley would have said, "She's probably just a pleasant young lady who found out she could earn a decent buck dancing around, showing everyone her giant tits!"

Each of the Cyclone's abnormalities had a tassel on the end that she could spin in tandem or independently of each other. Accompanied by torrid drum riffs, after each demonstration of technical expertise and quantum mechanics, she received spirited ovations.

Now winding her way among the audience itself—whirling, curving, cycloning . . . always keeping the tassels spinning like twin turboprops—she approached the man with the shoe. Cringing slightly, I realized what was about to happen. For a moment, I hoped that perhaps it would not, but I knew deep down it was wishful thinking. And as Cyclone Stevens stood there flatfooted, openly grinding in front of the man who had secretly smelled her shoe, it was just too much for him to bear. The dam broke, the center was breached, and he jumped up and snatched the tassels with a grand sweep of his hands and held them up triumphantly with the shoe— bouncing joyously and dancing to the applause.

11

Night washed over Echo Acres like swimming pools of pitch emptying overhead. Even a short distance away from the lights of the hotel, the world was in mourning with no stars and low-ceiling rainclouds that had relieved themselves and awaited replenishment from the west.

After the show, Kaplan and I had packed up our things at the bimmie shack and moved to our new lodgings in the old main house. Arnie had "come though" and gotten us a room with the rest of the staff on the third floor. In long forgotten years, this single building had been the entire hotel. Walking the two flights of worn carpeting and breathing in the dusky scent of times past, I was reminded of the Long Island mansion my grandmother had worked in as a maid for 50 years after emigrating from Norway. Both were remnants of a long forgotten world with echoes of untold guests, relatives, and strangers—all seeking respite from the maddening crowds.

Every door on the floor was closed, and Kaplan had to inquire at each to determine a vacancy: a chess match, a bed reader, and a jazz-charged room away, we found our lady—small, no windows, but again with comfortable-looking beds. We lay down and contemplated the flaking ceiling and the hectic day.

"So, what do you think about the gig?" Kaplan asked.

"Not bad."

"Hey, it's the fastest way I know to pick up a quick hundred or two, no questions asked, *and* no taxes."

I humphed agreement. "I have to admit. I think you're right. . . . So, what's on the agenda now—after feeding, pampering, and babysitting fifty and sixty year olds all day . . . not to mention, seeing the biggest tits in the world?"

"Now we enter the spiritual phase," Kaplan said sitting up, seemingly feeding on a new, unmined vein of energy. He fished through his small satchel and held up a partially filled plastic bag, as though it were the Ten Commandments. "Da-daaa! Lord Cannabis. Ruler of the universe. How do I love thee? Let me count the lays. . . . Accursed crutch and magic smoke. Elevator of the psyche. Oh, sap of hemp, down Mexico way."

I rolled off the bed and fell onto my knees, my face pretending confession. "Forgive me father of the hookah weed, for I have fooked. I said the word 'fook' a hundred and sixteen times since my last confession. I have not been to Fooque regularly. I think everyone is all fooked up."

Kaplan laughed through his nose. "Dere, dere, mah son a ma bitch. Say a Hail Mary full of grass. Then say it five times fast. Then do ten godfathers, four cartwheels, two turtledoves, and a jumping jack in a pear tree."

With that, Kaplan licked two pieces of rolling paper together, creased the new length along the bottom third, and began filling the trough with the contents of the bag.

"How much for the stuff?" I asked.

"Twenty-five an ounce. Want me to get you some?"

"Let me see what's back at Calypso."

"It's not super dope but it gets you off. Serviceable. Mellow. Puts you in a nice place. A good, safe shallow orbit."

"Hopefully, around Jupiter somewhere."

"You know, I always meant to ask you. What are you anyway?"

"What do you mean, what am I? Me man, earthling, human being, homo erectus. . . ."

"I already know you're a homo. I mean, what's your religion?"

"Why?"

His features scrunched together as he lit the joint. "Catholic, right?"

"I was told we were. But we never went to church or anything."

"So you don't believe in anything because mommy and daddy were hypocrites, is that it? Cut off your balls to spite your cock."

"What are you talking about? I'm supposed to believe some force said, 'I think I'll make me a world— here's a hippo, here's a tree, let there be light.' I just can't sign on to that whole spiritual, mystical, hocus-pocus, open sesame trip."

"Then where did it all begin?" Kaplan sucked in the words with the smoke.

"It didn't begin. . . . Who knows? Who cares? What does it matter?"

"But it does matter," Kaplan talked out smoke and passed the joint.

"Okay, there wasn't a beginning—it always was."

"How can you say that?"

"Because existence exists—always has, always will."

"I don't know, it seems like there should be something more."

"But that's the whole problem," I said. "That's ape-man shit. Something can't be explained or you're afraid, so what do you do? You invent something that explains it, lights up the unknown—a god, a totem, an angel, an enchanted mountain, take your pick. And to fill in all the cracks—it knows everything, it's everywhere, it's all-powerful, and it's much too profound for you to understand. It'll punish you if you're bad and reward you if you're good. . . . C'mon, man, it's ridiculous." The grass was unwinding me nicely. "If we have to worship anything, we should worship ourselves. Everything we have, everything we are, everything we'll ever be is because of us. Aren't you the most important thing in your life? If you don't feel that way, then you'll always be some simpering little hulk in the corner, always hoping desperately that things will be better—especially when you're dead. . . . Kind of pathetic, *n'est-ce pas?"*

"I guess. I see your point," Kaplan said, one eye squinted as he inhaled.

"I don't think so. You're a Jew. You can't help yourself."

We paused, both deciding to let the grass take hold. With no intrusions, it was a happy world.

"If you really need a god, then *I'm* God. I must be. I have to be. I . . . AM . . . God!" I stuck out my hand. "You may kiss my ring."

"And you may kiss my ass. . . . Okay, God, make Cyclone Stevens materialize right next to me, right now—without the cowboy hat."

There was a knock at the door and a twisting of the doorknob, which Kaplan had locked in his marijuana paranoia.

"Ooooh, ask and ye shall receive. I guess Cyclone heard the Lord's call," I whispered and pointed at the joint and the smoke.

"Who is it?" Kaplan asked, gesturing for me to put it in the ashtray.

"What do you mean, who is it?" came a female voice from the hallway.

Kaplan stuck the ashtray in a dresser drawer, and we waved our arms to fan the smoke away. Impossible—smoke did things at its own pace. He opened the door. It was Fran, his on and off girlfriend. As far as I knew, he wasn't expecting her. She was supposed to be working at a nearby hotel.

"From the smell of things," she began, "I seem to be missing the party."

"*Au contraire,* my little cabbage, still in progress, still in progress." He put his arm around her and locked the door with his free hand. "Can you really smell it from outside?"

"Can I smell it? I got wrecked just knocking."

"You're a sight for sore eyes."

"Hmm, I bet."

"No, I thought it was Mrs. Shindler. She's such a nosy bitch when she's pissed off."

"How do you know she's pissed off?" I said.

"She's always pissed off. It's in her DNA."

Fran unlocked the door. "Monica and Beeze are coming."

"Who?" Kaplan feigned innocence.

"Please. Monica and Beeze—the children's waitresses. Like you haven't noticed them."

"Oh, yeah, yeah, I know, I know."

They walked in casually. What a pair. Beeze: the physical essence of hamburgers and fast food, tough farm stock, wide-eyed, in your face—who had learned early on how to react to a man quickly and hungrily and to whom pleasure mattered more than substance or purpose. Monica: goddess of the west wind, sleek, Chinatown street gang girl wannabe, low affect and ultimately submissive—drawn to sex more as a bodily function than an emotional release. They were still wearing their dining room uniforms.

"Shit, I stepped in about twelve fuckin' puddles," Breeze said gruffly, looking down at her splattered white shoes.

"Oh, what a delicate way to put it," Kaplan said, removing the still-smoking ashtray from the dresser drawer. "You're just in time, ladies. Hawkes, close the door, please."

"Hello," Monica deadpanned.

"Christ, I could use a joint," Beeze said, running her hands like squeegees down her coily thick hair, forcing water onto the floor.

Monica sat down on the bed and crossed her legs as though for a job interview. Kaplan busied himself with the construction of a fresh joint while the old one circulated. What's going to happen now, I thought. Obviously, Fran broke up the happy quartet that Kaplan and I had half-anticipated. Of course, there was always the remote possibility of a *ménage* with Beeze and Monica, with me as the *trois*. What ancient pleasures did Monica know? Could she bind a man's genitals to prevent ejaculation and allow him to experience unheard of paroxysms of Mongoloid saturnalia? There was something intoxicating about her. She seemed no more than seventeen.

Beeze was wiping her shoes with the bedspread. "I have some booze in my room," she said. Was she already staking out her territory? Beeze, booze, boobs, I thought. "After we finish this we can go over there."

Nothing was said because we knew what would happen. There was the unspoken feeling that cleavage had already taken place: Kaplan would remain with Fran, and I would be tonight's jester for Beeze. Minutes later

Monica announced she was going back to their room. Goodnight.

Beeze patted me on the thigh and looked into my eyes. "C'mon, let's go over for that drink?"

"Sure," I tried to sound cheerful, even though I was very tired and very stoned. "I'll be there in a few minutes. Just want to wash up first—pry my eyes open."

Their room was at the end of the hall and was the same as ours except for two drooling windows. Fortunately, only a candle was burning on the night table between the beds. The overhead light in our room had been hurting my eyes. Monica was already in bed and, to my surprise, someone was under the covers with her. Even in the feeble light flickering on one side of his face, I could tell it was the MC. They sat up, reached for their drinks, and propped themselves against the headboard.

"How's it going, man," he said, grinned, and raised his glass.

"Hello," I said. Should I have said "man," too? Too late.

"C'mon, take a load off," Beeze said, slapping the bed beside her. "Let's catch up."

At first, the four of us talked—until the input of dialogue from Monica and the MC faded noticeably and soon the only communications came in extended sighs and rapid breathing. Even though their bed was only a few feet away, I pretended that I did not know what was going on and continued talking offhandedly to Beeze, who wore a bored expression and threw out fragments of speech like stiff left jabs: "getting' late," "got to get to work early," and "don't have all night." Time was at a premium again. Without warning, Beeze pounced off the bed, blew out the candle, and announced in a sultry voice, "Why don't I slip into something more comfortable, as they say."

I pictured her scratching herself in the darkness.

"Be my guest," I said and slid down the bed and stretched out luxuriously for the first time that night. I looked over at the other bed but could see nothing—still only rustling and breathing. I would have preferred Monica. At least there was still some mystery about her. Beeze came on like a dragoon.

After some noise and fumbling at the closet, a large weight depressed the other side of the bed, and Beeze's plump hand was on my hip—then radar guided to my crotch.

"There now," she said.

In the next few minutes something happened that had never happened to me before—I received the first physical sign that I was getting old—I could not perform on demand. Certainly age, creeping in its insidious death march, had caught up while I napped in youthful indolence—nipping out at me, showing that it was playing for keeps. It was like a big cat disemboweling its prey—gouging away at the soft underbelly with its powerful hind claws.

In any event, Beeze was not very moved either way. She took both my immediate and impending sexual extinction as just another happenstance, as though she might have to answer the doorbell. She stopped kissing me, which I did not protest because the symbolism of sticking her tongue into my mouth at the exact rhythms of her thrusting hips as she humped away, eluded me. Also, in the process, she had licked my entire face, and I estimated my chances were fifty-fifty that I would escape with nothing less than impetigo. The night before, brushing my teeth, I had noticed my gums were already bleeding.

Having abandoned her ingenious interpretations upon the soft impeachment, Beeze became involved with the problem at hand; namely, how to beat back the cycle of time and fill me up with fresh blood.

"There now," she said a few minutes later and crawled back up to kiss me. "That didn't take long, did it?"

Monica and the MC were giggling. There was a sharp knock at the door. It was Mrs. Shindler.

12

Two weeks later, I was sitting in the kitchen eating cereal a camper had left after spending two days at the apartment. I wasn't sure he had left the food as a token of gratitude for having let him crash, but judging by how little he seemed to care about anything, I guessed he simply forgot it when he felt the itch to move on and resume his summer wandering.

It was delicious. I tried to remember the last time I had had cereal. It must have been at the college dining hall, when I was still brimful of mother's admonishments to brush my teeth, eat three nutritious meals a day, and go to bed early—"You can't get in trouble sleeping . . . alone."

In the afterglow of finishing the cereal, I hunted for a cigarette, which I needed to make the meal a success. I loathed my weakness. I loathed cigarettes. I loathed the way I was dependent upon them, and how in my continuing daily battles with them I always lost, not to mention the coughing, chest pains, and greenish sputum—all of which were more frequent now. Even with the awareness of this, I went upstairs and took a few cigarettes from Davenant's Tareyton pack on the floor next to his bed. I returned downstairs to smoke in the same seat I had enjoyed the cereal. Here the afterglow was the strongest. I pulled out the folding metal chair very deliberately and sat down with a satisfied "Ahhh." Feet on top of the chipped enamel table, leaning back, a long stroke of a stick match against the underside of the table, I brought fire into the world and watched it flare up and cast away its harsh sulphur smoke. I welcomed the new day in peace. . . .

The moment was broken with the sound of a distraught woman running up the stairs. I anticipated her entrance a fraction of a second too soon, as she threw open the door a second later. It was Annie, our neighbor directly below us opposite Birdie, whom I had never said more than hello to.

"Oh, Dalton, could you please help me? My cat didn't come home last night, and I just found her out front. She'd dead! . . . Could you help me bury her? The ground's too hard for me to dig. . . . Please—the bugs are *eating* her!"

I brought the match deliberately to the Tareyton and, once lit, I slammed the chair down and followed her downstairs. There on the ground in front of the porch was the cat lying on its side as though it were sleeping. Bugs were clustered in its ear and crawling freely over its face. I half-expected it to get up, shake its head, and prance away. I touched where I thought the heart was and the body felt hard.

"Here, put her in this," Annie said. She was crying as she handed me a box with Official Lew Windsor Figure Skates printed on the side above a florid signature. Inside, pink tissue paper had been neatly arranged and folded into pleats like satin in a coffin. If she had been in such a hurry, I thought, when did she get the time to do this? I picked up the cat and placed it into the box. Clumps of dirt and grass and insects fell inside with it.

"Where do you want to bury her?"

"I started to dig over here," she said, pointing to a few scratches in the hard clay beneath a Rhododendron bush, the last living shrub adorning 42 Calypso's front yard.

"Is that where you want her?"

"Oh, I don't know. I'm not sure," she sounded troubled and looked forlornly at the ground. "What do you think?"

"Maybe there's somewhere better."

She wheeled and stalked towards the back of the house, where there was one small square of acceptable lawn left over after the backyard had been converted into a parking lot. A scraggily pine tree shaded the spunky scrap of green behind which sat my nine-year-old Valiant, unused since my graduation. I followed her carrying the box in front of me as though it were a cake for the queen.

"Here," I said, sounding certain and tapped the ground with my foot. "Let's put her here under the tree."

"Yes, that's better, that's good. . . . It's prettier here."

Unfortunately, I could not have chosen a worse spot. It seemed that this patch of ground had been the site of some old well or septic field long ago—hence the persistent green—and the deeper I dug, each shovelful unearthed whole or broken bricks and stones that had to be pried up or scooped out by hand. On a particularly difficult one Annie handed me a crowbar she had retrieved from her car. I could tell she wanted this done as quickly as possible.

Forty-five minutes later I threw the last spadeful of earth onto Lew Windsor and the cat, and Annie heaved a long sigh—nodding her head silently as if to say *amen*. Now she would mourn privately. I leaned on the shovel and looked at the grave, which had a noticeable depression. So many bricks and stones had been removed there had not been enough dirt left over to fill in the hole.

"Thank you, Dalton," she said and we walked slowly back to the front. She stopped on the porch, touched my arm, and kissed me quickly. "Thanks again. . . . Please come down sometime."

"Sure, Annie, I'd like that."

She went into her apartment and I knew we would never know each other.

No one else was home except Davenant, and he rarely awoke before noon. I decided to do some writing. The manuscript now stood at 121 pages, and without a concerted effort, was in no danger of rising. I always complained to myself that I just didn't have the time—although I always seemed to find enough daily rituals to take up the day. At one point I theorized I was destined to be a night writer—dripping candles, sleeping world, lonely inspirations—but that hadn't worked out either. In truth, I let myself be distracted too easily. There were always trips to the mountain, nighttime swimming parties, special drinking celebrations, trysts with Maxine (on the rare occasions she was in Old Ford), and doping to the point where I could barely stay awake—let alone be creative. And on those rare occasions I actually did find time to write, I was never able to push the manuscript forward more than a sentence or two at a time.

Then, too, there was the shame of finding it necessary to get high or masturbate before I worked. Drain or lose myself first, I rationalized—then coolly report things. To work on delicate, emotional scenes required the necessary skill to draw the reader along just right—without memories or sexual distractions—like Santiago and the marlin. Ultimately, even after forty days without a sentence, I knew grandeur was possible. It not only must be a great book but one that sells, too.

It was eleven-thirty when I put the pen and clipboard down and rubbed the strain of close work from my eyes. I stood up and arched my back, twisting against the stiffness, and walked into Mason's room. I scudded along his mattress and looked out the front window. I thought of my room where the only view was the peak and roof of the house next door. On rainy days I would watch how the raindrops hit the shingles, be seemingly absorbed, and then drip onto the next shingle below and so on like a rice paddy irrigation system—until the water fell into the gutter and down the noisy drainpipe back into the earth. From Mason's window there was a nice view of the other homes on the block and of the flats and the mountain beyond.

On the lawn across the street sat the retarded man and his mother. He sat hunched over grinning in the growing sun as though his dulled brain had ordered his body to relax every muscle completely. He always seemed engrossed in something. His mother sat patiently, still appearing very capable—though easily into her late sixties. He was pushing forty. I remembered her telling me how she was worried about dying before him. Would he still be happy when she was gone?

I watched two college girls pass by making their way down the hill into town. A thread of perspiration slid down, bumped aimlessly over my ribs, and was absorbed into my shirt—forecasting another hot day. Already my feet felt hot and swollen inside my boots.

"Christ, it's like Guam up there," Davenant's voice sounded above the slapping of his feet on the wooden stairs. He stopped in the doorway and cut a diagonal across the jamb. One hand hung limply and held a cigarette, whose trail of smoke went behind him up the stairs. "Jesus, do we have tsetses, too?" he said, nodding at the small dots and smears of blood on Mason's disheveled sheet and pillow.

"Jane used to sleep there."

Ray Mason's face had been scarred for life by a particularly malevolent case of acne—resulting in a mutilation of holes, slots, gouges, and pocked flesh of epic proportions. Once I had come upon him changing his shirt, revealing a cowl of peccant sores spread around his neck, down the planes of his shoulders, and across the squares of his chest—all seemingly in various stages of eruption and ooze—always manufacturing, always breeding, always plotting new destruction.

"Jane thought he was beautiful," I said.

Davenant's look was ambivalent, and he walked into the kitchen, sweeping a cloud of smoke behind him. "Flaubert said you shouldn't worry about pimples, it meant you were still young."

"Tell that to Ray," I said, following him to wash my hands and hold my wrists under cold running water—a trick my grandmother had taught me to cool down on hot days.

"What's there to eat?" Davenant's head was inside the dirty refrigerator.

"Nothing."

"That guy's cereal gone?"

"Yeah."

"Any milk left?"

"No."

"All right, let's go to plan B—reconnaissance," Davenant said reflexively and began searching the cabinets and drawers like a complete stranger—looking in places that anyone would have known contained mops and pots and kitchen cleansers. Finally, one cabinet held a small menagerie of cans and boxes. "Ah, I have a choice. What more can a man ask for in life? I got sauerkraut, breadcrumbs, dried prunes, and an open box of Chinese noodles. Weren't these here when we moved in?" And then reaching into the back of the shelf below, "Ah, looky here: poultry seasoning, elbow macaroni, and last but not least, canned botulism with no label," he announced and hoisted a badly bloated can.

"That's not a choice, it's a dilemma."

"I'm hip. You want some prunes and Chinese noodles?"

"I'll pass. I already had some cereal."

He laughed and sat down, prying a prune from the box. "If I can actually chew this thing, maybe I'll be able to take a decent shit. . . . Oh, before I forget, I think I have a way to make money for the rent."

"Already? What's today?"

"The twenty-first."

"You're kidding. The summer's flying by, man."

"Much too fast. Much too fast. . . . Well, at least we don't have to worry about the fall semester."

It came to me that I was no longer a student. "I wonder what I'll be doing in September."

"Who knows? Maybe you'll be looking for an agent."

"And you'll be England's Poet Laureate—and we'll all live happily ever after."

Davenant went to the counter and began fumbling with the box of macaroni. "How long do you have to let this cook? Is it the same as spaghetti?"

"Readith thy directions, Shakespeare. . . . So what's this money scheme?"

"A guy at the college wants his studio painted. Says he'll pay our rent. I figure you, me, and Mauberley could knock it off in two days."

"What about Mason?"

"He's too busy. Haven't you heard—he has a new lady friend. A Scandinavian. The skinniest chick I've ever seen."

"Jesus, he doesn't waste any time. . . . A bit unseemly, don't you think?"

"Life must go on, *mon ami*. When nature calls, who can refuse?"

"It's not exactly like taking a shit."

"When a guy hasn't gotten laid in a month, isn't it the same as constipation?"

"You do have a way with words." Deep down he was probably right.

"I think we both know Jane would have wanted it that way. Do you think she would've let any grass grow under her feet? . . . What's the point, really?"

After Davenant finished eating, we went to Gannon's, read the newspapers, and had a few drinks. One of the bartenders owed him money. We talked about sports and the upcoming rock festival that was gaining more and more attention in the media. We played a game of chess and walked back to Calypso, deciding we absolutely had to go to Europe next summer, no doubt about it. This time we shook hands on it.

"Shall we seal it with a kiss," Davenant joked.

"You wish."

He told me how he had gotten a brilliant idea for a "short children's book for adults," and if he worked on it hard enough, he could complete it by September. The only fly in the ointment was Tracy, his girlfriend, who was late with her period. It would just be his luck if she were pregnant—when he was trying to finish a book. But he had always been lucky on that score, he said, and tapped his knuckles on a passing tree to ensure a provident future. But Tracy was worried—she had never felt this way before. She wanted Davenant to arrange for a doctor, insisting it was his responsibility to make the appointment. Besides, she wasn't from around here and didn't know any doctors. When he had brought up the idea of an abortion, she wasn't sure how she felt about it. He had made an appointment for that afternoon. Back at the house, Birdie was tilted in a rocking chair with her feet up on the porch railing.

"Look at you," I said. "How acculturated you've become to the neighborhood—sitting out on the porch, watching the day go by, greetin' an' sayin' howdy to the good folk of Old Ford who might be moseyin' by. We've become such upstanding tenants. Nostromo would be proud."

"Welcome to the middle class, milady," Davenant said and laughed in his peculiar way—like the trill of a bird through his nose—and punctuated it with a little dance shuffle.

"What horseshit," Birdie said, her hands behind her head, each breast lying conspicuously on separate sides of her stomach and her toes pointing towards each other.

A breeze, the first of the day, rolled in behind us, up Birdie's green T-shirt, and ruffled her hair.

"About time. Where the hell did that come from?" she said. "If it would keep doing that, it wouldn't be so bad."

"Probably got lost coming over the mountain and smelled the Hudson," Davenant grinned. "Wanted to see kinfolk—river currents."

They looked at me. "Don't look at me. I'm just listening to you two morons. . . . Okay, it was a great wind—a provident zephyr from heaven. I bow to Aeolus, god of the winds."

"C'mon, it's hot as shit out here," Birdie said and thudded to the floor. "Let's go inside. I'll make some iced tea."

We followed her into her apartment, where it really was much more comfortable. She had three tiny fans going and the shades pulled down. Davenant and I sat in the living room. The furniture was nondescript. Birdie wasn't the type to worry about decor.

"Mauberley told me you had a monkey for a while," I called into the kitchen.

"Oh, Jesus, did we have a monkey." I could picture Birdie shaking her head. "After we got rid of it, it took me days before I could hear the phone ring. And the smell! Monkey shit's the worst. . . . And once the monkey was gone, I got rid of the ape whose dumbass idea it was to get it in the first place. I cleaned house—literally and figuratively."

"I'm gonna put a record on, okay?" Davenant asked, looking through a stack of albums.

"Sure."

I went into the kitchen and watched Birdie make the iced-tea. She used a powder that came in a white canister identified simply by a mauve colored oval label marked TEA in freehand. Adding a few scoops into a green plastic pitcher, she poured in cold water, added mint leaves, sliced lemons, stirred and poured the mixture into tall glasses with ice cubes—it was nectar. Calling Davenant into the kitchen, we all drank in appreciative silence to a slow, bluesy saxophone. Well into our second glass, Birdie went into the bedroom and returned with a small plastic bag of pot and a packet of rolling papers.

"Why don't you do the honors?" she said, tossing the raw materials onto the kitchen table.

I motioned to Davenant and continued sipping the tea. This obviously had been Nostromo's kitchen when he had lived here. It was big, airy, and cool. The cabinets were knotty pine but stained too shiny, hoping the wood grain would remain beautiful in a rustic way forever. On the windowsills and all available counter spaces on both sides of the sink were small clusters of pots with one skinny marijuana seedling in each.

"Layin' in this year's crop?" I asked.

"I was flooded out last year, Birdie said. "This year I'm waiting until after the rains. Hopefully, we've had the last of them for a while. I'll play it by ear. I have the perfect spot. I even rustled up a few bags of sheep manure. I could use some help."

"Sure," I said.

After smoking the joint, Birdie and Davenant talked about India: she, the practical matters of heat, insects, poverty, lack of sanitation; he, tranquility, chanting, spiritual awakening adventure. He lamented anew about not going anywhere yet this year. Said I copped out on him. I denied it. Birdie said she really had wanted to go with Zack, her old boyfriend, but he had made it clear he did not want her along. Since he was gone, she was angry, bored, and lonely. He even had the nerve to send her pictures from Kashmir.

We followed her into the bedroom and sat on opposite sides of the bed, as she sat between us and flipped through pictures Zack had sent, making interesting comments about experiences he'd recounted in his letters.

"I hope he gets the rot in Calcutta," she said.

It must have been Davenant who started it, because I simply have no memory of those first intimate moments—as suddenly both of us were kissing Birdie and touching her.

"There, there, don't feel bad. . . . We'll cheer you up," we said, soothing her, planting little pecks everywhere, and whispering what we could do to cheer her up.

"I'm warning you two," she said with her eyes closed, enjoying the attention. "You're going down a dangerous road . . . and pretty soon I'm gonna reach the point of no return."

We continued. . . . She threatened. . . . We continued. . . . Clothes were shed.

Soon Davenant and Birdie were making love, while I sat on the floor and played the guitar. At times I would try to coordinate the music with the progress of their lovemaking, but they were oblivious to my cleverness. There were no subtleties to Birdie's blandishments—tough, hard, fast-paced pelvic work, syncopated with lioness howls of pleasure. . . .

After they finished, Birdie beckoned wantonly to me, and I handed Davenant the guitar. He raised his eyebrows and smiled.

From the start, Birdie maintained her right to direct the operation. She dismissed my whispery teases to arouse her with a frown, "Dalton, I'm already warmed up and rarin' to go. I come fully assembled right out of the box. All you gotta do is flip the switch," and consumed me in the same way she had Davenant. In spite of her eagerness and aggressive appeal, Birdie's was a minor performance in comparison to Maxine or even Rachel. Nonetheless, it was satisfying and exciting—certainly a special memory of a hot summer day on Calypso Street I would always recall with a special smile.

The second time around, Davenant and I could have cared less about meaning, feelings, or purpose and let ourselves get caught up in the whirling dervish of Birdie—simply savoring the pleasure of two roommates selfishly making love to the downstairs' neighbor and confirming to the world that selfishness was a virtue.

At the end, the three of us stayed together in bed, eschewing the guitar and contriving ways for Birdie to accommodate Davenant and me at the same time. Only once did she speak— when I asked her how she felt, and she howled in delirium, "I feel like the Queen of Sheba! . . . I feel like the Queen of Sheba!

Finally, as the sun began to descend towards the mountain—having assuaged all loneliness, egos, and sexual fantasies—we herded into Birdie's glass lined shower, where she washed us, we washed her, and we all dried each other with lush huckaback towels. Afterwards she poured more iced-tea and we sat naked in the darkened living room, basking in the currents of the opposing fans.

"I feel like I should thank you," Birdie said, grabbing a pack of cigarettes off the coffee table and shaking one out. She looked sexy with her hair swept back to one side and the flame illuminating the side of her face. She squatted on the floor and shook her hair unconsciously and it fell straight on both sides. She was comfortable in her nakedness.

I think we could say the same thing," Davenant said, sounding as though he meant it. I knew we would talk about this later.

"I don't know, it's just one of those things that feels so good and right and that it should be like this all the time," she continued.

"Maybe that's why it felt so good—because it was so spontaneous and natural," I said.

"Maybe forbidden pleases are the sweetest." Davenant added.

"Maybe," Birdie said.

"Maybe," he said.

"Maybe," I said.

We laughed.

My attention fell to Davenant—sitting imperiously in a big stuffed chair with his legs crossed, one ankle resting on the knee of the other—the sparsely-haired chest, the denser forestry of the legs, and his stomach making three distinct folds above his insouciant-looking wilted flower.

"Hey, Hugh, put on the spindle and grab some of those old 45's. Let's dance! . . . Dalton, what's it called again?"

"*Le sacre du quarante-cinq!*"

"That's it!"

There was the sound of the needle scratching a record then a twisted sax and the voice of Fats Domino. Birdie jumped up in an earthquake of flesh and started dancing, inviting us to join her. I declined, saying I preferred to watch. Davenant needed no invitation and bounded in front of Birdie and cavorted lasciviously in his patented otherworldly gestures and gyrations. . . . After offerings from Bill Haley and the Comets, Little Richard, Elvis, Ray Charles, Chuck Berry, Bo Diddley, and forgotten groups with names ending in "Aires," "Satins," and "Tones," the coronation of the 45's ended with Birdie spinning in a whirlwind of carnality and flying hair.

"May I suggest another joint?" Davenant said out of breath, as though offering an after dinner Port.

"Yessirree," I said.

"Double yessirree!"

As I put on some contemplative smoking music, Davenant did the honors constructing a fresh joint, lighting it, and passing it to me. The end was wet. Brand new joint and he's slobbered it up already I thought—after one hit.

"Been hearing a lot about that festival," Birdie said.

"Yeah," Davenant said. "It was supposed to be over near Woodstock but the town turned it down because they didn't want to deal with a hundred thousand hippies. . . . Now *that* could be one happy family."

"That's what I heard, too—no drugs, no hippies, no tickie, no shirtie," Birdie added.

"I really want to go," I said. "It's our statement."

Davenant agreed. "Could be one helluva time— seminal, man—three days, great music, great drugs, great sex, great vibe . . . . Show the world what we're all about."

"I really think it's going to be something important," I continued. "There hasn't been anything like it. What a great idea—put the lid on the Sixties once and for all. Our coming out party."

"And what a way to do it," he went on. "An advertised bacchanalia! Hundreds of thousands of wild hippies, dancing like savages, smoking, screwing, freaking out—real hot shit! We'll blow their minds!"

Birdie coughed out some smoke. "Serve notice on the motherfuckers. Either you move over so we can sit at the table, or we're gonna throw you off the motherfuckin' train!"

More laughter.

"Hello, World, here I am—whether you like it or not." Davenant had a calm, glassy look in his eyes. "We're gonna change his-tor-eeee!"

"You just can't get away from symbols," Birdie said.

"Symbols, schmimbols," he blared. "We've been identified, classified, pacified, and decoded just like the rest of the rabble. We ain't symbols—we're the new edition, the next in line."

"But isn't that what everyone's gunning for— identity? Why settle for being just another number? Happiness *is* identity."

"Long live identity!"

Birdie sang Fifties-style, *"Hap-pi-ne-e-ess is i-denn-titty. . . ."*

We talked more, little things, but the pot was driving us inward, and soon the old music revival wasn't working anymore. We decided to call it a night or afternoon, whatever time it was—the world seemed dark behind the shades. Davenant and I retrieved our clothes and found secluded spots to get dressed, alone—strange after all we had just done together. . . .

Smoking a cigarette at Mason's window after dinner, I saw Tracy drive up, walk sternly towards the porch, and begin stomping up the stairs. I ran into the kitchen to warn Davenant, who was sitting at the table, mopping up the remains of a spaghetti dinner with someone's leftover bagel.

"Hurricane Tracy has arrived," I whispered, just as she burst through the door without knocking.

She took one look at Davenant and broke down. At first there were no sounds—like a child who had just started to cry but had not screamed yet.

"I'm pregnant!" she finally gasped and fell into a heap next to the cold spaghetti pot. Davenant continued mopping up his plate.

Not wanting any part of it, I said, "I have a game at Gannon's. Catch up with you later," and quickly left.

Happy to be out of the house, I started walking into town—just as Maxine's MG appeared beside me like an apparition. She beeped the horn. "Going my way, sailor?" I stepped inside without opening the door and took in the familiar leather/woman smell. Her tanned, sexy face smiled at me, and we were off. She was a breath of Provençal air.

"*Bonjour, mon ami.*"

"Hello, stranger."

"Did you miss me?" she laughed and the MG darted down Calypso Street, throwing me back against the leather seat.

"More than you'll ever know."

"That's what I want to hear—love and loyalty."

The MG chirped to a stop at the corner.

"Speaking of loyalty, am I the first person you've seen since you're back?"

"Let's be nice. It's unseemly to keep score."

"It's unseemly to be an afterthought."

"You *know* you've never been an afterthought."

"So, how was France? You have Gallic sun, sand, and surf written all over you."

"Oh, Dalton, it was glorious. . . . First, four days in Paris—I even looked up an old friend from my childhood days in Panama! Imagine! She took me places I never would have seen on my own. . . . Then I rented a car and drove down to Provençe. Just me and all these wonderful little towns—Ménerbes, Cavaillon, Roussillon, Gordes,

Bonnieux, Lourmarin, Avignon—each one more quaint and charming than the next. And the food and wine and cheeses! *Incroyable!* You must let me take you there."

"No argument here."

We smiled and enjoyed the rush of the night air. I took pleasure in watching her shifting and steering, feeling the acceleration of the MG along the narrow streets leading out of town. There was no hesitation in her manner and movements—pure Maxine.

After a drive up to the lookout, we came back to Old Ford and stopped at the Cacique for a nightcap. It was a slow night and, after hearing of Maxine's trip, Dutch regaled us with fantastic stories about Paris in the Twenties: the gardens, the bars, the street life, the famous people who were not famous yet—Hemingway, Joyce, Pound, Fitzgerald, Stein, Ford Madox Ford, Toklas, Picasso, Sylvia Beach—and so many others history had chosen to forget. He had known them all. It had been a happy time and there were more good memories than bad. The only thing he regretted was not having enough talent to be a first-rate sculptor.

"But I had a helluva time trying, I truly did." He paused as though conjuring a memory. "You know, Hemingway once said, 'Paris was a very old city and we were young and nothing was simple there, not even poverty, nor sudden money, nor the moonlight, nor right and wrong, nor the breathing of someone who lay beside you in the moonlight.'"

Dutch smiled and looked at Maxine and me. "You two remind me of the way we were back then. I thought we were a dying breed. . . . No, you two would have fit in just fine. You would have, you know—one of the beautiful young couples! . . . It's a glorious thing to be young and far away from home with talented people you truly admire and care about. . . . I consider myself a lucky man."

There were memories about boxing with Ezra Pound and going to the Luxembourg Museum and meeting Hemingway.

"Papa would stare at the Cezannes and say, 'Dutch, I'm learning how to write by looking at Mr. Cezanne's paintings.'"

He had visited Gertrude Stein's salon on the *rue de Fleurus* and had seen all the wonderful paintings—now masterpieces—done by her friends, most of whom were struggling and unknown. But they all knew they were gifted and believed sooner or later their persistence would win out and they would be recognized. That is, if something else did not get to them first—liquor, drugs, war, a destructive lover. . . . One had to be lucky and stay healthy or else all the talent in the world might not be enough.

Before we left, Dutch took our hands and looked at us very soberly and said, "A French writer once told me being young is a desperate business. It always has been. . . . Every generation has it despairs, but this life is worth its grief. . . . Find your light and the light in those you love."

That night I stayed at Maxine's. We talked long into the early morning hours—reveling in Dutch's stories and how we would have fit into Paris' glorious age of art and literature and American expatriates. Before falling asleep, I marveled at Maxine's hair swept across the pillow like a sable fan, almost blue in the bedroom's moonlight. Her clothes were tossed casually against the dressing table chair. I listened to the creaking sounds of the old stone house and its wide-beamed floors forever settling beneath the Hudson Valley's night sky—its summer stars calling down to two lovers with ancient light spoken long before time began.

I came back to the apartment house a little after nine the next morning. As far as 42 Calypso Street was concerned, it was still nighttime. The hall light was on in the dilapidated foyer, and as I flicked the switch, a moth darted up to the ceiling and stuck there. Not wanting to disturb anyone, I walked softly up the stairs and found the entrance door ajar. To my surprise, Davenant was standing at the kitchen window, smoking a cigarette in quick motions. Tracy was bent over the stove, stirring at something in a dented stainless steel pot. She wiped her forehead with the back of her arm. I stepped down a few steps out of the line of sight.

"I just want to get away for a while," he said. "Christ, I'm twenty-six and I haven't been anywhere. I want to see a few things—at least see the country before it turns into one big, goddamned parking lot."

"I'll show you some pictures," Tracy said, stirring harder.

"Give me a fucking break."

"And what about me while you're off seeing the world? You know and I know that if you leave, I'll probably never see you again."

"What's that supposed to mean?"

"Just what I said."

"That's crazy."

Davenant walked over and from behind put his arms around Tracy's waist. He hugged her for a long beat and made a grunting sound as he held her. She sighed and leaned her face against him. She turned and they kissed.

Tracy pulled away and looked down. "What's wrong with things the way they are? I'm happy. Aren't pregnant women supposed to be happy? Aren't you happy?"

"It's not that I'm not happy. There's nothing wrong. I know you're pregnant. I'm the father, remember?"

"Hugh, I really don't want to be here without you." She sniffed loudly. "And what about getting married? How long have we been putting off *that* talk? Don't you think it's about time, especially now? You promised, remember? . . . I want things settled in my life. I want to be happy. I want my baby to be happy. I want you to be happy."

"I haven't forgotten. . . . But, Trace, I know what it's like to be married, you don't. It's not the easiest thing in the world."

"What are you talking about? It's not like going to the moon."

"I just want some time to think and to sort my head out. I want to make sure what I'm feeling . . ."

I coughed and made a noise on the stairs, waited a moment, stamped my feet, then pushed through the door. They looked at me, startled. Tracy's face was wet and puffs of steam rose off the stove.

"Hey, cowboy, come on in. We were just talking about you," Davenant said and turned to Tracy. "How much longer 'til we eat, honey?"

She looked back at the stove. "Soon."

"Great. Set a plate for Dalton. I'm going down to the Post Office. I need to get some poems out today. We'll be right back," Davenant said, beckoning me with his hand.

"Okay, but hurry."

"Hello, Tracy."

"Hello, Dalton."

"Goodbye, Tracy."

She tried to smile. "Goodbye, Dalton."

Davenant put the cigarette between his lips and slapped his pockets. "Honey, do you have any money for stamps?"

"In my pocketbook."

"Where?"

"Probably upstairs."

I followed him upstairs and watched as he fumbled through Tracy's purse.

"She's starting in again with the marriage shit," he said in a low voice. "What the hell am I supposed to do?"

"Do you love her?"

"Shhhh! Sure, of course . . . I guess. But I don't want to be tied down again—not like last time. . . . What can I do—she's pregnant."

"It takes two."

"Shit, not you, too."

"Well, tell her then. Tell her how you really feel."

"I try but she makes it sound like she'll die if I leave. She goes on about how much love she has to give—to me, to the baby, to our lives together."

"Leave. She'll have to deal with it."

"There're a few flies in the ointment. I don't have a job. I don't have any prospects. I can't pay the bills. She pays for everything. . . . I need time until a book deal comes through."

"Will it?"

"I'm hoping. My agent's enthusiastic," Davenant said, emptying coins from a small change pouch into his palm and funneling them into his front pocket. "I just want to get away for a week or two without this sword of Damocles hanging over my head. Get things in perspective. Stop the world from spinning out of control. . . . Come with me."

"Jeez, not again."

When we left the house, it was pleasant outside, but I could tell from the sun and the sky that it was going to warm up quickly.

"Look, I feel for what you're going through, I really do. But I got my own issues with Maxine—playing her boy toy when the mood hits her."

"You gotta be kidding me—servicing an older, Class A piece of ass with no strings attached. Boo-hoo for you! When you're through crying, sign me up, *amigo*."

"Okay, okay, it's not quite the same, but Tracy's your business, your problem. I can't get mixed up in it. Besides, I need to stay put for the time being—figure out my own shit."

"Yeah, yeah."

I stopped and pulled his arm. "Hey, you forgot your poems."

He looked frazzled. "See what all this is doing to me. I don't know whether I'm coming or going. . . . The hell with it, I'll do it tomorrow. It's not the end of the world. I just had to get some fresh air. I may as well check and see if there's any mail."

The Old Ford Post Office was a small brick building that sat very close to the road. An American flag hung limply out front and two big blue mailboxes sat on each side of the door—one marked "Out-of-Town" and the other "Old Ford."

"Do you think I'm being a bastard?" Davenant asked, sounding contrite. He jingled Tracy's coins around in his pocket as he walked.

"No. Should I think you are?"

"I don't know. I just keep thinking that, in the end, our first duty is to ourselves."

"Ah, yes, seeking God and finding yourself."

He nodded and looked up at the sky—large, cloudless, western-style, stretched over the mountain.

"Hey, want to get in on a game tomorrow—speed chess? A few townies've been hanging around lately. Probably belong to the high school chess club or something. I think there's a few shekels to be made."

"Sure. Always like taking young buck money."

Davenant walked ahead of me into the Post Office, and I watched as he turned the tumbler on the large cubbyhole mailbox—a gift from Tracy to accommodate all the expected correspondence he would receive from his writing. It was empty.

13

That Sunday, now a month into summer, I finally hooked up a tiny black and white television I had rescued from a snooty neighbor's spring yard sale—put out close to the road away from the good stuff—with a brightly colored sign that read: "I'm free and I work!"

Since moving to Calypso, I had noticed an antenna clamped to the chimney above the roof—with a parched wire that dangled down the side of the house and slapped against the dirty clapboards when the wind blew. Snagging the wire and pulling it through the attic window, I had hooked it up—at the same time trying to boost reception on the TV's built-in antenna with aluminum foil, a bent metal hanger, and framing wire. The result was a picture that looked like an agitated, snowy paperweight, which no amount of fiddling in the world could reliably focus the fuzzy blobs and blips that danced across the screen. And just like my old television, the volume fluctuated involuntarily between a roaring din and near silence—all at the diabolical whim of a useless sound control. But it was a television, and I had placed it on top of a small telephone company cable spool that we had been using as a table on the roof of the front porch. In the end, serendipitously, none of this mattered, as we could always say that we were watching it live on TV—when man first walked on the moon.

In the lead up and preliminary talk—in which Mauberley, Davenant, and I marveled at the large gouts of high-minded nonsense of the commentators—we still could not help feeling that it was an extraordinary technical achievement. The sheer scientific know-how and engineering was staggering—especially in the short time since Jack Kennedy had announced it in 1961. Yet nagging in the back of our minds was the fact that this was an American monument to the world and we hoped they would not do something stupid—leave a discarded Coca-Cola bottle on the lunar surface, bury human waste under the pristine moon dust, or hit a golf ball into the rarefied atmosphere. We hoped NASA understood this—that it was a sacred mission—and represented man's initial inquiry onto the surface of another planetary body. To us, the Moon had to be approached like a fragile child. She had to be respected and understood, and we had to be worthy enough to accept her gift—as two American men inside a sophisticated alien toy were descending upon a virgin and cuckolding the Earth.

In truth, we were only half-listening and were more interested in talking about women. In particular, I was lamenting about Maxine and her Siren-like effect on me. How she made me feel hesitant and unsure how to approach her at times—like the Moon. How despite her assurances, she would look at me, then pull back and study my face—as though deciding whether I was worth her time and would keep her interested. How she possessed an intoxicating, heartbreaking allure of love and sexual promise that somehow seemed offered and withheld at the same time. How to explain her European sensitivities, whose unique sense of life made me defensive and wary—feeling she could walk out of my life forever without a care in the world, without shedding a tear.

We watched the blizzard, as Neil Armstrong began climbing down from the lunar module.

"*. . . at the foot of the ladder the left footpads are only depressed in the surface about one or two inches. . . .*

the surface appears to be very, very fine-grained. . . . It's almost like a powder. I'm going to step off the LEM now."

"Stepping into the abyss!" Mauberley bellowed.

"Let's see how tranquil this sea really is," Davenant laughed.

"That's one small step for man, one giant leap for mankind."

"Nice line," I said.

"With just enough portent and mystery for the occasion," Davenant added.

We watched the blip hop down. . . .

"How old is Maxine, anyway?" Mauberley asked.

"Mid-thirties. . . . You know, it's hard to tell with foreign women."

"Definitely true, my man. They definitely got that thing about 'em."

"Who cares how old she is? She's hot. What else do you need to know?" Davenant said.

"Yeah, but sometimes I feel . . . I don't know. . . . I just wonder how she sees me. I mean, I don't even know if I'm good-looking enough for her."

"Oh, Christ," Mauberley moaned and laughed his Wicked Witch of the West laugh. "Hey, pretty boy, don't expect me to sit here and tell you how good-lookin' you are, okay," and chortled again.

He was right. Deep down, I knew I was handsome in a Marlboro Man way, and I knew women found me interesting and attractive. How many times had I gone to a party and watched women suddenly go to the bathroom to freshen their make-up or shake out their ponytails at my arrival? I was used to the smiles of perky sales clerks and the chatty conversations of shop girls—catching them looking me over and whispering to each other as I walked by. I had never forgotten when my best friend's mother—returning home a little tipsy one night—had caught me staring at her and taken me aside. "I really shouldn't tell you this, Dalton . . . but you know you have it—I mean with women, right? . . . It just comes off you—that *it* factor or whatever it is—and we pick up on it like animals. I guess it's like some kind of natural attraction, a scent like catnip, and it stirs us all up and we can't resist. . . . One thing's for sure, you're never going to have trouble with the ladies," she laughed and kissed me on the lips. Thinking back on it now, how many times had lady friends, relatives, casual acquaintances, and even some women I had just met—kissed me on the lips as they greeted me or said goodbye?

"The surface is fine and powdery. . . . I go in only a fraction of an inch. . . . I can see the footprints of my boots and the treads in the fine, sandy particles. . . . There seems to be no difficulty in moving as we suspected. It's even perhaps easier than the simulations."

"I wish I had your problems," Davenant mused.

"No, I'm serious. Sometimes I look at myself and I think I look like a monster. Like everything is distorted and brutish. It's freaky."

"You're in love, sweetheart, face it," he said.

"But if that really bothers you, bunky," Mauberley offered, "I could always arrange for a good beat down— you know something Medieval—make that pretty face of yours look like you had a serious industrial accident."

We laughed.

"But sometimes I'm not even sure how to *act* with Maxine."

"Shit, man!" Davenant exploded. "What is this— the Calypso School for Young Gentlemen? You want us to tell you how to act with chicks? Jesus Christ, how old are you, anyway?"

I was tempted to say he did not always appear so mature and actualized with Tracy. Instead, I looked him in the eye with an intensity that implied I knew things he didn't think I knew.

"I guess we all can get into things with women that are hard to figure out."

Davenant looked at me quizzically, a half-smile trying to gauge my meaning.

"It's a very soft surface, but here and there where I plug with the contingency sampler collector, I run into a very hard surface . . . it appears to be cohesive material . . . It has a stark beauty all its own. It's much like the high desert of the United States. . . . It's very pretty out here."

"Why screw things up?" Mauberley said and crushed his cigarette into an ashtray. "You have a good thing going. . . . Besides, everyone knows she's in love with that painter dude anyway. Enjoy the ride while you can."

"Yeah, I know," I said. "Guess it's second fiddle city for me."

"But that's the point, man—no strings, no lies, no demands, no bullshit necessary. . . . You have the perfect setup: a beautiful woman you can screw with no guilt, no responsibility, and no head-trips. Stop your bitching."

"I guess you're right."

I was thinking I did not want it that way with Maxine. I wanted her to fall head over heels for me—like the others. I knew how to handle that. A few nights before she had said in her trademark lilt, "Dalton, I do love you, you know," as though she instinctively knew that was what I wanted to hear. She was right—that was exactly what I wanted to hear.

Aldrin: *"OK, I'm at the top step. It's a very simple matter to hop from one step to the next."* Reaching the surface. *"Beautiful view!"*

Armstrong: *"Isn't that something? Magnificent sight down here."*

Aldrin: *"Magnificent definition."*

Armstrong: *"Isn't it fun?"*

The volume was so loud that it was vibrating the plastic sides of the television and jarred us to it. Davenant got up and pounded the plastic chassis. It worked. He turned and shook his head.

"What's the matter?" I asked.

"I was just thinking. I can't even name all the astronauts."

I thought for a moment. "Well, there's Armstrong. I think he was supposed to walk out first. . . ."

"What about the other two?"

"Got me," Mauberley said. "It could be the Three Stooges for all I care. As far as I'm concerned, all this spaceship junk's for the birds. What a colossal waste of bread."

"Who are the other two then?" I asked Davenant.

"I don't know. That's just it. Shouldn't we know?"

"Jesus, we can't even name the first men to walk on the Moon."

"It's like porno flicks," Mauberley laughed. "Who pays attention to the actors? You see one blowjob, you've seen 'em all. You see one space jerkoff, same thing."

"I'll read the plaque. . . . First, there's two hemispheres showing—two hemispheres of the Earth. Underneath it says, 'Here men from the planet Earth first set foot upon the Moon. July, 1969, A.D. We came in peace for all mankind.' It has the members' signatures and the signature of the President of the United States."

"Let's light one up and celebrate," Mauberley offered.

We smoked and soon after started dozing off with the screen rolling, tossing its snow from one frame to the next.

President Nixon: *"Neil and Buzz, I'm talking to you by telephone from the oval room at the White House, and this certainly has to be the most historic telephone call ever made. I just can't tell you how proud we all are . . . For every American, this has to be the proudest day of our lives. And for the people all over the world, I am sure that they, too, join with Americans in recognizing what a feat this is. Because of what you have done, the heavens become a part of man's world. And as you talk to us from the Sea of Tranquility, it inspires us to redouble our efforts to bring peace and tranquility to Earth."*

14

We were in the woods and Mauberley was walking in front of me with a shovel slung over his shoulder. We were following Birdie to the area she had picked out to plant her new marijuana crop—a large expanse of woods at the base of the mountain and well beyond a horseshoe of collapsed farm buildings that had long ago given up the ghost. Birdie said she knew the niece of the landowner who was in his 90's and probably hadn't walked these former pastures for a generation.

She was carrying a pallet filled with small pot plants in drinking cups. Besides the shovel, Mauberley was hauling a bag of sheep manure and complaining the whole way. I trailed with two other cartons of plants, each in one hand over my head like bus boxes of dirty dishes— which also doubled as shields against the branches Mauberley absentmindedly kept snapping back into me. I chided him about how he would have made a disgraceful Indian.

We had taken a previously well-trod footpath until it intersected a stream, and from there charted a desultory trail along the bank—until it unexpectedly opened on old tractor tracks whose gashes through the trees were still visible.

"Let's rest a second," Birdie said, holding up her hand like a cavalry sergeant.

"Yes, *Memsahib,*" I said and placed the pot cartons down gently. I stretched out on the grass and looked up at the hazy, thin blue sky.

"Hot, hot!" Mauberley complained, then started laughing in an exhausted, silly way. "Birdie, where you taking us—Oz?"

"Don't worry, it's just at the end of this path. Wait 'til you see it. It's beautiful. Perfect for a small pot farm."

"I don't care what it looks like—just as long as it has a water fountain."

"On the way back, we'll cut over to the stream."

"And drink some brackish swill that'll keep me on the throne for two days? No thanks."

"Stop being such a baby," I said.

"How about *you* carry the sheep shit and *I* lug the plants?"

"If you can't handle it, I'll carry the manure, too."

"'If you can't handle it, I'll carry the manure, too,'" he mimicked. "Sure, now that we're almost there."

"You're right, it was all a plot—to get you to do as much work as possible, especially the heavy stuff. Wait until you have to dig. You think this is tough."

"Bull-shit."

The view was indeed worth the walk, as the tractor tracks led to a five-acre meadow hidden ever since the farmer had left it fallow years before. Miraculously, it hadn't grown over. I wondered how many people had ever even seen this place—we were certainly part of a select few. The hay was deep and we cut waist-high paths as we walked straight into it. One side of the field sloped sharply down from a line of craggy shagbark nut trees and was dotted into puzzle pieces by swatches of yellow chickweed as though painstakingly placed by the hand of some pointillist.

"Monday Afternoon on the Grande Meadow," I announced.

Birdie and Mauberley ignored the allusion and drank in the wonder.

In the center of the field, a large boulder exposed its massive side like the bulge of a sleeping mammoth in the shade of a pair of stately pine trees. Fanning out from the base of the rock was a low, level area, and it was here Birdie planned to, according to Mauberley, "till the ancient land in the ploughman's tradition begun long ago by a handful of brave Huguenots."

As we walked, I recited the opening of my novel, which I had once spent a week committing to memory for an occasion just like this:

"One might never link a heritage from the small northwestern town in Brittany, Concarneau, to another in Massachusetts; however, it had been ordained. The bridge, sometimes over bleak and afflicted moments, had been completed one misty afternoon in 1886 with the arrival of the vessel, La Cathédrale Engloutie, duly blessed at the Pardon de Paimpol, and Hélène Dusine, wife to Étienne and almost mother to Paul, taking the first step onto the New World. It was the year which resulted in her perennial summer "distress," always felt but never mentioned, contracted somehow during the crossing. . . ."

"Preach, brother, preach!" Mauberley urged.

"The ship, born in the Bay of Douarenez, was ominously christened after the old legend of the lost city of Ys, which was destroyed when it was covered by the waters of the bay as a result of the treachery of Princess Dahut. The princess became a mermaid, and even today legend-minded sailors and fishermen claim she haunts the coasts off Brittany.

"The foot, once that of a ballerina, gracefully arched and tested the rickety wharf and pronounced it safe for the family's disembarkment. The Dusines had become immigrant Americans. . . ."

"We are the new Dusines!" Birdie exclaimed and started walking faster.

Mauberley and I hastened our pace to match hers.

"Étienne and Hélène had decided to give Paul a new world as a present for his birthday, more than the March to October itinerancy of a fisherman. If a girl, Hélène did not want her to gaze intently out to sea, her eyes reflecting the mood of the waters, watching the sailing vessels inch forward to the horizon bound for the cod grounds off the Newfoundland banks. The brightly colored sails smoothing in and out of tiny harbors, the fishermen in their blue berets and orange sailcloth suits, and the distinguished pale blue nets dripping dry from the masts would all be memories and stories for their child. In America, the women did not carry the day's catch in baskets to the neighboring canneries. . . ."

Reveling in my own words as I trotted behind—I barely shouted out the final paragraph.

"Hélène had paused on the gangplank, looking at her reflection in the muddy-brown water; she still wore the black dress topped by a brightly colored apron and white lace cap that her grandmother and great-grandmother had worn. At times she would miss the moors and grey skies of the rough coasts, but perhaps most of all, she would miss the droning skirl of bagpipes at the Pardons. Never again would she see the Breton women kneeling at the wayside Calvary Crosses, praying for the safe return of their husbands, sons, or lovers. It had been on one of those patches of sedge that she had decided to join the destiny of a land beyond the glittering fleece of the horizon. . . ."

Birdie and Mauberley cheered my recitation and we ran gleefully through the hay.

Like my story, I wanted to link myself with something—some path, some world, some meadow, some past . . . no matter the consequences. This is what I expected of the summer. Sometimes I felt as though I were several people and no one of them dominant. Yes, I could function and get by without much pain, but I didn't want to find myself in Maxine's position—anxious, adrift, and waiting for a promised rescue to make everything right and which might never come. I didn't want to write poems to myself asking the same questions I had asked five years earlier—content with occasional distractions and petulant reprisals with younger lovers—all to prove that I had not lost my youth and beauty or, more important, that I mattered to someone.

But there was something tragic about placing one's faith in a new season. Was it realistic to expect the world to grant me a hearing, to help me find my potential, and to guide me accordingly? That I was a young man of talent, a budding artist who felt things in his bones, I had no doubt, nor did I question a certain superiority—which sadly made me curse my present doldrum and the squandering of my gifts all the more.

The virgin meadow, which Mauberley and I were turning over and folding in sheep manure, represented the untapped potential energy I felt. I remembered meeting an old school friend in Gannon's one night—I had not seen him in years—and after we had greeted each other and made small talk, he asked, "So, what's your purpose in life, Dalton?" Such a pompous thing to say, I thought. Purpose. Is a man measured by his purpose? Now in retrospect, maybe the fool had had it right all along. Wasn't that what I was looking for? Perhaps. . . . Only now, I felt I needed a success to validate my purpose. What was more moral than an uncompromising man who believed totally in himself and became successful in his work? Success breeds morality and purpose. Let my success make the noise. Give me a cab driver with a million bucks and watch how moral he becomes. But then again, morality can apply only to those who have a choice.

The more I thought about all this, the more I realized that mine was the most common case of all—I was in love and it was not the best of times to be in that condition. I was in love with Maxine Cooke, that much was certain. It was very easy to say, but why didn't I feel it in my bones the way I felt I should? Why didn't I want to admit it to others? Had that process somehow been drained away by how I had been brought up and taught how to attend to my emotions? But Maxine knew. That's why she never failed to say she loved me. In our little game, she was both my lover and my enemy. She knew the path she must follow and, sadly, I was only a brief part of it. I had to accept that.

Oftentimes there were no words. We understood there could be no boundaries—to impose restrictions would imply a loss of freedom and strength, and it was precisely our individual freedoms that could never be compromised. They were what had brought us together in the first place. Freedom and its manipulation were what made our relationship work and gave it an excitement I had never experienced before. Perhaps part of that excitement was born out of the knowledge that I resented Maxine, maybe secretly despised her. Her money and poise had been given to her as if a grade school exercise, which she had practiced and learned like the times tables and wore so casually, almost swaggering at times, unfurling it out like a bolt of fabric. . . .

At the end of the day, we stood there looking at Birdie's marijuana field and the small plants twittering in the soft breeze brought on by the waning sun.

"I wonder if we'll have some in time for Woodstock," she said and kissed Mauberley and me for luck.

"Why did it take you so long to kiss me?" Maxine said one night not long after, as we embraced in her living room after dinner.

"I don't know. Maybe I don't kiss until after I've eaten."

"Cute. . . . C'mon, what is it? What's darkening that brow of yours, Mr. H?"

"I don't know. Maybe I want to punish you."

"For what?"

"For being who you are, what you are. . . . For expecting to have everything when you want it. . . . For saying you love me and still hoping Maurice will leave his wife for you."

She pulled back and smiled. "Well, *that's* quite a mouthful. . . . I was wondering when this would come." She took both my hands and placed them on her breasts. "But you want it, too, *n'est-ce pas?*"

"You know I do."

"As much as I do."

"More."

"Then what's the problem?" she said and laughed with her head thrown back, a powerful chord running the length of her neck.

I didn't like her laughing at me like that.

"The problem is you use people up and discard them . . . turn them against you. Why?"

"I guess every girl needs a little sadness."

"But you make it your passion, your mission," I said, pressing her breasts and watching her eyes wince slightly in pain.

"Oooooh, feeling powerful," she smiled and pushed me back roughly onto the couch, quickly undoing my clothes. "You want to rub in a little dirt, don't you? Take me down a notch. Maybe make me make a little noise . . . howl like some teenage slut giving it out free to the football team? Is that what you *really* want, Dalton? Just tell me. . . . I'll say and do anything. All you have to do is ask."

"That's right. . . . I want to hear the words coming from your mouth—the filthiest, sickest, dirtiest things there are. . . . Say them. Say them in Spanish—as if you're drunk on a beach in Panama with one of your cabana boys. . . . And you'll love it, too, won't you?"

"More than you'll ever know," she moaned in a lascivious way.

"You're a bitch, you know that—a real solid gold bitch."

"Yes I am, and that's why I want you to do anything you want, Dalton, anything—whatever you like, wherever you like, whenever you like. . . . Come to me when you feel the most depraved, when you want to hurt me the most. . . . You do want to hurt me, don't you?"

"More than you'll ever know—let you feel what I feel."

"Ha-ha, that's good! . . . And that's when I'll open my arms the widest, darling . . . and my legs and my mouth. . . . I only want to please you—because I love you."

"No. Because you know by pleasing me, you'll only be hurting me more."

"Don't you see? That's the way it has to be with us. . . . Am I frightening you, Dalton?"

"Shut up," I said, tearing at her clothes, forcing her beneath me.

Completely naked, Maxine crossed her hands behind her head and stared into my eyes a languid beat. "What took you so long?" she said.

BOOK III

Its Hour Come Round

15

On the morning we were leaving for Woodstock, I was awakened by a young girl stroking my cheek. I was not startled. I simply looked up at her. I had never seen her before. Immediately, it came back to me I had slept in Mason's bed because Davenant and Tracy had wanted to talk and she would be staying the night. Technically our room at Calypso was Davenant's studio, which he told Tracy he absolutely needed in order to write effectively—so since Ray Mason hadn't come home, I was like a man without a country.

Besides this strange, disheveled girl, I had a severe ache in my neck and the realization that I had purposely slept funny—to avoid those parts of Mason's pillowcases and sheets covered with dried smears and flecks of blood from his murdered pimples. In truth, I had been so stoned, I had been lucky even to find the bed. I looked back at the girl who was kneeling primly next to the mattress. Her thin arms looked like flesh colored sticks propped against her knees.

"Why did you do that?" I asked, gauging that she could be no more than fourteen/fifteen.

"I wanted to wake you up. I thought that would be a nice way."

"I guess it's better than most. What time is it?"

"I don't know." She spoke softly in a contrived kid bravado that could not camouflage her apprehension. "It's early."

"Why did you want to wake me up?"

"I wanted to talk with you."

"Do I know you?"

"No."

"Okay, sounds logical. I mean, why can't strangers talk with each other like anyone else, right? The world would be a better place. . . . So talk."

"A guy told me you were going to Woodstock. I want to know if you could give me a ride there. "

"Who told you?"

"A guy who picked me up last night. I was hitchhiking from Kingsbridge."

"What's his name?"

"I don't know?"

"Didn't your parents tell you not to get in cars with strangers?" Her innocent awkwardness was making me impatient. "What did he look like?"

"Tall, old, about twenty-five, twenty-six . . . had a big red car. He snorted when he laughed."

"Shit, probably Kaplan—the asshole," I muttered and sat up and rubbed the back of my neck. This kid's conception of age was amusing.

"Will you?"

"Wait. . . . Hand me my pants and things there."

I watched her pick my clothes off the floor. It all looked outsized next to her. Wonderful, we have a runaway, I thought, throwing back the covers and standing up to get dressed. I watched her as I did it—her expression trying hard not to show any signs of embarrassment—as though she had resigned herself that in running away and travelling alone, she would have to watch men get dressed and undressed in front of her. It probably had been the biggest decision of her life—a lot for someone so young. She was not a pretty girl.

"Boots, too," I said pointing and sat back down on the corner of the mattress. "Here, you want to rub something, rub my neck, it's killing me."

She silently obeyed and I felt her little fingers kneading away amateurishly at the muscles sheathing my neck and shoulders.

"Up higher. There! That's it. Good."

"What's all the blood from?"

I was tempted to say, that's where we play with little runaway girls, but bowdlerized it to, "My roommate has terminal pimples," wondering if she knew what 'terminal' meant in that context.

"My brother has a lot of pimples, too."

"Does your bother know you ran away?"

"Yeah . . . by now, I guess. He's up with the cows early."

"So he'll be looking for you, worried about you."

"I guess so."

"What about your parents?"

"What about them?" She stopped massaging.

I tested my neck. Surprisingly, it was better. "Thanks," I said and stood up and knocked down my pants by stamping the floor. "Do you drink coffee?"

"Maybe, I mean, I don't know. I've never really done it much."

"How about milk?"

"Yeah."

"Good, let's have some and decide what I'm going to do with you." She followed me into the kitchen. "What's your name anyway?"

"Cynthia."

"Cynthia what?"

"Just Cynthia . . ."

"Hey, look, 'just Cynthia,' we can't start off by playing games. You level with me; I level with you. No one asked you to come here."

I took a carton of milk out of the refrigerator and poured her a glass.

"Thank you," she said.

"You want some potato chips? They're fresh. I brought them back from a party last night. I tossed a half-filled bag on the table and began making coffee. I heard the bag crinkle and thought it was a good sign—at least she was eating.

"My name is Cynthia Correault—it kind of rhymes with asphalt."

"Well, Cynthia Correault, my name is Dalton."

"Dalton what?"

I laughed. "What are you a wise guy?"

"You said no games."

"So I did. Okay, Cynthia Correault, I'm Dalton Hawkes. Glad to meet you," and shook her little hand as though meeting a niece.

I watched her sip the milk and stuff potato chips into her mouth. She smiled meekly as she chewed—specks of salt and chips gathering in the corners of her lips.

A minute later, my water whistled and I poured it into the instant coffee, then sat down and added sugar and milk from the container. Over the brim of the cup, I looked at the young girl sitting across from me. . . . Probably life was rushing at her all at once: getting hair in places she had never had it before; legs taking on definition; a figure appearing as if overnight . . . she was ripening.

"Are you going to tell me why you ran away?" I asked, half-expecting a litany of standard woes: mother and father separated; mother drinks now and has a mean boyfriend who beats the kids . . . no money, accuses her of being a tramp . . . in love with a boy name Ritchie.

"I left home because it was ugly there."

"Ugly."

"The farm . . . my mother and father . . . the family—we don't get along. Never did. They're mad at everything I do. They don't really . . . love me."

"Some heavy reasons," I replied softly. "How do you know they don't love you?"

"Because I don't love them. Because we don't love each other. I know—I live with them. Don't you think I'd know?" She was on the verge of tears.

"So by going to the big love-in with hippies and drugs and rock and roll, you'll find something better, is that it?"

"I guess so." She looked down.

"Hmmm." I sat back and took a long guzzle of coffee. I lit a cigarette and she eyed the pack when I threw it and the matches onto the table. I gestured for her to take one and watched her light up in a practiced way. I should have been formulating logical reasons to convince her to return home.

"So, why are *you* going to Woodstock?" she asked.

I considered everything for a moment. "I guess for the same reasons you are."

"What, are you crazy, man?" Davenant barked later, looking as though he wasn't sure whether to laugh or cry. Gone was his ever-present caftan in favor of odd, tight-fitting jeans, a leather vest with no tee shirt, and almost effeminate-looking reddish sneakers. Was this really happening—taking a stray young girl to the festival with us? It was absurd. "It's not even worth discussing," he said.

He and Tracy had come downstairs, discovered what had landed on our doorstep, and immediately broke into two camps: Tracy whisking Cynthia into the bathroom presumably to clean her up and chatter about girl things—hearing their high, singsong inflections through the bathroom door; and Davenant, who was thumbs down from the minute he laid eyes on her.

"They'll hang us by the fucking balls!" he bellowed. "I mean, we're getting into Federal shit, man—kidnapping and . . . and . . . and *knavery!*"

I couldn't help laughing. "How about promoting *gusto picaresco?"*

"That, too. Go ahead, laugh, but the kid goes."

The issue was confused further when Mauberley appeared and complained about all the shouting. What was going on? I told him the story and his reaction was typically Mauberlerian.

"What's she look like?"

"Why ask him?" Davenant said. "He doesn't give a shit one way or the other."

"Back off, Tinkerbell . What's with the new duds?" Mauberley snickered, then blared at the bathroom door. "I'll tell ya' one thing—if you two don't get out of there pretty soon, I'll show you how much of a shit I give about all this!"

We sat around and drank coffee until Tracy reappeared with the girl, brandishing her about like a stiff refugee. Her cheeks had been scrubbed to a dull patina and her clothes somehow made more orderly. Tracy had gathered her hair and arranged it nicely. Now she looked like a presentable, albeit ordinary looking, young waif.

Mauberley humphed and began looking for cigarettes. Now that the kid was plain and even younger than he had thought, he was indifferent to the whole affair.

"Where do you live, kid?" Davenant snapped.

"Kingsbridge."

"You know we're going to have to call your house and tell them you're here."

Cynthia looked at me, then to Tracy for a desperate moment, and then at the floor.

"Stop it, Hugh. Hasn't she been through enough without you having to start in?" Tracy said, making a face at him for being so hard on the girl. "And, Dalton," she continued, "what's the matter with you? Are you crazy? Why did you give her a cigarette? My God, she reeks of smoke. Of all things, couldn't you think of *anything* else?"

"I gave her some milk and potato chips."

"Oh, wonderful. . . . You're really something, you know that."

"I smoked when I was her age," Mauberley said and sauntered into the bathroom.

"And look how *you* turned out," Tracy said after him. "C'mon, Cynthia, let's go downstairs and see if Birdie has something decent for you to eat," and led the girl away, closing the door harder than necessary.

"What's the kid's story? What's her name?" Davenant asked.

I told him.

He frowned.

"It rhymes with asphalt."

"Not really," he said, reaching for the phone and dialing. "Now we're going have to deal with the family. . . . Kingsbridge please."

Thirty minutes later a dark blue pickup truck rumbled to an abrupt halt in front of Calypso. Hearing it, Mauberley called out the window to the driver that he should come upstairs.

Standing on the landing, Davenant watched as a large, sandy-haired, young farmer bolted through the open front door and clambered up the stairwell.

"Are you the people who called about Cynthia? Cynthia Correault? She's my little sister."

"Yes, yes, I called you," Davenant said, pouring himself another cup of coffee. "Don't worry, she's fine. She's having breakfast downstairs. . . . She showed up here this morning and said she wanted a ride to Woodstock."

The brother's nimbus of short, light, untrimmed beard hair bristled from a formidable array of scars, seams, and dents left in his face from a hideous adolescent complexion. Everything moved up and down as he spoke in an earthy vulgarity. He appeared to be working a plug of chewing tobacco.

"I knew it," he grunted. "That's all she's been talkin' 'bout—this Woodstock thing, listenin' to nigger music . . . papers fulla things about drugs and hippies and . . ." he trailed off and glared at the three of us individually. He walked over to the sink and spit out a dollop of tobacco juice.

Mauberley snickered. "Make yourself at home, fella."

"I'm the one who found her," I said evenly, diverting his ugly stare.

"Why'd she come here?"

"My friend just told you—she wanted a ride."

"You ain't tellin' me nothin'! I still ain't found out why my fourteen-year-old sister is hanging out inside a . . . a hippie house!"

I laughed and shook my head at Mauberley.

"What can I say?"

"You listen," the brother pointed at me. "You ain't outta trouble yet, not by a long shot. After I bring that little whore home, the first thing I'm gonna do is call

Judge Tex, who runs this whole goddamn college hippie town. He's a friend of the family, and I'm gonna ask him why kids run away to a hippie house like this. . . . That's for openers."

There was a momentary silence—for some reason, all expectant of me.

"Now, *you* listen to *me!*" I boomed. "I don't know who the hell you think you're talking to, but you can take that shit and shove it up your Holstein ass!" I paused and saw Mauberley and Davenant smiling proudly at my metaphor. "Now, let's start again. . . . Your sister ran away. She ran away for a reason. Maybe 'for openers' you should try to figure out why."

"I know why."

"You don't know shit. All you know is how to bulldoze your way in here making threats, asking stupid questions, and accusing people. . . . We did you a favor, man. Maybe the next person won't bother to call."

"Ah," the brother flicked his hand at me and ran down the stairs. We heard him bang on Anne's door, trying to open it, but it was locked. He stormed over to Birdie's.

"C'mon, this guy's crazy," Mauberley said and bolted out of the kitchen. Davenant and I hurried after him.

The brother emerged from Birdie's apartment, dragging Cynthia away by the arm.

"Asshole!" Birdie screamed after him. "What the fuck's the matter with you?"

"She was just eating!" Tracy yelled from inside the apartment.

At the curb, he opened the truck door, threw his sister in like a limp toy, and slammed the door shut. The truck gunned away, swerving and whining in every gear.

We all watched from the porch.

"I feel sorry for her," Tracy said.

"Me, too," said Birdie.

"No, ladies, the big takeaway here is Hawkes," Mauberley crowed. "You should have seen him dressing down Old MacDonald there. . . . Jesus, I got a hard-on just listenin' to all that testosterone."

In the weeks preceding Woodstock, local newspapers and radio stations had announced jobs were available in the festival's food concessions. Mauberley and I decided to apply for work, and in the process solve our main problems of paying for tickets and food. Tracy had no problem ponying up for her and Davenant, while Maxine eagerly wanted to explore and experience everything Woodstock had to offer—to me, an ominous portent.

The plan was to drive up, check out the preparations, nail down the jobs, come back to Calypso and get whatever we needed—then load up the next morning and spend a couple of days camping before the real crowds came. We also had to see if we needed a tent, as there were rumors Old Ford would have a huge tent where anyone from the town could stay. If that were true, it would make things a lot easier. On the down side, under the cloud of a bad luck Tuesday for some unknown past transgression, everyone else's car was either too small or in various stages of repair—so my ill-tempered Valiant was designated to make the trips back and forth to the "Tents 'O' Israel," as Mauberley anointed the gathering of "the hippie clans." Getting the Valiant roadworthy, it took me two hours to wash off the grime and tree sap that had been accumulating and another hour to replace all the fluids and finally get the motor to turn over. It was going to be an adventure.

A little after one-o'clock we were off—the bottom of the Valiant scraping out of Calypso's uneven driveway—bogged down from the weight of Davenant and Tracy in the back seat with Mauberley squeezed in between, and Maxine and me in the front. Two miles out of town the muffler was sheared off negotiating a hump on the flats, and suddenly the car sounded like a dump truck going up a steep hill. In the rearview mirror I watched the muffler skid across the road behind us and tumble to a rest in the weeds along the shoulder.

"To hell with it," I shouted above the cacophony and gunned the engine even louder.

"Let's get this party started," Maxine called out, her hair ribboning back in the wash of the open window, enjoying herself like the night I had watched her from the Cacique. She produced a pocket bottle of Wild Turkey and passed it around.

As I drove towards the mountain, the sun broke through the overcast sky and imbued the cliffs with a golden warmth that reminded me of Yellowstone Park. It was a good sign, I thought—until minutes later we began our ascent and a new bank of clouds rushed in quickly and cast us back into gloom.

The sunless sky matched Davenant's black mood. For him to go through with the festival now—under the pall of Tracy's ever-present anxieties about being pregnant—sent discordant shock waves through his normal love and anticipation of adventure. Before leaving, he had confided to me that Tracy was intensifying her demands about settling things between them.

The heavy mountain air was cool and we rolled up the windows—happily insulating us against the rocketing of the broken exhaust. We sat back and enjoyed the dark beauty of the forest, raw and unblemished, save for this lone road that ran through it. I noticed the turnoff for Fallen Rock and one word flew to mind, Jane—no thoughts, no memories, just Jane.

"You know, I was thinking," Davenant said. "Maxine, you could have saved us a helluva lot of hassle and hard work."

"How's that?" she said, turning around to him squarely.

"Well . . . with all the Cooke millions—surely you could have subsidized a small excursion like this, a tiny little fiesta, with a proper vehicle . . . and all the trimmings."

"That's rude, Hugh," Tracy said.

I looked in the mirror. There was a cocky look on Davenant's face. Mauberley was asleep next to him.

"I don't control all my father's money. Besides, he was a believer in people taking responsibility for their own lives."

"He seems to have set you up pretty nicely."

"You don't know me. You don't know anything about me."

"Well, I know . . ."

"Hugh, stop it! What's the matter with you?" Tracy scolded. "What are you trying to do? We've just started and already you're trying to ruin the trip. . . . We all know you're mad because you really didn't want to go and how you feel I dragged you against your will."

"Tracy, don't," he said.

"What's your point? What are you trying to prove?"

"I said drop it, okay. Just drop it."

"Thank you, Tracy," Maxine said, "but you don't have to defend me,"

"I know, Maxine, but it's just mean. It's uncalled for."

Maxine turned back to Davenant. "Yes, Hugh, I come from a very rich family. Yes, my father was wealthy, and because of all that I have the luxury of not having to do many of the things others have to do in life.

I'm not making any kind of statement. It's not snobbery. It's just a fact of my life. I have complete freedom. I can do what I want, whenever I want, wherever I please. I can have virtually anything. . . . Yes, I have unlimited funds!" she said swinging an arm through the airspace of the car. "Is that what you want to hear? How rich I am? How much money I have?" Her voice cracked perceptibly. "My father loved me . . . and he supported me in any way I chose to live. Though I'm sure you think that's ridiculous, I am very grateful and appreciative for what he gave me and for all the freedoms I'm allowed. . . . But what I'm not going to do is apologize to anyone for what I have. Nor am I going to accept for a second that you or anyone else can make claims on me. . . . Before he died, my father told me we have to take responsibility for our own lives—no matter what the circumstances."

Davenant snickered and turned to the window. I drove on and let Maxine's words settle.

I recognized the small towns I had driven through with Kaplan weeks before: the simple rows of dumpy storefronts lining both sides of the road and cars parked diagonally into the raised sidewalks. In several villages, the same policemen were directing traffic at the same blinking signals, as their partners sat in nearby squad cars eager to scream after any interlopers—especially a car full of hippies with drugs and no muffler. Luckily, I saw all these potentially dangerous encounters well in advance and devised a method of touching the gas pedal ever so slightly, so as not to tax the broken exhaust system into too loud an argument—then coasting past the constabulary, the unmuffled engine piping with seeming power and nothing more.

I noticed one patrolman eying us a bit longer and watched in the rearview mirror for him to give a sign to his partner, but it didn't come. Once in Pelhamville, I took the turn towards Monticello.

Later on, as we cruised the large meniscus around Monticello Raceway, a huge gaudy pink sign suddenly intruded on the afternoon. It was surrounded by a rectangle of blinking colored lights that reminded me how Times Square always seemed to add garish artificial light to daytime. Black plastic letters inserted by hand spelled out the newest spectacle to come:

PLAYBOY ROOM
Excl. Area Engagement!
Wed. Aug 13 – Sun. Aug. 17
Back by Pop. Demand
CYCLONE STEVENS!!!

"Hey, I know her!" I said pointing proudly.
"I'll bet," Tracy laughed.
The first thing that came to mind was how she was going to compete with Woodstock. Then again, she attracted a decidedly different clientele. I pictured her cavorting in a smoky spotlight in front of a bank of liquor bottles, tired but needing the money, and shaking her assets for all they were worth. In an odd way, I didn't want to share her with anyone else.
"Shit, I missed the turnoff," I groaned, as a sign LEAVING BETHEL drifted past. I stopped at a roadside fruit stand and Maxine inquired about directions.
"Three roads back then make a left," she said. "He called it 'Yasgur's Farm.'"
The road into Yasgur's Farm started out well paved but gradually deteriorated into a narrow, unkempt side road between two ditches that wound and pushed its way through lightly wooded sections until without warning a great cleared field appeared—upon which a nascent city was being raised before our eyes.
"Welcome to Oz, my pretties," Mauberley intoned.

Ogling and proceeding very slowly, we made our way past clots of bare-chested workers with ponytails and headbands. Whining trucks were scattered everywhere in confusion. People lay in the shade, looking lazily at the sky. Couples kissed while smoking pot, the smoke rising incongruously against the trees. Dozens of cars and vans were parked haphazardly among brightly colored tents. Piles of silver posts for chain-link fences sat shining in the sun as everything and everyone made preparations. It was the skelter of a great marching band that would somehow materialize into recognizable form. Despite all the activity, there was still a sense of serenity—a hot afternoon waiting patiently for the passage of the clouds.

"God, do you believe all this?" Maxine marveled.

"It's fantastic," said Tracy. "This isn't a rock concert anymore, it's a . . ."

". . . Monster!" Mauberley interrupted in a British accent. "We've created a monster."

"It's almost overwhelming," I whispered. "Look they're drilling wells."

"Water shall flow in the desert!"

"And over there, portable toilets, Tracy said. "There's gotta be hundreds of them."

"Hey, kid, this ain't a piss-in-the-grass affair," Mauberley joked.

"They're supposed to have a hospital, too," Davenant said, breaking his petulant silence and joining the excitement.

Up and over a little rise a stage materialized at the bottom of a saucer-shaped corner of the huge field—upon which a castle, a fortress, a massive unfinished temple was rising up out of the alfalfa that sloped gently down to it. Scaffolding towers stood on both sides like skeletal turrets. Behind the stage was a cluster of house trailers—presumably home to promoters and temporary quarters for performers. Inside the gaggle of vehicles, a naked woman dove into an above ground swimming pool.

Coming to a crossroad, one dirt fork was a ceaseless line of roaring trucks circling around to the rear of the stage, which Mauberley informed us eventually led back to the town of White Lake. The other road ended in a parking lot with a miscellany of cars from as many states, some as far away as New Mexico, Oregon, California, even Alaska.

We parked and there was the unspoken feeling that the word had been spread well and all the tribes of our generation had sent large delegations to pledge their support in a show of solidarity—for who we were and for how were choosing to live our lives. We walked along one of the paths leading away from the parking field, and Mauberley asked a stoned, bare-chested man where we could sign up for work. Following his slurred instructions, we trudged the perimeter of the field beyond the concession platforms—to where a few recreational vehicles and tables were fashioned into a makeshift receiving center. A queue of applicants lay in the grassy shade to be processed and hired. Mauberley and I went to the end of the line and sat down.

"You don't have to wait for us," I said to the others. "Go check things out. We could meet back at the car in an hour or so."

"I anticipated the doldrums," Davenant said and produced a pregnant-looking joint from his shirt pocket and fired it up.

"Hugh, haven't you smoked enough for today?" Tracy said.

"I can always count on you for the definitive chastisement, can't I?"

"Oh, don't be so sensitive. It wasn't a put down. It was just an observation."

Mauberley stood up. "Save place, comrades. Must take shit," he said and started walking towards a stand of portable toilets behind some tractor-trailers. He shook his head as he walked away.

The joint was passed around, Maxine demurring, taking a brief tug then recirculating it quickly. As I watched her, I understood how she liked her decadence raw and unfiltered—to look Gorgon straight in the eye.

I took her hand. "What do you think of all this, babe?"

"I'm really very happy about everything."

"You sound as if you're surprised about it."

"In a way, I guess."

"Aw, come off it, sister," I said in my best Bogart, "you know you've gotten under my skin," and leaned against her. I wanted to feel her against me.

A scruffy, handsome man from a neighboring group walked over, inhaling grandly. "Mind if I join you?"

"Be my guest," Davenant said, happily passing the joint. It seemed as if he wanted to cram as many diversions into this adventure as possible—maybe to keep Tracy off balance reacting to new experiences. One thing I knew for sure—he wasn't going to get married again, kid or no kid. We all watched the man cup the joint inside both hands and draw the smoke inside his fist with a mighty pull of air.

"I see it's your first time," Davenant joked.

The man nodded, his mouth full of precious smoke, which he began drawing into his lungs in short bursts.

"The first one's free, kid."

Despite everything, I was glad the grass was mellowing Davenant out.

The new man, his name was Cade, was a sturdy, roustabout type whose lack of personal hygiene tarnished his initial impression. His hair was matted and had a dull sheen from not having been washed and was tied back in a Chinaman's braid. He was barefoot and sat cross-legged, exposing dirty, kidney-shaped footprints on the bottom of each foot. I could see the dirt-clogged pores under the hair on his ankles.

It seemed he had seen some prodigious feats of marijuana smoke inhalation in Jamaica, the mention of which piqued Maxine's attention. "The cats there are freaky, man. You think this is a joint?" he laughed. "I met this guy, a native who worked at one of the hotels. He would take a sheet of newspaper or a brown paper bag, roll it from corner to corner into a giant cone, and then fill it with ganja, man. I mean, the thing must have been this long and this fat," he illustrated with his big hands and long blackened fingernails.

"Hmmm," Maxine fetched a sigh. "I enjoyed Jamaica, too," she said, insinuating Caribbean wonders of her own.

Davenant looked at her sternly, as though to say, *you sicken me.*

"I'm telling you. This cat did the whole fuckin' thing, man. I couldn't fuckin' believe it. The whole fuckin' joint, I swear to God," and made the sign of the cross.

It amused me that he must have thought the religious gesture would give his story a plausibility that was beyond question. Anything said in the name of the Lord was established law—beaten furiously into tablets by a twenty-four hour standby crew of rock chiselers.

"And the cat's eyes were incredible. They didn't have any whites—just yellow, I swear—deep yellow like an egg yolk. And bloodshot! Whoa!"

We all laughed.

"Anyway, he rolls this spliff for me and I work myself up to take a big toke, and it barely makes the ash glow! Incredible. . . . Later on, he asks me to go up into the mountains to score some hash with his friends. I tell him no, because I say to myself, 'Self, you go up in them mountains, you ain't comin' back.' You know what I mean," he said tracing a headline in the air, "White American Missing in Jungle. . . . Hey, I'm talkin' Mau Mau country," he laughed and snorted.

"I went up into the mountains, and I lived to tell about it," Maxine smiled.

He looked her over a beat. "Yeah, well, I ain't exactly built like you. . . . Anyway, after we smoked, I started talkin' to him about what it was like livin' in Jamaica. He told me the local officials hassled the young people there, just like here—didn't like long Rasta hair, beards, the whole nine yards. . . . So, I whip out this picture of me in the snow, holdin' my dog, when I had a beard. First, he laughs and laughs and then he stares and stares at the picture, and points, 'This white everywhere. Is that what they call snow?' I say, 'Yeah, that's snow, man.' Can you believe it? Then he says, 'How does snow work?' So, I say, you know—snow. Kind of like frozen rain. When it gets real, real cold. . . . And I'm thinkin', how do you explain snow to someone who's never seen it? Finally, he blows my mind and says, 'I don't recall ever getting' cold, mon.' I mean, he didn't even know what fuckin' cold was!"

"I know exactly what you're talking about," Tracy said. "I roomed with a girl from Uganda."

"Yeah, people are strange, man."

". . . She didn't even know what an electric light was. I had to show her how to operate the switch."

"Now, *that's* heavy," Cade said, seeming to want the floor back. I wondered if he felt he was weaving some kind of storytelling magic over us. "I roomed with a cat from Nigeria," he paused to let everyone catch his enthusiasm. "A Muslim. Had five wives—and then one dies while he was over here. Went nuts. . . ."

"Where was this?" I asked.

"At school—State University at Old Ford."

"Are you kidding me? We all went to Old Ford— well, most of us. We live there now."

"No shit. . . . You know, there's an Old Ford tent here."

Behind Cade, Mauberley was returning.

"When did you go there?" Davenant asked.

"Graduated four years ago. . . . What are we—in some kind of moon phase or somethin'?" he laughed. "Same college, African roommates. . . . This is getting' freaky, man."

"We finished in June," I said.

"I was there when you were there," Maxine said. "Funny we didn't run into each other at some point."

"Yeah, well, I lived off campus."

"But students weren't allowed to live off campus until senior year. What dorm were you in before that?"

Cade paused awkwardly. "Well, I paid for housing . . . but I lived off campus anyway. My roommates were cool and played along.—covered for me."

"What was your major?"

"Art. . . . I'm a painter."

"Now, *I'm* getting scared," Maxine said. "So was I. *I'm* a painter, too. Whom did you study with?"

"Who else?" Davenant interrupted. "Maurice White was the main man, right? Number one poon hound at Old Ford. "Maxine shot him a hateful glance. "So, what ever happened to the Nigerian?"

"Cracked up. Ended up in Bellevue the last I heard. Never got over losing his wife," Cade was smiling now that he was back on familiar ground.

"That's terrible," Tracy said.

"Yeah, I felt sorry for him. . . . I remember one Christmas everyone decided to buy him a present—the same guys who hated him and busted his balls and called him the 'live-in savage' for a year. . . . But they were in the Christmas spirit, I guess, and they decided to get him a transistor radio and wanted a dollar from everyone. I refused to donate because I thought they were all hypocrites and a radio was ridiculous. The cat had trouble speakin' English let alone listenin' to some hyped-up disc jockey. He didn't even have a winter coat: I had to give him one of mine. . . . One time, I remember him tellin' me that he hadn't been properly prepared to come to America. He said that at the airport in Nigeria some of his friends gave him religious stuff from his old tribal religion. He said he didn't believe in it, but he took the things anyway out of respect to his friends. Then one day he asked me to help him destroy all the shit—little leather balls sewn up the back and filled with some kind of sand, pieces of beads, and straps . . . stuff like that. I told him, 'Look, all you have to do is throw it away.' He insisted it couldn't be done like that. He was scared, even though he kept tellin' me that his tribal religion meant nothing to him. I told him to flush it down the toilet, and he looked at me like I was crazy. Anyway, in the end, I had to cut everything up very precisely with a razor blade and then dispose of it in certain ways. It was freaky. . . . After it was all done, he said something I'll never forget. He said, 'You must understand that I am a Christian, but I also know there is no place for a black man in Christianity.'"

"That's so sad," Tracy said.

Davenant lit up a fresh joint, and we smoked while Tracy told us about her Ugandan friend. Afterwards, Davenant said to Cade, "It's interesting that you went to Old Ford and you hadn't heard of me—I was the Bard of Old Ford."

I drove home that night with Maxine. Since the Old Ford tent did exist, it was decided I could return to Calypso and get a few things that we and the others needed. There really was no necessity for everyone to go, and there were enough blankets in the trunk to get through the night. It seemed logical, and I gauged the Valiant had at least a hundred miles left in her.

"I want you, Dalton," Maxine said on the way home.

"You got me."

"No, I *want* you, want you."

"Well, I want you, want you, too."

"Dalton, let's just let it happen between us," she said. "Let's try to keep it fresh and exciting and see where it takes us. . . . No have-to's, no schedules, no regrets— only when we want to—every day, every week, whenever it's right . . . . We really have had a damned good time together."

"Yes, we have."

I pulled into Maxine's driveway, the gravel under the tires playing a counterpoint to the rumbling melody of the muffler. I shut the Valiant down and suddenly the world was peaceful again. I looked at Maxine, who smiled back. We had accomplished a lot today, and if nothing else, we knew we would be spending the next few days together. She moved to me and we kissed.

16

In the daytime the Old Ford tent was absurd.

"It looks like a giant baggie," I said, standing with Maxine on top of the rise overlooking the Visqueen monstrosity that was stretched and stapled between freshly cut saplings and had OLD FORD written in black tape across one side of the roof.

"Well, it's stood for a couple of hours," she said cheerfully. "It should hold up for a few more—I hope."

We clasped hands and plummeted down the slope—the duffel bag of things I had brought back from Calypso slapping against my side. Quite a few tents and crude temporary shelters had been built even in the brief time we were away, and we had to zigzag and pick our way through the encampments—avoiding small campfires, drying clothes, and coolers of food. There were huts made with leafy branches; three-walled shelters made with bikes or motorcycles perpendicular to a rock or vehicle and a tarpaulin draped overhead . . . teepees, igloos, one-man tents, mummy bags, large cardboard boxes broken down and taped together—all part of the motley assortment of slapdash structures that dotted the landscape like a hobo clan gathering. Inhabiting everything were bare-chested men meditating in yoga positions, blissful women stretching and trying to feel the sun on their faces, children playing in the dirt, and loose dogs barking and darting after each other in unsupervised abandon. Like the ragtag army of Spartacus trying to pursue freedom and a new way of life, somewhere inside all the activity was the anticipation that we were going to succeed where he had failed.

It had rained again during the night.

I stuck my head inside the tent and instantly felt the change in temperature. "At least we'll get up early or else fry to death," I said to Maxine. "Jesus, it's like Guam in here." It was Davenant's line.

Maxine stepped inside after me. "Oh, my God, it must be twenty degrees cooler outside, and it's hot out."

Tracy was squatting next to Mauberley in the middle of the tent. He was resting on one my blankets from the car, and it was obvious he had just gotten up. Tracy looked upset.

"Oh, Dalton, I'm glad you're here," she said, looking up at me as though my mere presence was enough to ease her pain.

"Shit, it's like Guam in here," Mauberley grumbled. The hair ringing his forehead was dark with perspiration. He glanced up at Tracy and fell back laughing. "You should see your face. You look like you just lost your best friend."

"I have." She plopped down on a vacant bedroll.

"What happened?" I asked.

Maxine went over and sat next to her.

"Hugh didn't come back last night . . ." she stopped, fighting back tears. Maxine pushed away stray hairs from Tracy's face and handed her a tissue. "He didn't come back. He's gone."

"Where did he go?" I asked.

"I don't know. After we ate, he just got up and walked away."

I turned to Mauberley. "What's going on?" Why did all the evils of the world always seem to gravitate to me? I was only twenty minutes back in Eden.

"Who the hell knows? This is all news to me. . . . He didn't say anything to me about leaving."

I tried to make sense of it. "Tracy, he must have left for a reason. What happened to make him leave? Did you have another fight or something?"

"Yes." She sank deeper into Maxine.

"Why didn't you say that?" I was trying to sound calm but it was coming out petulant and singsongy. "Don't you think that's an important piece of information we should know? I mean, why make things into a soap opera and make us guess? . . . Okay, Davenant left because you had a fight. Not so hard to understand."

"I'm hip," Mauberley chuckled in his dirty way.

"Can't you two show a little compassion? Can't you see she's upset?" Maxine said.

"Yes, she's upset. . . . But is she upset because Davenant left or because he didn't come back or because of something he said or . . ."

"All of them!" Tracy blubbered, a hopeless expression on her face.

"What did you expect, Trace? Really. It's been a constant harangue about trivial things—all because you're insecure about the baby. He hasn't forgotten you're pregnant."

"That's not it."

"That *is* it."

"It's not, it's not . . ."

I waited a moment and proceeded calmly. "All right, I'm going to be very honest with you, Trace, and tell you exactly what I think and what I've seen and what I know other people have seen, too. Maybe it's none of my business, but you're my friend, more than a friend, and I need to say it. . . . To my mind, ever since you've learned about the baby, you've been clinging to Davenant every second. I mean, *every second!* It's been hard to watch. You're smothering him. And the funny part is, there's really no need for it. He hasn't said anything against the baby—he's been all for it from the start, hasn't he? He said he'll be with you when it happens. What more do you want?"

"Then why did he go away?"

"Who knows? C'mon, when *isn't* Davenant thinking about a trip somewhere? He always wants to go places and usually ends up just talking about it, you know him. He asked me to go to India with him before any of this business happened. . . . That's when you'll know something *is* wrong—when he *doesn't* want to go somewhere. Besides, he told me he would be sticking around for a while anyway—he working on something new."

"Working on something," Tracy threw out the phrase. "He's always working on something. Working on what? Does he ever show you anything he's working on?"

"Not always."

"He doesn't show it to me either. Really, not to show your ideas and stories and poems you've been working on for months, *years,* to someone who shares your life, who's having your baby. . . . Don't you think that's kind of odd?"

"No, it's normal. I don't show my stuff to anyone either."

"Why?"

"Because you'll lose it if you talk about it. . . . Serious writers don't go around telling people what they're doing—and talk the whole thing away. Most of the time people aren't interested, and if they are, they usually don't get it anyway. Why ruin it?"

"I'm not stupid."

"No one said you were. It's not a matter of intelligence."

"Them what is it a matter of?"

"It's a matter of being a writer. Artists don't stop in the middle of what they're doing to discuss what they're doing. You can destroy the juice if you talk about it, analyze it, and dissect it. It's working then, too. It's always working."

"All you need is a violin," she said.

I smiled. "I told you I didn't want to talk about it. . . . Let's put it this way: an artist's personal life controls the explosion that's going on when they're working. Lately, you haven't exactly been helping to control things as much as fuel them."

"Oh, so I shouldn't upset the delicate, artistic balance, is that it?"

"Yeah, in a way."

"But what you don't get, what men don't get—is sometimes there comes a point in a relationship that *needs* attention, sometimes *immediate* attention. There are such things as priorities. What could be more important to Hugh than his child?"

"You'd have to ask him that question."

"I wish I could. He's not here!"

"Now we're back where we started," Maxine interrupted in a soothing voice. "Let's look at it this way. All his stuff's here, right?"

"Yes."

"So, he has to show up sooner or later. And he can't go anywhere—Dalton drove."

Tracy looked at the three of us and took a deep breath. We were all perspiring. "Okay, let's wait and see what happens. . . . I'm sorry."

"Don't be silly," Maxine said. "You have every reason to be . . ."

". . . And everyone lived happily ever after," Mauberley interrupted. "Now let's get the hell out of this prophylactic."

Maxine and I had returned to the festival just in time, as upon inspection the Old Ford tent had scant vacancies. With some shifting and sliding of blankets and sleeping bags, we secured places near the middle of the tent for maximum heat and protection during the night. That settled, Mauberley suggested we drive into White Lake for lunch.

Walking back to the car and driving along the road behind the stage, we saw how many people were truly coming to the festival. There were thousands. The long sleeve of hill adjacent to the green and white striped hospital tents overlooking the small lake behind the helicopter-landing site was dotted with dwellings and people and machines, resembling a pilgrimage on the move, a modern crusade. Work was continuing on the stage as we inched by in bumper-to-bumper traffic—too late to turn back. We were caught in the inexorable movement of men and materiel pushing us along. Eventually, it spewed us out onto a back road, which unfortunately prevented us from cutting over and reaching White Lake from behind. Going back we would have to take the main drag, whose traffic we could only imagine. There was no other way open now, and I knew we would never be able to park anywhere near the stage again. It was foolish for us to have gone.

In town, the White Lake Superette was doing a land rush business. Hastily written signs and new prices labels announced drastically higher prices for everything due to limited supplies. The proprietor stood nervously at the cash register, constantly having to check a list because he did not know the new prices yet himself. Outside, two local policemen stood waiting for any sign of trouble and kept people moving along the sidewalk. No one was allowed inside without a shirt and something on his feet.

We mingled with the others waiting on line, and the mood was openly hostile over the ridiculous mark-ups. When the owner was challenged about his ethics and forced to defend his actions, he would reply in different variations of the same trilogy: "I have to think of the townspeople. . . . No one's forcing you to shop here. . . . I have to eat, too, you know." In effect, we were waiting on line to be cheated and robbed.

"I can't believe it. That guy was evil, man, really evil," I said slouching back behind the steering wheel to eat my hero sandwich. I flipped open the glove compartment and gestured for Maxine to use the underside of the flap to put our drinks on. "See, this is the whole thing right here. . . . First, everyone was so afraid of all the hippies getting together. Then they screamed that it was dangerous and unhealthy and that there'd be drugs and drinking . . ."

"The three D's," Mauberley said. "Danger, drugs, and drinking."

". . . and then what happens—*they're* the ones acting like assholes and raking in all the bread they can grab. How fucking evil is that? And on top of it, the guy was smug about it."

Mauberley laughed. "What did you expect, integrity?" He was chewing and smiling. His teeth were small—I had always called them marmot teeth—and were greenish in the seams.

"I hope we can make it back all right," Tracy said.

"Me, too," said Mauberley with his mouth full. 'There's supposed to be something at the Hog Farm tonight,"

"What's the Hog Farm?" Maxine asked.

Mauberley took some time to swallow. "I heard they're some commune from New Mexico . . . feeding people . . . have a band . . . whatever."

"Sounds great," Maxine said and shimmied in her seat.

"If it doesn't rain."

The road leading back to Yasgur's farm was closed. Two whistle-blowing attendants stood in front of makeshift police barriers, waving people away and telling them to park in the fields across the street. We tried to explain we were workers, but the mantra was, "No more cars, period." We parked in the wet fields where row upon row on vehicles were slowly sinking into the soft ground. As we crossed the road on foot, I hoped that I would be able to find the car again. It was obvious there would be no more driving until the festival was over. Walking back down the road we had driven unimpeded the day before, I saw why. A solid wainscot of metal lined both sides. In the narrower spots there was barely enough room for three people to walk abreast. It was the beginning of the sensation we would experience for the next few days with increasing intensity—the impression that you were following someone and that everyone was following everyone else. One was simply part of a flow now, a piece of the ooze, and therefore indistinguishable.

Back at the tent that night, we ate extra sandwiches we had bought in town. Davenant still had not shown up and Tracy was feeling low again. Maxine and I took a walk and said we would meet the others later on at the Hog Farm to listen to music. We could not help but marvel at the activity.

"I'm really glad we're here," I said, holding her hand as we walked.

"Me, too."

"It's almost as if I feel *proud* being here. We'll be able to tell our grandchildren, 'Yes, children, we were at Woodstock in 1969.'"

"I know. I have the same feeling. . . . *Our* grandchildren?"

"Oh, forgive my impertinence. Don't get excited now—it was just a daydream. . . . But now that you mention it, I wonder what our kids *would* look like?"

"Beautiful, of course."

"Of course."

Climbing the slope higher, above the trees, we could see the last glow of sunlight—bands of pinks and reds and subtle violets illuminating the line of the horizon.

"You have it pretty bad tonight, don't you?" Maxine said, staring at the sunset.

"Maybe."

"I'm sorry."

"Don't be sorry. I don't want you to feel sorry for me. . . . Didn't you say sorrow is an emotion, and that was a rare commodity in your life right now—that you didn't want to 'overdraw your emotional account?'"

"Okay, okay. . . . You always have a way of rubbing my words back onto me—especially when they don't fit into your . . . your neat, little plans."

"My neat, little plans." For a second I thought, why shouldn't I rub it in? Why shouldn't I try to hurt her the way she hurts me. But truth be told, she'd been honest with me from the beginning. I wanted things my own way, I was not getting them, and I resented it. "Wanna fool around?" I asked.

"Right here, right now?"

"Why not?"

"Yeah . . . but where?" she laughed and looked around.

"I'll find a place," I said, feeling happy that at least she wanted it as much as I did."

We walked along the crest of the rise until it reached another line of trees. Beyond the trees, it was darker but we could still see a field that eventually bordered the back road we had taken to White Lake. On the far side there was an old barn sagging badly into the ground. Below us was the Hog Farm. In front of a few painted buses, some men were building a one-step platform for musicians and their equipment. In a way, it looked like a lecture center amphitheater. Woodstock was now a college whose only semester would end Sunday: no tests, no grades, no books, and no instructors— everyone would learn for himself.

We passed an imposing milk trailer truck that had "Drinking water" printed on its chromed sides and two self-serving spigots in back. The ground was muddy and the garbage cans were full of paper cups gone to overflow. Farther on, was a sculpture of teepee poles with thick ropes that hung down from the center, supporting a huge stone.

"How does it hold it up?" Maxine asked.

"I guess the weight's distributed just right."

She walked up and passed her hand along the rough granite. "Where did all these boulders come from?"

"Probably from glaciers originally—terminal moraines. Farmers probably took them out of a field a long ago."

"Amazing. And they didn't have tractors back then."

Maxine stroked one of the thick ropes. Night had fallen. "What do think about Tracy?"

"Just what I said—she's been like an anchor on Davenant. She needs that I guess."

"But she *is* pregnant. And now *she* has a built-in anchor . . . and maybe no ship."

"Maybe. . . . Davenant has been acting a little overwhelmed under the pressure—like the way he started in on you for no reason."

"Oh, with me he had a reason."

"What do you mean?"

"Let's not get into it. . . . I think deep down you know the reason."

"What are you talking about? . . . You brought it up. Finish what you started."

"I didn't start anything." Even the annoyed look on Maxine's face didn't mar her beauty.

"Just give me the Cliff Notes version then."

She paused. "I agree with you that Tracy can get a little hysterical at times—especially with the baby coming and all—but that's only part of the situation with Hugh. . . . He's also dealing with something about himself that's scaring him much more than the baby."

"Now this is getting interesting."

We had reached the information booth at the crossroads, and the vast dusky saucer in front of the stage lay before us. Nighttime seemed to have pushed all the people and noise to a distance. We walked out to the middle of the field and sat down facing the stage. Five steel girders glinted dully above it.

"It's wonderful here," Maxine said.

"Yes, it's nice," I said, looking at the storybook city rising before us. We allowed ourselves to be taken in by the open space, the high grass, and the lights in the tents inside the trees. A gibbous moon watched from over the campfires on the hill.

"As you were saying, what's this big secret Davenant has—and that you know, too, and that has him howling at the moon."

"Do you really want to know?"

"Yes, he's my friend."

"I assume what I'm telling you is confidential."

"I'm incommunicado."

She hesitated. "Hugh is homosexual . . . at least bisexual."

"What? You're crazy."

"Maybe I am, but I'm certain about this."

"Davenant, gay? No way! . . . He was married. Tracy's pregnant." I laughed and it thudded out into the openness. "Look, you're beautiful, Maxine, and I'll believe almost anything you say, but I live with Davenant. Don't you think I'd know? . . . Or maybe *I'm* a homo, too?"

"You can make jokes about it but I know what's happened, what's been said, and what I've seen—there's no mistake. . . . It's no big deal."

"What happened? What did you see?"

"Do you really want to get into this? . . . There's a whole bunch of things."

"Tell me one."

"I don't know—this is beginning to sound very catty."

"Go ahead. Just tell me."

Maxine took a deep breath. "The first time was that night at Fallen Rock. At some point before the accident, I went over to introduce myself to Rachel, but she ran off when I got there. Anyway, Hugh was very direct with me and said we both were 'promiscuous types.' I asked him what he meant, since he really didn't know me, and he laughed and said we both liked to 'get down and dirty with boys.' I'll never forget the smirk on his face when he saw my reaction."

"Ah, he was drunk. We were all drunk."

"He wasn't that drunk when he asked me about Panamanian men and boys and how he believed 'the darker the berry, the sweeter the juice'—and how it was his fantasy to be with someone exotic like that. . . . He kept pressing me to describe what their bodies were like and how they responded to Americans. It was creepy—wanting all the dirty details and the way he kept trying to shock me."

"You know what I think. I think he was pulling your leg, trying to get you to open up about your wild days in Panama—maybe put it in a poem."

"I don't think so. Do you remember a couple of weeks ago when we were in Gannon's?"

"Christ, we're in Gannon's almost every night."

"It was when your friends from Paris called. They had come down from Montreal unexpectedly."

"Sure, I remember."

"And do you know Roger who's a waiter there once in a while?"

"Roger. Sure. . . . Wait, not the Roger, the fairy bartender? . . . Stop."

"Let's just say that Hugh and Roger were getting it on pretty hot and heavy that night and they were digging it. And they were getting off that I saw everything. . . . Dalton, there's no mistaking this for anything else. I saw it all the time on the beaches in Panama—the suggestive looks, the tiny kisses, the puckers, the gestures. . . . Hugh was even rubbing the back of Roger's leg when he brought the drinks over to our table."

"Give me a fucking break," I said, shaking my head, wondering if there was any significance that it was Davenant's pet phrase.

"Dalton, they even went to the bathroom together, and Hugh grabbed his ass and waited until I saw him before they went in. . . . He gets off watching me watch him."

She stopped, the stillness returned, and the spaces of the festival sounds around us grew wider. Nearby, two crickets were communicating in low register couplets—both using the same eighth notes.

Maxine had reason to feel angry towards Davenant, but the surety of her manner was convincing, and I had never known her to lie.

"Well . . . I'm sure all of this is *possible*, but I think there must be another explanation."

"What do you mean, 'possible'? Either it's true or I'm lying. It's as simple as that."

"But I haven't seen it. No one else has seen it. You're the only one."

"I know. . . . And he's doing it on purpose, right in front of me."

"Why would he do that?"

"Because he's never liked me, and if I said anything, it would mean I was spreading vicious slanders about him, which I'm doing now—but *only* to you. . . . I had to say something. I was beginning to think I was going off the deep end."

"Well, it's certainly news," I concluded. "But in the end it's his business, not ours."

"Of course, I agree. It is what it is. Let's not talk about it anymore."

We sat and looked at the huge tarpaulin sagging over the stage like a drooping banner over an ancient castle.

"You're really something," I said and kissed her. She was warm and there was the pleasant rush of her smell that could only be described as a mixture of fresh herbs and a new day. "I love to look at you . . . and the way you move. It's all incredible to me. . . . I feel at home with you, Maxine. . . . And when you're gone, I lose it at times, but as soon as you come back, it's always there again."

"And my eyes are magenta pools shimmering in the moonlight like lambent coals," she orated and laughed. "Remember that spot we were looking for? How about here?" she grinned and pulled me gently into her.

"You're a constant wonder."

"I'll be the virgin and you'll be the conqueror, and you have to sacrifice me to the gods."

"They will be pleased and the village will rejoice."

"To the spirits of Woodstock," Maxine whispered and lay back, opening herself up like a morning flower.

At the Hog Farm that night the music was a good spunky rock that coincided with the tempo of the evening—light punctuated phrasing pumping everyone up for what was to come. It was a cool evening and a gentle mood prevailed.

The four of us, for a pleasant change in affairs, weren't concerned with Davenant's absence. Conversation drifted back to the metamorphosis of the festival and that the entire world was watching. More and more we came to realize we truly were in a moment of time that was in history rather than of history. Mauberley said it was a work of art—something that had its time and place indelibly cast and was therefore ageless, existential, and free of the dilemma of having to live and die.

We smoked a few rounds of Israeli hash, gifted by a baldheaded black man, then a joint courtesy of another stranger. As usual, Maxine and Tracy were reluctant when it came their turn to partake and declined more often than not. The music penetrated everything it touched—soaking into the ground and rustling the atmosphere like a gas jet playfully operated by a child. I liked to let the drugs work into me. With the hash there was a mellow feeling of lightness—lying back, relaxing, feeling the drift of my mind and marveling at the tricks my senses were playing—no constraints, no demands, no weight, no anxieties, no responsibilities . . . snatches of sounds barely audible inside the boom of the moment. I lit a cigarette and blew the smoke at the sky. I didn't want to have to move another muscle ever again. I wanted to feel the smoke and sink into the earth and sense the ground against my back and move with it as it spun wildly through space. Such a fragile thing our planet, I thought, an absurdly minor attendant without the vaguest idea about anything. I had strapped myself to the earth as Ahab had to the great white whale and had bummed a ride to immortality. . . .

A quick darkness blotted out the stars above me and spoke. "Are you still with us, fella?" It was Maxine's voice.

I took my time answering. "Oh, very much so. Only don't ask me to move."

"What are you thinking about?"

"Nothing." I closed my eyes. It seemed I would be able to formulate answers better that way. It was like picturing a mental pencil and paper.

"Is the company that dull?"

"Well, you can only work with what you have."

"Very funny." She lay down next to me. Our hands touched.

"You know, every time I feel you, you're warm."

"My engine always run a little hot. . . . You know what they say: warm hands, cold heart."

"I never liked clichés."

There was the scent of fire. I sat up slowly and saw Mauberley shielding a flame poking up timidly from a scattering of leaves. The band had stopped and an older representative of the Hog Farm was at the microphone as similar shaggy stagehands prepared for the next performer, one apparently not needful of drums or amplifiers. The Hog Farm, he said, was going to try to feed as many hungry people as they could while their supplies held out. There would be yoga demonstrations tomorrow morning. I watched the glowing cigarettes moving jerkily in the dark, and in the tongue of trees behind the buses, countless lightning bugs were tinseling the blackness like tiny Christmas lights. I rolled over and put my arm around Maxine.

"Look at these two," Mauberley said, "cavorting like a couple of wood nymphs."

"Mock on, Voltaire, mock on. . . . Let us cavort," I said, stroking Maxine's breast on the shadow side of the fire.

Mauberley turned to Tracy. "Tell me, my dear, do you come to Woodstock often?"

"Yeah, quite often, what's it to you?" she replied like a streetwise teenager. "Ain't you the lucky stiff?"

"But, Miss . . . isn't that your line of work—stiffs, I mean?"

Tracy tried not to laugh and screwed her face into insouciance. "Yeah, that's right, super balls, but this cow pasture ain't exactly dee-lucks a-kom-moe-dayshins. . . . An' I got news for you—you ain't gonna be sleepin' next to these tonight," she laughed and bounced her breasts independently in her palms.

We all roared.

"That is regrettable, my dear," Mauberley continued, "However, allow me to say that you have two of the foxiest guacamoles I've seen in quite a while. . . . May I feel them for a second?" he said and reached out for her like Frankenstein.

Tracy cringed melodramatically and crisscrossed her arms against her chest. "Back off you load of nuts and bolts—or I'll take a monkey wrench to your ass!"

Maxine couldn't stop laughing. It was good to see her so happy and free.

The thin-voiced folk singer was a rank amateur in comparison to the tight knit rock group that had preceded him—hitting wrong notes, forgetting lyrics, and forced to improvise with silly noises to fill in the awkward voids. Impatient with his mediocrity, the audience was loud and raucous during his performance, and when his set was over and he walked off stage, no one bothered to clap.

We all sat around looking at the fire, watching Mauberley place twigs and small branches strategically into the flames where they would be the most advantageous. The wood was green and hissed and bubbled as it tried to burn.

"Behold the Hippaneezee!" It was Davenant.

I looked at him and turned to Tracy. She watched him coldly.

"A tribe that worships the fire triangle of air, fuel, and heat. Unfortunately, their average life expectancy is only nineteen because of the staggering incidence of smoke inhalation," he joked.

Mauberley was laughing in his peculiar way, and he had me laughing just watching him. Despite the circumstances, it felt good for the three of us to be laughing together again. Maxine and Tracy remained stoic.

"Neither hunters nor gatherers, the Hippaneezee must rely on the only food acquisition they know, which hasn't changed in millennia—they wait for animals to be entranced by their flames and, hopefully, stumble into the fire and die."

"Welcome back," Tracy said loudly. "Long time no see."

Mauberley was coughing from the imbalance the laughing had caused to his Pall Mall enslaved respiratory system. I was holding my stomach, making sorrowful faces to indicate that I knew it was a serious moment, but I couldn't help myself.

"Hello, Trace," Davenant said, seemingly unfazed by the reference to his absence. He bent down to kiss her. "How are you?"

She allowed herself to be kissed and then turned away quickly. "Fine. Yourself?

"I'm well. I'm good, thanks. . . . Hello, Maxine."

She nodded.

"Well, isn't this nice—all back in the bosom of family," he said.

"Hello, hello," I managed brightly.

"Wow, it's really happening, isn't it?" Davenant's eyes were glistening in the firelight as he scanned the tents and the unseen thousands in the darkness. "I think it's already more than anyone expected."

"Let's all talk like Davenant," Mauberley said, mimicking Davenant's newfound speech and lip condition. It was not exactly feminine, but it was definitely softer—sounding like a variation of the standard hippie dialect inflected with lispy rhythms. "Entranced" was now "entrahnced" and "Maxine" became "Mahkzine." Shit, maybe Mahkzine was right.

"Sorry, I chipped a tooth on a soda bottle last night," Davenant said, running his thumb along the ridge of a front tooth.

"Sounds more like you got kidnapped by Liberace."

"Let me see it," Tracy said, offering to examine his mouth at close quarters. Davenant bent down and bared his teeth like a horse. "I don't see anything. It looks like it always has."

Davenant stood up and smiled at Maxine. "You look nice tonight."

"Thank you. . . . It's good to see you, Hugh. We were all worried."

"Well, I'm a big boy now."

"I hope you didn't catch cold in the rain last night—while you were chipping your tooth," Tracy said. "You didn't sleep out in the open, did you?"

"No, no," he smirked and knelt down next to the fire. He knew what Tracy was driving at, but he didn't want to tell her. Let her sweat it out; she'd caused him enough grief. Now the fire was growing enough to warm all of us. Davenant whispered something to Mauberley and then turned to me.

"Hey, Dalt, I saw the crew from Gannon's. They got a great spot near the woods behind the medical tent. And guess who's staying with them?"

"Who?"

"Ernie Parks."

"Ernie Parks! You're kidding!"

"Yeah. He wants to see you."

"Ernie Parks, I don't believe it. How is he?"

"Fine. Lookin' good."

I looked over to Maxine. "The only guy who went through Vietnam and didn't come back messed up."

"Unless you consider going down the dirt road normal," Mauberley said, letting the remark hang there.

"What?" Maxine was confused.

"Steve, has a thing about gays," Tracy said.

"Oh," Maxine said and shot me a knowing glance.

"Ernie's good people," Davenant said softly.

"So, why aren't they staying with us?" I asked.

"You're missing the point, my man," Mauberley said snickering. "How are they gonna play grab ass and hide the salami with a bunch of breeders like us around?"

"Are they all there?" I asked Davenant.

"Yeah, Gene, Tiny, Marcel, Roger, Ernie . . . all of 'em."

"And nary a lass between them," added Mauberley.

I stood up. "Max, you mind if say hello to Ernie? Who knows when I'll see him again?"

"You don't have to ask me."

"I'll go with you," Davenant said. "I have to hit the bathrooms anyway. I'll show you where they are."

"We'll be right back," I said and started up the slope.

A new band with several guitars and banjos struck up a sound like a child's walking toy. The hillside was alive with music again.

"Is she mad?" Davenant asked once we were out of earshot.

"What do you think? Yeah, she's mad."

"Shit. . . . I knew this whole thing was going to be a downer."

"You aren't exactly being a big fucking help, you know."

"Yeah, I know, but I've had it, man. I just had to get out. I'm sorry if I messed up things for you and everyone, but I needed it for my head. . . . In a way, even though it's a huge hassle, I'm glad it happened. Now I know exactly what has to be done and what I'm going to do."

"What's that?"

"Some of the guys from Gannon's are taking off next week for San Francisco. I'm going with them." He sounded excited. "I got the itch bad this time. Roger has some friends there . . . then by October or so, we'll settle into Aspen for some winter skiing. Get some good slope work in before the Christmas crush."

"Sounds like a plan. . . . Kind of sudden though, isn't it? I thought you were working on something."

"I am. It's almost done."

"That was fast."

"Hey, man, I don't fool around. I figure I can do the final rewrite in Colorado. . . . Dalt, I'm excited about it. I think I've caught it just right—one of the best things I've ever done. The Bard of Old Ford is back."

"Great, I'd like to see it."

"I'll send you a carbon."

"I'd like that. . . . What about Tracy and the kid?"

We found separate port-o-johns in the line of toilet shacks near the parking field. The acrid urine smell hung inside the booth and almost made me gag, as I tried not to splatter my boots and pants in the dark. Back outside, zippering up, I gulped down the fresh air and waited for Davenant.

"I'm not going back with you," he said, returning.

"What should I say to Tracy? . . . Look, I don't want to tell you how to live your life, but don't you think you owe her an explanation?"

"Yeah. Tell her . . . tell her not to worry and that I'm going to be a great father."

Davenant spoke about how he was planning to see a psychologist friend in Colorado because there had been some rocky moments recently that had freaked him out. On top of everything, he was becoming paranoid. A week ago he thought Tracy was trying to kill him with poison mushrooms, and there were times he felt like he couldn't trust anyone, not even me.

"Who doesn't have freak-outs?"

"I know, but it's just that sometimes I feel as if I'm not in control. . . . There've been some big changes going on."

"No, shit. We lost Jane. You're going to be a father. . . ."

We stopped along the way and watched a couple dancing inside a circle of people who were clapping loudly and encouraging them on. Apparently, the woman took all the exuberance as a signal to disrobe, and now she gyrated in red bikini underwear and a well-occupied tee shirt with "Lick it" stenciled on the front. Judging from her teasing movements, the shirt was next in line for removal.

Davenant turned to me and looked directly into my eyes. "I guess we won't be seeing each other for a while, partner."

"What about Ernie Parks?"

"I just said that to get away."

"Jesus."

"Gimme a hug, man."

We hugged not knowing the future.

"Good luck, Hugh," I said smiling and meant it.

We looked at each other and sensed the goodbye was incomplete.

"What?" he asked.

"Look . . . I can give you an explanation about how and why I'm going to ask you what I'm going to ask you, if you want, but since we won't be seeing each other again for a while—I'd like to settle something. I know it's none of my business . . ."

"The answer is yes," Davenant said and smiled.

"You don't even know the question."

"Yeah, I do, and I think by now Maxine has probably told you something about it."

"Should I say congratulations?"

"Yeah, sure, why not? It's one of the few good things that's happened to me in a while." He paused to light a cigarette. "Hey, don't worry, it's not catching, and I'll spare you all the theatrics. . . . I've finally accepted the fact who I am—I'm gay. It took me a long time to say that, but I know now I always was gay, and I'll always be gay. . . . For the first time in a long, long time, I feel good about that. I feel clean and happy and loving . . . yes, even loving, believe it or not." He paused and looked at me through the haze of cigarette smoke.

"Roger? From Gannon's?"

"Yeah, I'm in love with Roger, can you believe it? And we're going to go away where no one knows us and try to see if we can make it together. All I know is that I'm happy. . . . About everything else that's going on, it'll work itself out because it has to. And I haven't forgotten the baby. Believe me, I'll be the best motherfucking queer daddy in the whole goddamn world." He shook his head. "Who would ever believe this—divorced writer living off an older woman knocks her up and then finds out he's homosexual and runs off with the first blond that comes his way . . . vowing he'll be a terrific father to the unborn child. Ha-ha, how's that for a story?"

I smiled. "Hugh Davenant, The Bard of Old Ford."

We laughed, shook hands, and clasped each other in delight.

"Writer's destiny, I guess," he said.

"Whatever—if it's good and it feels right."

"Wouldn't it be great—one of these days, me at the top of the poetry charts and you number one in fiction."

"At some writer's conference at the Waldorf."

"Both of us sneering at the whole rotten planet and getting paid for it!"

"Talk about poetic justice."

"And they'll keep buying our stuff and begging for more."

"Wouldn't it be pretty to think so?"

"There you go quoting Papa on me. . . . C'mon, say hello to Roger. Give us your blessing."

Just before we reached Gannon's tent, Davenant stopped. "I was thinking. I think I'll name my kid Jason or Pierre."

"What if it's a girl?"

"Nonsense! Impossible! . . . True writers, potentates, Hawkeses, Davenants . . . We don't make girls, only men!"

That night it rained again. This time it was more urgent than before, but it lasted only for a brief stretch and stopped. A few minor drippings notwithstanding, the Old Ford tent weathered the storm in style—even though it seemed as though any second everything was going to crumble into a heap of plastic and sticks on top of us. The wind had snapped the Visqueen like a sail that had not yet caught the air properly and drove bullets of rain against it. Everywhere was the wet musky smell of blankets and damp dungarees. People came and went throughout the night.

Maxine and I slept with our clothes on, while others had made a large ceremony of undressing—so many people doing the same simple thing in so many different ways. Not long after the last flashlight had been extinguished, came the cries of Carla—an Old Ford lady friend with the body of a Greek statue and the face of a gargoyle—who prepared for sleep by loudly screwing a thin Jamaican near the entrance to the tent. Her deep, sighing grunts and his syncopated choo-choo notes of ecstasy blended perfectly with the outside sounds of the festival.

Don't stop the carnival.

17

"Howdy folks," a cowboy said the next day, holding back the flap of the Visqueen door, a large dark blob in the effulgence of the morning. He had not been the first cowboy or intruder to visit the Old Ford tent. He was holding a small suitcase that looked as though it could have belonged to his grandmother.

We all had slept a little late and everyone was still straightening out bedrolls. There was the warm feeling of a contented cavalry unit coping with the inconveniences and unpleasantries of a three-day scouting mission. Before the cowboy, we had been discussing how we probably would not be getting back until late that night—with so much to do and see and so little time before the concert. Mauberley suggested that we have breakfast at the Hog Farm—check things out and "get the lay of the land"—then eventually work our way over to the workers' meeting that afternoon. He figured by the time we scrounged up supper and ate and digested properly with a little weed and wine, the music would be starting at the Hog Farm. This time it was decided we would hang out by the bandstand and dance with the rest of the crowd. I groaned at the idea. Dancing was never my cup of tea and, to my mind, it was simply an atavistic ritual in preparation and anticipation of sex. Maxine and I were beyond dancing in our courtship; however, she loved to move her body to music and loved having people watch her.

Word was that the Hog Farm had moved and was setting up operations on higher ground near the woods and the water trailer. Supposedly, it had joined forces with Ken Kesey's Merry Pranksters, and together they would continue feeding the masses before the concert—a population that had grown by some estimates to fifty thousand.

"I hear you folks're from Old Ford," the cowboy said loudly, as he stepped inside the tent. He was a big, tall, good looking, young Texan in jeans and a tight, pearl-buttoned western shirt that barely concealed an impressive arrangement of taut muscles. Instead of a ten-gallon hat, a flat Confederate army cap was pulled down almost to his nose. He was smiling and chewing gum vigorously.

"Well, I spoze, we is—seein' what the tent says," Mauberley drawled like an Arkansas bushwhacker. "You reckon you'll be needin' a place to hunker down for the night?"

"Yes, sir, surely will."

"Well then, best you stow your gear wherever you can, fella—dig out a spot—an' downwind if you don't mind." Mauberley flicked his arm like an indifferent cavalry sergeant. "C'mon, boy, don't just stand there!"

The cowboy complied, giving Mauberley a long stare.

"You're terrible, Steve," Tracy said. "And what's with that awful southern drawl?"

"Just don't want some drifter from Texarkana lookin' for an easy score, ma'am. . . . Hungreh, boy?"

Despite his politeness and youthful innocence, the young Tarzan looked as though he could scream "Kreegah bundolo!" and smite Mauberley asunder without the slightest trace of emotion.

"Yes, Sir, I believe I am."

"Good, let's eat. Hut-hut!" Mauberley ordered and stormed from the tent. We and the gangly man/child followed.

There were lines at the Hog Farm but no one looked annoyed. It felt good to stand in the half-warmth of a diminished sun and watch the new city awaken as miraculously as it had appeared—eager for the new day, eager to grow and to continue evolving. Last night in a drug-induced soliloquy, Mauberley had pontificated about how Woodstock was a kind of pseudo-event: "It's a social experiment. It's planned, reported, and prophetical—to see what impulses can be generated from the imagination, the spirit, the dream. Its very ambiguity is symbolic of its mythology. . . . Woodstock is a bard, a visionary, my friends—Yeats with trees." We just let him go on.

At the feeding pots, the great unwashed were fed and ushered along expeditiously with an aura of a quasi-ordained decentralization of authority—producing a working, viable creature that knew its needs and was taking care of them. I stared at the two emaciated women shoveling food from green plastic tubs resting on wooden pallets and nudged up and whispered into Mauberley's ear, "Talk about 'Double, double toil and trouble.'"

He looked over. "Not to mention, 'Fire burn and cauldron bubble.' . . . Wouldn't it be freaky if one of these hags told you were going to be Thane of Cawdor?" Mauberley chortled and stuttered off a clip of laughs. Then he wheeled and faced the cowboy. "Some vitae, boy, vitae. I'm the recreation director at the Old Ford tent, and I'm charged with getting the scoop on everyone. . . . Give it to us straight, son, no drivel."

The cowboy's big walnut eyes squinted in the sun. Was this skinny hippie guy with hair down to his shoulders funnin' with him? "Sure. What can I do you for?"

"Who are you? Where're you from? What's your journey? There are no secrets at Woodstock—no secrets except in its very own mysticism. . . . You're among friends."

"Well," the cowboy began hesitantly, still not sure what this fast-talking hippie wanted, but he had understood the phrases *Where're you from?* and *What's your journey?* and in tortured rebelese revealed he had run away from home. It was the first time in his life he had been "more than fifty miles in one day" away from Lubbock, Texas. He was proud he had planned and executed his hitchhike to arrive at the festival ahead of time. His parents probably knew he was here because they had argued about his going with friends. When the friends had suddenly backed out, he was still determined to go. His mother had said if he did, she would track him down and give him a tarring in front of everyone that he would never forget. That was a week ago. His name was Sam Branch.

"Well, Sam Branch, be careful—cultural odysseys and generational rites of passage like Woodstock ain't always a bed of roses," Mauberley warned.

Breakfast was a paper plate with a modest mound of a raisin, oat, seed, and honey mixture over wilted lamb's quarters. Close up, the hags proved to be older hippie women with hair bound in two ropey braids down their backs and wilted from the rigors of serving. Past the food pots was another line waiting for water from two galvanized casks siphoned from the water trailer. Inside the Hog Farm compound were tables of freshly picked loose strife that children had gathered—to be brewed with mint into tea. A few men stripped to the waist were completing a wooden framed geodesic dome as women stapled sheets of plastic over the completed parts of the exoskeleton. Elsewhere: children and dogs ran after each other; traces of coffee and breakfast drifted in from other campsites; and a yogi was teaching acolytes how to stand on their heads, a few of whom tumbled laughing into the grass. . . .

"I got good feelin's from these people," Sam Branch said softly, conveying clumps of food to his mouth with his fingers. "I sure hope my mama don't come up here chasing after me, 'cause if she does, I'll have to make a fool outta her. . . . It's a terrible thing if you hafta make a fool out of your own mama."

"I know how you feel, Sammy, my parents are assholes, too." Mauberley sounded thoughtful. "Look, your mammy is probably well intentioned, but she just don't understand where things're at. . . . Most of the time our mamas are harmless old charwomen happy to accept things the way they are. But remember, they're still assholes. My father once told me, 'Boy, once an asshole, always an asshole, and if you find an asshole, leave him as such.' Words to live by."

Sam spoke loudly in his teenage baritone. "I'd never call my mama things like that."

"Yeah, yeah, I know, but you will. It's sad but true. I mean, if so many mothers are saints and inspirations—then there's got to be a few fuck-ups left over, right?"

The cowboy looked hurt.

"It's too bad, but what can we do? . . . Oh, when they die we'll feel bad, might even cry a tear or two. But the truth is—they may have been all right but they could have been better—much, much better." Mauberley folded his arms and smirked like a contented Buddha.

"I love my parents," Tracy said.

"I did, too," Maxine said and looked at me.

We all went on eating.

The truth was I never really thought about my parents very much—until they called me and we went through our family phone rituals, usually forgetting what we had said five minutes after I had hung up.

I smiled at Maxine. "You look wonderful in the morning."

"Go on. I'm ragged."

"Not to me."

She leaned over and whispered. "I really wanted to be with you last night."

"Sorry. I got back late from seeing my friend. I didn't want to wake you."

"I wasn't asleep."

"It's not the end of the world."

"For me it is."

"Why didn't you say something?"

"If we have to say it, then it's not right. We shouldn't have to say anything."

"Okay, okay . . . Christ, doesn't this game ever take a time out?"

"If it does, then it's over."

I sighed. "How about a swim after we eat?"

"Sure, why not?" She smiled weakly and looked down. "I'm feeling funny again, Dalton."

"You look funny, too,"

"No, I'm serious. . . . Will you at least see me through the festival?"

"Of course. . . . Where's all this coming from?

"I'm starting to feel, you know . . . the wanderlust again. . . . Promise?"

"I promise," I said and nervously watched the sun gather on the plastic dome.

"I christen thee Janus," Maxine intoned, standing naked and delicately applying her toe to the waters that ran down a narrow rock sluiceway, joining a small pond at her feet. "The god of good beginnings and good endings."

This place was off from Philippine Lake, gotten to by a narrow trail that opened onto a wonderful pool—fed by stream and perpetuated by overflow. Mauberley had led us first in clumps and then single file, wearing a white pith helmet and singing dirty blues melodies. He wielded a stick, which he used to beat down impudent branches that deigned to block his passage. It was worth the effort.

"Pure bucolicism!" he'd announced and waved down to the score of people below us, all naked: men and women lying on blankets, sunbathers, readers, swimmers, standing nudes, smoking nudes. . . . So moved by the sight, he had clawed away his clothes and run down to find a place among the rocks and flesh.

"That's why January's the first month," Maxine continued. She was shaking her foot in the water and watching it foam the surface.

Seeing her like that, so innocent and precious, I just wanted to hold her and tell her I loved her.

"You're such a bundle of information," I said, hugging her.

She hugged me tighter. "C'mon, we must walk straight in. No turning back. Let's go," and she pulled me into the cold water against my will.

"Shit, it's freezing!"

"There's no stopping us now—once we're set in motion—it's irreversible. Keep going, keep going. . . ."

Finally, there was that last frozen moment when I was standing on my toes, feeling the water consume the last inch of my thighs—until the flood came and we were treading water, facing each other.

"Oh, my god! . . . What do you want to do for fun now?" I said, squeegeeing water off my face and hair. "Tie weights to our ankles and see how long our last breath of life will last?"

"Hmmm, sounds delicious."

"You really *are* a sadist."

"I thought you knew that already." She dipped under the water and returned with her face breaking the surface, sweeping her hair back like a rich dark fabric. "You once called me a masochist, remember."

"You're a masochist, too."

"God, I'm so bloody rotten, Dalton,"

"To the bloody core."

"How does anyone stand me?" She moved closer and felt me beneath the water. The muscles in her cheeks bunched into a smile.

"That tickles . . . immensely."

"It's supposed to." The rest of her body drifted closer and our warmths came together.

"You're such a cockteaser."

"C'mon, you have to see how long you can take it."

"Why?"

"Because you must."

"Maxine, I'm telling you. If you keep that up, I won't be able to get out of the water for an hour."

"I don't care if we stay here all night."

Still holding me, she led me over to a grassy outcropping beside an overflow that tumbled down a jagged wrinkle of rocks and splashed among some smaller stones. In the shade of a tree, a man and woman sat Indian-style, meditating, and sharing a joint.

"You're such a party pooper," she laughed, releasing me and hoisting herself onto the ledge to lie in the sun. Her breasts settled into two perfect mounds like clay centering on a potter's wheel. I watched the dying rivulets and beads of water roll off her skin—joining the pluming water and splashing below . . . endlessly.

I marveled every time Maxine was naked. She enjoyed her body—content with its beauty and happy with its effect. She truly had been made to attract and provoke men. To me, everything she did was suggestive, and I always felt skittish with anticipation around her. As I stood there looking at what was offered to me so freely now, the sun played through the leaves and speckled the water—illuminating the center of the stream. There were bodies of other people I didn't know and would never see again. A portable cassette concealed somewhere higher up on the ledge gave music to the glade, and I returned the friendly eyes of those standing above the pool.

Subtly, as though accompanied by a harp glissando, the figure of Mauberley broke into the fleshy tableau above us. He stood looking down, debating whether to dive into the pool. He looked around to see if anyone was watching.

"Behold Mauberley," I said.

Maxine rose up and shielded her eyes. "He looks like a nude scarecrow."

"Doesn't he? I was thinking more along the lines of a hairy white umbrella with an extremely ugly penis."

"You're right! My god, it *is* ugly. What's the matter with it?"

"Nothing. It's uncircumcised."

Maxine sighed and sat up straighter. "I know that. But his is all bent somehow."

"No doubt about it—one ugly pecker."

We both laughed and Mauberley waved and started to pantomime a man afraid to dive.

"How come he wasn't . . . fixed?" Maxine asked, watching him clown around.

"It's not exactly like spaying a dog."

"I know but . . . where was he born?"

"New Jersey."

"Really? I thought maybe he was from Asia or something. A roommate of mine had a German boyfriend who was like that. She called him 'the anteater.'"

"Anteater. That's funny."

"She always joked about it, something like, *der ameisenbär, der ameisenbär!*"

"Ole *der ameisenbär*," I repeated, unable to conceal the thought that maybe she was making up the whole story and that it had been her boyfriend.

"I miss them," she sighed. "I should try to see them again."

Mauberley pressed his hands together, stuck his elbows out awkwardly, faking an old-time dive.

Maxine waved and cupped her hands around her mouth. "Nice tan, Steve. Dalton says you look like a hairy white umbrella!"

Mauberley gestured that he could not hear.

Maxine signaled him with a twist of her hand—for him to jump.

Saluting, Mauberley belly flopped into the water, surfaced in the roil, and began swimming inelegantly over to us.

"Christ, you're one terrible swimmer," I said.

"Oh, what a pleasant thing to say—especially after I put my life on the line."

"No, I'm serious. Going swimming with you could be dangerous."

"Well then, I'll cross that off my Christmas list. . . . Water's never been my element, anyway. Is it my fault I was deprived of a normal American childhood—my parents never took me to the beach. . . . And I could never go into the basement because it was always full of water. I detest water. We fell prey to a crooked contractor."

Maxine laughed. "Tortured by a wet basement. . . . Did the ceiling leak, too, right on your forehead—no matter where you slept?"

"Yes, how did you know? . . . America doesn't realize it, but it's the general contractors who've ruined our minds—made us embrace drugs and mindless music. .

. . So many shitty houses and buildings—all that cement and steel and asbestos and mold—not to mention, having to live with the thought of an atomic bomb decimating all those substandard structures. Everything reduced to homeless dust, riddled with nuclear radiation, and rendered uninhabitable for thousands of years."

"Oh, you poor baby," Maxine cooed and kissed Mauberley on the forehead.

"Thank you for caring, darling," he said dramatically. "Let's face it, we're an isolated, displaced generation—like the lost souls of Pitcairn. We'll breed among ourselves until the young reject our ways and no longer want to stay. Soon, we will have been just a pretty experiment." He shook his head. "We are the first cold war people. We must warn the world what it's doing to itself. All our weapons are obsolete, just tools of posturing, and it's no longer important how many everyone has. We must realize that the Earth is beginning to betray us because we have violated her. Soon money will become meaningless, just like our weapons, and then there will be only one thing left."

"What's that?" asked Maxine.

"Ideology! Everyone will become a political visionary and freedom will have become merely an abstract idea everyone used to talk about on the way to the shoe factory or the rice fields. America, capitalism, it's already paving the way."

"Pithy," I said.

Happy with his analysis of the world, Mauberley pulled himself up onto the grass, and we all lay silently in the sun until he suddenly got up and splashed away.

"You've changed me," Maxine said after a while, still looking at the sky.

"*I've* changed *you?*"

"Yes, and I really didn't think it was going to happen."

"Why?"

"Because of who I am, how I live my life, my ways. . . . It's my fault."

"Why is being together anyone's fault?"

"Because it can't . . . be."

"It can if you want it to."

"My poor lost boy." She paused. "If you want to leave me, I'll understand."

"Did I say that?"

"No, but it's there. I know you."

"What do you know about me?"

"That you want us to be what you want us to be."

"And what's that?"

"Monogamous. . . . Lovers. . . . A future with some American version of a white picket fence."

"Can I help it if I love you?"

"Dalton, I'm not worthy of your love. You know me. You know who I am. I told you not to fall in love with me."

"Why don't you let me worry about that?"

"I don't want to hurt you . . . and I know I have."

"Whatever happened to our spontaneous, trip the light fantastic arrangement?"

"It not right for us, for you. I have baggage."

"Like what?"

"You know what I'm talking about."

"Okay, then. Maybe I should talk to Maurice and see what he thinks."

"Is that supposed to hurt me?"

"It is what it is—but it still doesn't stop me from loving you."

"Shouldn't it?"

"Love doesn't ask for rewards."

"Is that from a poem, too?"

"No, it's from a movie. . . . I love you, Maxine."

She hesitated. "And you know I love you, too—in my own way."

"What kind of love is that?" I said and stood up and dove into the water—letting the cold envelope me.

We gyred and gimbled until the verdant wabe grew dark and we joined the others up on the slope for the last rays of the sun. Lying there, stretched out fully under the trees, we all felt a silent satisfaction about being a part of something greater than ourselves.

Nearby a group of French-speaking teenagers told us in cute English that they had just completed their student exchange program at SUNY Old Ford and were returning to France after the festival. Woodstock would be their last impression of America. We told them that we lived in Old Ford, knew almost everyone at the college, and Mauberley spoke disparagingly about one of their professors. I couldn't help noticing how foreign they seemed to me. It was in their faces: odd expressions, alien eyes, unexpected gestures and reactions. But they were interesting. The Germans we were told—they were the ones who fooled you. I wondered if we appeared as conspicuously different to them.

They spoke about Vietnam, which was strange coming from foreigners—although they, too, had been occupiers—and their familiarity and condescension about the war almost gave me the urge to defend our policies. Who were they to criticize us? . . . Ever since I was a kid, Europe, the Middle East, Africa, Asia were just points on a mental globe, and places where things happened in magazines and on television. It made me think—were Americans that solipsistic or were we truly the center of the world for the time being? We shared a joint with them.

One of the girls, her name was Monique, was youthfully beautiful and the quintessential French tease, giving even the most innocuous subjects the suggestion of sex—like all French women, seemingly offering it and withholding it at the same time. It's what drove American men crazy and made us appear stupid and naïve. She told us in intriguing accents on the wrong syllables about an old tree house up the river a few hundred yards. She offered to lead us there. I accepted and Maxine quickly grabbed my hand—not wanting to let me out of her sight. The others said they would catch up after sharing another joint.

Maxine and Monique walked in front of me, and I exalted in the way the muscles in their buttocks and the backs of their thighs worked to propel them from rock to root to water. Monique's flat-chested litheness flitted forward with barely an effort, while Maxine's voluptuousness swayed sexily but still with an athletic grace of movement for a larger woman. There was moss on the rocks near the bank, and I could not help thinking about Jane and Fallen Rock. In the difficult spots, we chose our route carefully until we finally cut back onto land, where a shady trail humped with tree roots followed along the stream as it wound alongside us.

Somehow, walking naked through the woods, feeling the loose trail dirt between my toes and watching spots of sun move up and down the bodies of Maxine and Monique—it all seemed very natural. Wasn't that a sign of something—something extravagant, something marvelous, something unifying? I realized I was very excited and very stoned.

We passed a naked man walking in the opposite direction, and everyone greeted each other as though the world was finally on an even keel and clothes-wearing humans were the anomaly. As I considered this, possibilities building upon one another like a gathering wave, I envisioned the opportunity of being with Monique and Maxine—both seducing me and my satisfying them completely. I pictured how their faces would look, what sudden expressions would erupt, and the way their bodies would move to the nuance of gesture and touch in our lovemaking. It would prove that I had the power and desire enough for two women—like Birdie had been with Davenant and me—and how happy and depleted they would be. I wondered if Maxine would go along with something like that. What would Monique do? Had Maxine done things like that before, perhaps with her sister in Panama?

"You better watch where you're going there stud," Maxine chided and lowered her eyes.

I looked down. I hadn't realized.

"Oooh, la la!" Monique said and laughed in a French way.

The wind had picked up and the sound of it through the trees sang in the air above us. Parts of the stream rippled on top and slow vortexing pools were created by the running water being trapped against peninsulas of rock. Maxine's hair was blown to one side and exposed the back of her neck. Suddenly, Monique stopped and her little girl breasts came to repose. She gestured and there before us was a tree house in the crotch of a Chinese maple that forked into three boughs like a turkey foot. Inside the crook was a square frame of wood whose walls were half windows and half enclosure. It looked like the press box at a high school athletic field.

"It's so breezing now. It's absolutely super!" Monique cried and climbed the ladder nailed into the tree trunk. I followed behind Maxine, who hesitated, then negotiated the rungs sidesaddle.

The hut was cramped but afforded a pretty view of the stream. The floor was littered with pine needles that had eddied into clumpy lines from indirect winds. There would be no lovemaking here.

"Where did you learn English?" I asked.

Monique closed her eyes to the wind. "In school. I have been studying it for many years, but I cannot still speak it the way I must."

"Don't be silly," Maxine frowned. She leaned against one of the corner posts and crossed her arms and legs. "You speak it well enough and you know you do."

"No, no, no . . . not really."

"Do you think in English?" I asked.

"In about half sometimes."

"That must be hard," I said to Maxine, "to think in another language."

"I did when I was in Panama."

"Oooh, Panama, how *exotique,*" Monique said. "The grand Canal Panama."

"Do you dream in English?" I asked.

"Sometimes," Monique said and looked around. "I am starting to be cold."

"How do the French feel about Americans?" Maxine asked. "You don't like us, do you?"

I could tell Maxine was getting into one of her moods—when she looked almost numb and would start feeling sad about her life and her world, and how she did not care what happened to her. In was in these times she could become most cruel and most dangerous. She made a beautiful whipping post.

Monique looked at her nails. "To answer you, yes. Most French do not like Americans. We do not like the things that Americans do. We do not like their bourgeois ways . . . and their faces of superiority. "

Maxine's face was beautifully hard. "Isn't there anything else we can talk about?"

"You brought it up," I said.

"*I* brought it up?"

"Okay, forget it. It's my fault. I'm to blame."

"Well, it's just that it's a bloody bore to have to listen to someone telling you how millions of people hate your guts."

"How bloody is it?" I asked sarcastically.

Monique did not say anything, as though thinking—let the American bitch make a fool of herself. It is truly too beautiful a day to have to deal with a jealous American woman.

Maxine just stared at her.

"Monique, what do you think of the concert so far?" I asked.

"Are they always so big?"

"No, this is a kind of special concert."

"Will the land by the music be filled with people?"

"They say so."

"And they will be selling ham-bur-géres and hot dogs and po-ta-toes, yes?" Monique asked childishly, suddenly reduced from Paris *vedette* to riverbank *clocharde.*

Maxine laughed knowingly. "The bigger they are, the harder they fall."

"Let us return to the others now, no?" Monique said, a bit petulant and confused at Maxine's laughing.

"Yes," said Maxine. "Let us return."

I looked at both of them. *"Allons y!"* I said, holding up my hands in surrender and began leading the way back.

That night we sat in the saucer and watched as the construction gangs continued work. Men were hoisted into the air by formidable hundred-foot cranes—positioning speakers and spotlights inside the scaffolding towers that were clustered about the stage like a high-rise apartment complex. There were four spotlights to a tower, while other desultory lights played out into the night that spoke of rain. The moving light beams made it seem as though it were nighttime at a gaudy national monument. As men called to each other with tinny megaphones, a vastly powerful machine was in its final stages of assembly and tomorrow its engines would be tested for the first time. We all hoped it would be a sweet thunder.

Davenant still had not shown up by the time we had gone to the workers' meeting that afternoon. It had been very perfunctory: general remarks, vague working times were allotted, food would be purchased with tickets, and everyone left with the sense that it was not going to be a moneymaking venture. We would be working only for a few hours each of the three days. The work idea could turn out to be more of a drag than anything else. Then again, we didn't have to pay for tickets—$18 prepaid, $24 at the box office.

Afterwards we had walked around and saw the brightly tattooed buses with plastic bubbles, the encampments in the woods, the funky head shops where incense burned around the clock, trails marked with wooden arrows that read "Gentle Path," Groovy Way," and "High Way." We had stopped and watched an unimpressed cow lying in a small corral, her big, blasé mooneyes half-closed, as though nothing unusual was happening around her. "What cheek!" Mauberley had brayed. Many people just sat alone or stood against trees and stared bewildered at some invisible horizon, their vacant looks wondering what to make of this brave, new world—just like the cow.

Back at the tent very late that night, we were exhausted, and it seemed that everyone went to bed at the same time—and, thankfully, without the histrionics from Carla and her wormy Jamaican.

Officially, tomorrow was the first day of the festival.

BOOK IV

To Be Born

18

On Friday, August 15, 1969, we awoke to what would be by the end of the day, the fifth largest city in the state of New York. An extraordinary "flood" had begun during the night and was continuing at a staggering pace—as everything associated with man had reproduced wildly until all usable space was occupied by some definition of a dwelling, a body, or a vehicle. It was the old nightmare come true—when the world had finally populated itself to the point when everyone would be allotted a square foot of land because that was all that was left for him on the planet. Like the shifting of vast continental plates, great masses of multi-colored crowds gnashed against each other from all directions—all hoping to sit in the shallow saucer fronting the stage of the Woodstock Festival aka An Aquarian Exposition. Everywhere was the movement of bodies—blood cells in the capillaries of a greater organism, oozing from 10, 50, 100, 1,000, 3,000 miles away, clogging every road, every path, every highway—all driven towards a phenomenon most of whom would never get any closer to than a few miles away. Apparently, that was enough, as they drove on. It was on a scale much larger than Max Yasgur's farm and beyond anyone's wildest expectations.

Getting up, walking over to the Hog Farm, waiting on thick spiraling queues that strung out from the encampment like old radio wires, ultimately to receive a quarter of what we had been allotted yesterday—took hours. The server at this meal was a disheveled Ginsburgtype who rationed out the food like gruel and repeated at irregular intervals, "Bring back anything you don't eat! . . . Bring back anything you don't eat!"

We ate, did not bring anything back, and slipped into the woods whose linking paths to the stage luckily had not yet been discovered by the multitudes, whose greatest concentrations were on the outlying roads and in the fields. Ironically, we passed Davenant's new tent— with Mauberley, Tracy, Maxine, and Sam Branch in complete ignorance, I in silence. I saw Davenant standing in front embracing a streaky-blond haired teenager who appeared to be wearing nothing but an oversized tee shirt. They touched foreheads, kissed each other lightly, and then hugged again. Davenant looked up and saw me. His face cautioned there was nothing that could pass between us beyond a glance. I diverted everyone's attention to a scruffy-looking man sitting behind one of the head shop tents and announced that it was Abbie Hoffman. No one was very intrigued by this middle-aged hippie slumped over his breakfast, whoever he was. Even a supposed revolutionary star was pallid next to the nova of Woodstock.

There was also a young Leftist presence everywhere, which had interpreted the festival as a sounding board of sorts, but they, too, seemed sucked into the undertow of impending music and sense of event that was irreversible. Their leaflets were limp from the rain and humidity, their prose seemed clumsy, and their proselytizing lacked conviction. They seemed content to hand out their philosophy like a tired hawker on a New York City street corner. Accepting a pamphlet, Mauberley concluded with disdain, "Silly philosophical rantings of harmless malcontents," and quickly deposited it into a trash basket full of discarded broadsides.

I didn't know why, but ever since last night, I had the sense something was going to happen with Sam

Branch—some kind of violence. He had finally stood up to Mauberley—after being lackeyed for a day—and announced rather inelegantly but leaving no room for doubt, that Mauberley was no longer to order him around or tell him what to do, ever again. If Mauberley did, Sam said he would "beat the living shit" out of him. Mauberley took the warning in stride and went into windy discourse about all he had done for the "waif" and how it was a disgraceful way to treat someone who had taken a stranger into his tent and out of the cold. But in "Christian fashion," he would forgive Sam and accept him as a peer, though Sam's "traitorous and ruthless nature" was shocking and would "scar him forever." With that, he'd clasped the Texan's hands in both of his and said, "Samuel, I am sorrier for your treachery than I am for my peril at your hands. . . . It profits me nothing to offer my home to a stranger, to a cretin, and yet you reward my largesse with threat of violence upon my person. . . . Yes, I realize you have limited cranial endowment, and I accept that, but betrayal knows no class, no culture, no birthright. . . . I weep for your soul."

Satisfied he had made his point, Sam smiled back.

As we trekked on, at one point we realized Sam was no longer with us. Turning, we saw him glaring down at one of the leafleteers, who apparently had not been content to merely distribute radical literature but also felt obliged to offer a loud, annoying hard sell as well. Sam was holding the papers as though rags, bellowing something, and then he balled up the sheets and threw them down at the man's feet. Perhaps emboldened by the spiritual value of his politics, the man cursed and shoved Sam hard in the chest. The Texan stared at the man a long moment, understood what he must do, and simply stepped back and assumed a loose boxer's stance—ominously authentic to the Leftist—as it was evident Sam knew what he was doing. Without warning or seeming effort, Sam banged two stiff left jabs into the man's face. The startled revolutionary rubbed his hurt cheek, became livid, and with bulging eyes made a strange, high-pitched whinnying sound before charging at Sam, flailing his arms like a water sprinkler. Anticipating the man's response, the Texan deftly sidestepped the amateurish assault and sent the radical headlong into the mud via a pointy cowboy boot to the ass. Mauberley and I ran back and formed the last part of the circle that closed around the two fighters. Deciding the best way to defeat Goliath was to put him on defense, the anarchist sprang back and framed himself into an exaggerated European boxing stance and began peppering a flurry of punches that all fell three feet short of the giant.

"Peace!" someone yelled.

Sam was on his toes now, circling to his left, purposely throwing a slow series of feeder jabs, waiting for the communist's feeble left hook he knew was imminent. When it came, he pulled his head back at the last possible instant, letting the blow miss his face by an inch, and took advantage of his reach by coming over the top of his assailant's left arm and slamming home a ham roast-of-a-right into the man's left eye. Another hook, the nose. Another, a crack to the cheekbone—each a short, crisp, clean punch thrown with chilling precision. Wobbly-legged, the radical stood dazed, his face glistening with a smear of blood and more sputtering from his mouth as he gasped for air. Unconsciously, he plopped down to one knee, as if to ponder the godforsaken reason he had gotten into this suicidal mess in the first place.

"Peace! Peace!" the chant grew around them.

Sam looked around confused—he had simply defended himself and looked to the crowd for an answer.

Frightened and bloody, the pamphleteer seized upon the cowboy's moment of hesitation, jumped up, and tomahawked Sam on top of his head. Sam wheeled around indignant and glared down at the man before driving home two classic, evil-intentioned body shots to each side of the man's midsection and punctuated them with a picture perfect right cross to the neck. The man slumped back down in agony.

"Peace! Peace! Peace! Peace!" everyone chanted now. Mauberley and I joined in, "Peace! Peace!"

Eying his handiwork, Sam lowered his farrier arms slowly and the anger visibly drained from his features.

"Peace!"

He shrugged and walked over to his bloodied adversary and extended his hand in friendship. The beaten revolutionary recoiled at first and then accepted his defeat grudgingly.

"Peace!" the chant continued.

Sam hugged him and he hugged Sam back. Everyone applauded as Mauberley and I raised Sam's arm in victory and pulled him from the ring. As we made our way back to the others, someone yelled, "Faggot!" Mauberley raised a middle finger and we continued on through the woods.

For days, there had been the rumor that Bob Dylan might show up, as he lived close by in the town of Woodstock and often recorded there with The Band. Many felt his presence was necessary and his absence might diminish Woodstock as a generational statement. Mauberley thought this absurd. For him, Dylan had never been a hero. "A serviceable songwriter, granted," but "an abject amateur musician" whose voice was "the piteous ululation of a whining dog" that broke and cracked and wheezed—"all seeking exit from an Hebraic gibbous nose and a Maginot Line of Semitic sinuses." As far as Mauberley was concerned, "Dylan has done nothing for our generation. He's the vanguard of nothing and nothing has come from his music. He's just another created hero who happened to be at the right place at the right time—and now he's like an old punch-drunk sparring partner, who still refuses to fall—plodding on obscenely year after year after year."

"That's bullshit and you know it," I said.

"Joan Baez can hold up the folk contingent just fine. And she can sing. "

"You're just jealous."

"Of what?"

"That he does his art. That he doesn't suck up to anybody, and he doesn't feel any obligation to a public."

"Maybe he should. . . . Go to Washington Square and you'll find a dozen Dylans. Heaven knows he hasn't gotten where he is on his good looks. I'm amazed anyone still buys his crap."

"That *crap* is going to win him the Nobel Prize someday."

"Tsk. Right, and Twiggy's gonna grow a pair of forty-four double D's."

"Mark my words."

"Win for what?"

"For literature. For poetry."

"Jesus. Man, when you fall, you fall big time. . . . I can see it now: Dylan's dying—of course he would have to be crucified as befitting his station—and you're clutching the cross, splinters gouging your hands, looking up at his balls hanging out from his filthy loin rags and cursing Golgotha and the folly of man who had not understood his genius. . . . Then seeing his lips move feebly, trying to speak, you grip the cross even harder, craning to hear the maestro's last words, pleading, 'Yes, Bobby, I hear you, I hear you! Speak to me, Bobby, speak to me!' And finally shuffling off the mortal coil, with a last sweep of his shaggy mammoth head, he leans down to you and says, 'Hey, Hawkes, my balls are blowin' in the wind. The answer, my friend, is my balls are blowin' in the wind,'" Mauberley said and giggled venomously.

We emerged from the woods, forded the current of people on the road, and moved along the perimeter of the packed saucer. The sun had run through the early part of its day, and looking out over the crowd in the grainy light, there was a sense of volatility and purpose. Many people just stood in one place, their hands on their hips or arms crossed across their chests, and stared portentously at the fortress of the stage with its five incomplete-looking turrets—storey upon storey of yellow metal scaffolding towering over ill-defined shadows of bodies moving below them. The concert was running late. Behind the stage were the tents on the hill, formless explosions of trees, and the purple brushstroke of a distant mountain. Seating was impossible. Someone had mentioned that there would be balloons marking where everyone from Old Ford would be watching the concert together. We looked but saw no balloons.

"Why don't we go to work now," Mauberley suggested. "This thing's running late, and it doesn't look like it's going to start anytime soon. We can work until five or so. We're not going to get close enough to see anything now anyway. Sooner or later, a lot of these newcomers will have to leave to find a place to stay tonight."

We agreed, and after talk of a rendezvous, we went our separate ways—with the mandate that each of us was going to try to scrounge as much food as possible. For the next couple of hours, I collected tickets and doled out hamburgers, and in a way, it gave me a sense of purpose. I was more important than a spectator. I was part of the production. People probably wondered how I got the job. How was I chosen over so many others? As I worked, I smiled down at the faces with their outstretched fists of tickets. On one occasion a hand held no tickets and the plaintive face behind it smiled as though to say she was hungry and it was regrettable she could not pay for food. . . . I passed out hundreds of hamburgers: free, semi-free, and overcharged. I just grabbed at tickets and threw them into a shoebox behind the counter. Sporadically, I would divert my rhythm and incorporate what the workers called a "third grapefruit," a hamburger of my own, which I consumed as quickly as possible. I ate three hamburgers in the first hour, always guided by the thought this could possibly be my last meal until we got back to Old Ford. It was evident that the concessions and the Hog Farm would never be able to feed everyone, and with the roads snarled the way they were, it seemed impossible fresh supplies could be trucked in. A silent proviso dictated we try to survive the best we could.

As the sun waned, everything was tinged in red, and the powerful system of amplifiers rumbled to life like a rousing monster electrifying the air with its thunder—Woodstock's voice. Now, finally, after all the hassles, everything was plugged in and its hour had come around at last, slouching towards Bethel to be born. A man banged on a microphone.

"TWO, THREE . . . HELLO, HELLO . . . MORE ON THE GUITAR MIKE, MIKE . . . GUITAR MIKE, MIKE, MORE ON THE GUITAR MIKE, MIKE. . . ." The sound system was powerfully sensitive and picked up surrounding noises from around the stage: whistles, rumblings, laughter, the voice of a cop . . . "PLEASE KEEP IT MOVING . . ." Another, "LET THE VAN THROUGH." Someone near the stage was screaming "SHIT, MAN!" More banging on the microphone." "C'MON!" A kazoo, a helicopter, a voice in mid-sentence:

". . . COMFORTABLE . . . JUST HUNKER DOWN IN THERE. YOU SEE, MAN, IT'S LIKE THIS—IT'S A PUZZLE AND EVERYTHING'S

GONNA START TO FIT TOGETHER JUST RIGHT PRETTY SOON. YOU JUST WAIT AND SEE. CAN YOU DIG THAT? . . . HEY, YOU KNOW . . ." A second later, an immense buzzing washed over the saucer and thousands of people covered their ears. The buzzing stopped and there was more tapping on the microphone and announcements from a bare-chested, longhaired, bearded hippie wearing a string of beads:

". . . HOLLY HAS YOUR BAG WITH MEDICATION."

". . . HELEN SAVAGE, PLEASE CALL YOUR FATHER AT THE MOTEL GLORY IN WOODRIDGE."

". . . THE WARNING THAT I'VE RECEIVED— YOU MAY TAKE IT WITH HOWEVER MANY GRAINS OF SALT YOU WISH—THAT THE BROWN ACID THAT'S BEEN CIRCULATING AROUND US IS NOT SPECIFICALLY TOO GOOD. IT'S SUGGESTED THAT YOU DO STAY AWAY FROM THAT, BUT IT'S YOUR OWN TRIP. BUT PLEASE BE ADVISED THAT THERE IS A WARNING IN THAT. . . ."

It's actually happening, I said to myself. Max Yasgur's farm was filled and poised, and portentous voices like Aztec priests were calling for willing sacrifices. Our lives were being eclipsed by something greater than our worlds and we were made greater by experiencing it. There was an incredible excitement as the sun glowed on the backs of the audience and the renascent stage quivered with activity. Everything was ready to burgeon to life. Then at 5:07 in the afternoon . . .

"LET'S WELCOME, MR. RICHIE HAVENS!"

A tremendous roar rose up. A guitar began pulsating with congas, both lunging perfectly on the downbeat. Then the rhythms stopped abruptly and there was the tuning of a guitar and the plinking of strings trying to match pitch. For the moment, they became the most important sounds in the world— with everyone desperate for them to synchronize. . . . All tuned, the layers of sound came back again, melding into one, as though the music had never stopped but just evolved.

I threw off my apron. I had to find Maxine. I needed to be with her. Struggling through the sheer density of people proved almost impossible, yet the songs urged me on: "From the Prison," "The Minstrel from Gault," "Get together," "High Flying Bird" . . . Finally, a gaggle of balloons quivered under the muted sunlight, and as I moved closer, I could make out words written on them—OLD FORD bobbed into clarity above all my friends. Maxine saw me and called my name and we rushed into each other's arms. We kissed and embraced just as Richie Havens began "Handsome Johnny," about a young man who had gone to war in the fields of battle: Concord with a musket, Gettysburg with a flintlock, Dunkirk with a carbine, Korea with an M1, Vietnam with an M15, Birmingham, Alabama, with a defiant, clenched fist—waiting for the bullets to start whistling before he could be free. . . . Here comes a hydrogen bomb, here comes a guided missile. What's the use of singing when no one is really listening?

Havens walked away from the microphone—still strumming with that unique, long thumb, open tuning style of guitar playing, weaving among the people on stage as they clapped to his artistry, a huge swath of sweat darkening his orange robe.

"WHAT BETTER WAY TO START THAN WITH THE BEAUTIFUL MR. RICHIE HAVENS."

Cheers and love rained down everywhere.

Maxine and I hugged tighter, feeling the import of the song and hearing the festival's plea.

"We're all going to hell!" Mauberley boomed. "We're all going to hell!"

No one listened to him.

"Say something sweet," Maxine said intimately, as if we were the only ones standing in the field.

Her face looked radiant, and I looked into her eyes in a way that made her take notice of my seriousness.

"You're all that I want. . . . You're all that I need. . . . You fill me up and make me whole . . . and when I'm with you, I'm home."

"Oh, Dalton," she said with that heartbreaking foreign lilt in her voice that always made me so happy when she said my name. She touched her forehead to mine and we stood like that until the announcer called Havens back for an encore. . . .

"FREEDOM, FREEDOM . . . FREEDOM, FREEDOM . . . FREEDOM, FREEDOM . . . FREEDOM, FREEDOM . . ." he sang in a pleading, rasping, tired, wailing, insistent, sore-throat-of-a-voice with a base note somehow always lurking in the background—the misshapen mouth of a world-weary black man preaching call and return—airy, plaintive, feeding back on itself, words bursting from his mouth as though through a rent in his cheek.

"SOMETIMES I FEEL LIKE A MOTHERLESS CHILD . . . SOMETIMES I FEEL LIKE A MOTHERLESS CHILD . . . SOMETIMES I FEEL LIKE A MOTHERLESS CHILD . . . A LONG WAY FROM HOME . . . YEAH, YEAH, OHHH . . . FREEDOM, FREEDOM . . . FREEDOM, FREEDOM . . . FREEDOM, FREEDOM . . . FREEDOM, FREEDOM . . . FREEDOM, FREEDOM . . ."

The audience clapped in half notes to each measure, as many in the crowd swayed, closed their eyes, and nodded their heads to the sweet refrain. Spontaneously, bodies jumped up and danced in rapture. Clothing was removed and twirled in circles above people's heads. Frisbees parabolaed back and forth, their owners never to see them again.

"FATHER . . . MOTHER . . . SISTER . . . YEAH, YEAH, BROTHER . . .

The song ended and a cheer-applause-roar united the stage and the audience forever.

A short while later during a lull between acts, I made my way back to the concession stands and resumed my hamburger duties—promising to rendezvous as soon as possible. Back to routinely passing burgers down to the outstretched hands, one unexpectedly held on. I was surprised to see the young runaway girl from a few days before smiling up at me—somehow older and prettier looking. She was going to be an attractive young woman in a way I had not seen before.

"Cynthia! What are you doing here?" I said and smiled down at her. "Then again, why *shouldn't* you be here?. . . I'm glad you made it."

She laughed and covered her mouth with her hand as many women do—almost in an act of shyness. Her mouth seemed fuller now with a sensuousness beginning to form. I was amazed at the metamorphosis. I conjured the scene with her brother. There was no doubt that this kid had had some kind of instant course in growing up. It was incredible.

"I'm here for the same reason you are," she said. "I thought we went through this last time."

"So, we did." She hadn't forgotten a thing. "Listen, meet me around back, I'm going to quit now. You want any more hamburgers?"

She shook her head.

Tossing my apron into a hamper, I grabbed a grease-spotted shopping bag filled with "third grapefruits" and walked out. When Cynthia turned the corner and saw me, she ran and I caught her just as I put my bag down. I pulled her against me avuncularly and she squeezed back and kissed me on the cheek.

"That's the second time you've done that, only this time I'm awake. You have something for my cheeks?" I kissed her back.

"Yeah, and it's catching."

"C'mon." I retrieved the bag and guided her away, our arms around each other. Christ, I thought, I'm getting on better with this kid than I am with most of the others. I felt she needed to feel safe and I wanted to make her feel that way. Some kid.

"What's in the bag?"

"Food. I'm not sure how much there's going to be left after today."

"It's so exciting. It's unbelievable, isn't it? I knew it was going to be like this."

"Yeah. Did you have any trouble getting here?"

"Nope. Hitchhiked to Monticello and caught a motorcycle right here. Where we going?"

"To meet up with my friends, give them some supper, and listen to the music. Where're you staying?"

"I don't know."

"Good, you can stay with us."

"Really? Thanks. How are your friends doing?"

"Well, except for Davenant taking off for parts unknown and Mauberley being threatened by a runaway Texan. Sorry, I guess I shouldn't use that word. . . . And Maxine—you don't know her; she's the lady I brought here—well, she's been acting a little strange. And Tracy cries on and off about Davenant. And there's a leak in the tent above my feet. Other than that, everything's perfect!" I squeezed her and smiled down at her happy face.

"Sounds just like Calypso Street," she said.

"What are you, some kind of wise guy?"

"No, it's just that someone who looks like you told me never to play games."

"Your friend sounds like an extremely intelligent person."

"I wouldn't know—I've only met him twice."

We regrouped with the others, and everyone was glad to see Cynthia, even Mauberley. The food scrounging had been successful: Maxine had commandeered some soda; Mauberley, bags of pretzels and potato chips; Tracy, cigarettes, a six-pack of beer, and a package of hot dog rolls—"croissants for our morning coffee," if we had any.

"Where'd you get the beer?" Mauberley asked.

"A potter friend. Has a trunkful of it."

"He just *gave* it to you?" Mauberley continued. "He didn't ask you to come over and see his kiln or his hanging planters?"

"Of course. And his ladles, too!"

Even Mauberley had to laugh.

"I'd like to meet this friend of yours. Sounds like my type of guy."

"Yeah, both bullshit artists," I said. "Let's try to find a place closer to the stage."

Mauberley had been right—the realities of the chill, impending darkness, and the threat of more rain had induced many to investigate how they were going to spend the night. Now, even though the entire bowl was crowded, a few empty spaces of trampled grass could be seen. Two aisles had been established and ran from the stage to the concessions and were being kept clear by members of the Hog Farm—recognizable by their Woodstock tee shirts: a hand playing a guitar and a dove sitting on the neck of the guitar. Also noticeable were cops from New York City, who were providing security, despite the fact they had been ordered not to work because it would constitute moonlighting. Even though the Hog Farm had somewhat taken their place, the cops stayed on and were conspicuous around the stage and concession areas—not bothering anyone, mostly directing things, and looking as if everything was under control. If nothing more, they were visible reminders that complete chaos had not set in. The Hog Farm people were low key and intuitively realized that at an unprecedented event like this, it was important to have the facade of order in the face of a potentially volatile situation. We had not heard of any arrests or even any trouble. Peace and love.

As we walked down the aisle, Maxine spotted a red balloon with GANNON'S painted on it in white. It rose up from a very concentrated area near the stage, and it was certain we would not find any room there. For Tracy's sake, I didn't want to run into Davenant and his new boy toy, and Maxine agreed. We followed Mauberley like ragtag sojourners in a reprised Canterbury Tales.

Even though night was setting in, there were so many fires, flashlights, car headlights, spotlights, matches, cigarettes, and sundry other luminous objects that the saucer had the subdued lighting of a wine cellar, an outdoor Cacique. People always seemed to be walking towards us—the women seductive in the chiaroscuro. It was obvious that many in the audience intended to camp there rather than relinquish their spots in front of the stage. It was a good idea, barring rain; however, I knew weather was coming because the old scars on my back were itching. They never lied. Even my bad thumb—an old baseball injury from a circus catch against a centerfield wall—was acting up. Either it was going to rain or else my body had irrevocably fallen from grace in concert with the elements. A man passed us wearing nothing but two cartridge belts X'd across his chest and another around his waist—most of the loops filled with small vials, packets, and cachets of drugs, or so he chanted like a short order cook. "I got hash, sunshine, acid on a tab . . . best rolled joints money can grab . . . seconals on the bottom, speed on the top, makes your mind go flippity-flop."

A drunken woman sitting along the aisle reached up, pulled his penis like a train whistle, and slurred something about his being the Good Humor man, ringing his chimes.

It was insane: People in outrageous costumes or no clothes at all, open sex, and the ever-present sweet smell of marijuana. A joint was passed to Mauberley as he walked. He tugged on it, passed it back, and back again and again until it reached me. I returned it to original owner as I passed by.

"Thanks, man."

"Anytime, man."

We finally sat down and started to eat. It was in between sets, and following the precedent thus far, a time filled with messages and renewed warnings and reports about the state of affairs of the new country of Woodstock.

"IT HAS COME TO OUR ATTENTION THAT MANY OF YOU ARE CONTRIVING FALSE EMERGENCIES TO LET YOUR FRIENDS KNOW WHERE YOU ARE, AND WHERE YOU'LL BE OR WHAT HAVE YOU. . . . PLEASE, WE CANNOT BECOME A COMMUNITY BULLETIN BOARD FOR HALF A MILLION PEOPLE."

Cheering.

"WE ASK THAT YOU GO TO INFORMATION BOOTH, WHICH INFORMS US THAT IT HAD JUST SET UP A MISSING PERONS BUREAU, AND WE WOULD APPRECIATE THAT YOU DIRECT ANY INQUIRIES OF THIS NATURE TO THEM. . . . I HOPE THESE ARE LEGITIMATE: WILL MITCHELL PLEASE MEET HIS SISTER AT THE HOG FARM, SHE HAS YOUR JACKET WITH THE INSULIN. . . . BARNETT, YOUR LITTLE BROTHER IS NOW IN POLICE CUSTODY. PLEASE CONTACT SERGEANT PIERCE AT THE WHITE LAKE POLICE STATION. . .

. BERNIE SIEGEL, YOUR MOTHER CALLED AND YOU ARE ASKED TO MEET YOUR UNCLE SIDNEY AT THE MONTICELLO RACE TRACK—IT'S EXPREMELY IMPORTANT."

Another man walked out from the rear of the stage, and there was the sound of the microphone pinging as it jostled from one man to the other.

"Do you have a cigarette," Maxine asked. We had not talked much since I had gone back to see her to celebrate the beginning of the festival. There seemed to be no specific reason, except she decided we should not talk to each other for a while. It was her most conspicuous virtue—predictability in her unpredictability.

"You didn't eat much," I said, offering her the cigarette pack with my thumb holding back the flip top. She took one, put it to her lips, and waited for a light. I lit hers then mine in one sweep of the flame, and she blew it out the match with her first exhale. "How was work today, darling?"

"Shitty, sweetheart."

"Oh, what a poetic way to put it."

"Very funny."

". . . MAYBE WE CAN GET BACK TO WHAT WE WERE TALKING ABOUT BEFORE. . . . MY FRIENDS, THERE SEEMS TO BE A BAD BATCH OF BROWN ACID CIRCULATING AROUND THESE PARTS. HAVEN'T HAD ANY PERSONALLY; HOWEVER, MANY OF MY FRIENDS TELL ME IT'S A BUMMER, SO WATCH OUT FOR THAT ONE. . . . HEY, IT'S YOUR OWN TRIP. I'M JUST PASSING THE WARNING ON TO YOU, MAN. IF ANYONE DID TAKE BROWN ACID AND IS HAVING A BAD TIME RIGHT NOW, PLEASE GO TO THE GREEN AND WHITE STRIPED HOSPITAL TENT DIRECTLY WEST OF THE STAGE. OR GO TO A HOG FARM REPRESENTATIVE AND ASK FOR IMMEDIATE

TREATMENT. YOU CAN TRUST THESE PEOPLE, SO PLEASE, IF YOU FEEL YOU NEED IT."

No sooner had we begun to put the food away, than Sam showed up hungry and lonely—with the news that he had seen a woman who looked like his mother. . . . He promptly diminished our reserves—"The Great Hunger" Mauberley called it—by three hamburgers, a bag of pretzels, and a bag of potato chips, which I considered a modest tithe considering what he seemed capable of consuming. And it was when he was eying a fourth hamburger, he saw Cynthia. The instant look on his face spoke of joy and fulfillment—of dragging this heifer back to Lubbock and showing her off as his very own "New York hippie lady."

For her part, Cynthia's big eyes spoke of having never seen anyone like this young Texan before—tall, leathery. dungareed, booted—at once parts cowboy, altar boy, and self-effacing athlete. In the lambence of the saucer, his teeth were drops of milk set inside perfect bezels and honed to a straight line on genuine, grain-fed, Lone Star steer. Cynthia smiled back coyly, her teeth dull and pitted from neglect—to Sam, a temporary flaw in an otherwise spectacular, female Tadzio.

"Oh-oh," Mauberley said, seeing the electricity. He was lying down with his head propped up on his pith helmet. "Sizzle the griddle and catch the preacher, the cowboy just found him a god-danged creature."

"I'm warnin' you." Sam pointed two thick fingers like a gun at Mauberley.

"Relax, Sammy," Mauberley said and held up his hands in surrender. "Isn't one fight enough for today?"

"Then why don't you stop instigating?" Tracy interrupted. "I swear, you sound like an old lady half the time."

"Who's instigating? I'm just extolling the wonders of nature, the natural attraction of the species . . . pondering the Mendelian possibilities."

"That's what I mean—what you're doing right now—instigating."

"Me? Nah."

"Sam, this is our friend Cynthia from Old Ford," I said.

"Hello," Sam said in a soft, kind voice.

"Hi," Cynthia said cheerfully and smiled—just lips, no teeth.

"Ah, the bond of runaways. You know Cynthia's a runaway like you, Sammy," Mauberley continued.

"C'mon, man," I said. "Enough is enough."

Mauberley swiveled slowly towards me and glowered, "I don't tell you what to do, man. Don't start telling me. Dig?"

Immediately, even as I replied, "Dug," I thought of a physical confrontation between Mauberley and me. He was certainly taller at six-two. But I had street savvy from the Bronx and Long Island. Coupled with an all-county wrestling championship in high school and a short-lived stint thinking I could contend at the Golden Gloves, I felt I held a decisive edge over him. I had always been told that I looked tough, which I guess helped in situations like this, but I also knew that if someone forced me into something I couldn't back away from, I could give a good accounting of myself. I was willing to bet that Mauberley had never even been hit in the face before, let alone smashed someone else's face. He had been weaned more on the genteel, upper class, Caucasian kind of violence of his scientist father— duplicity, backstabbing, and innuendo. Looking at him now, I knew he was stoned. I could murder him if I had to. A fresh joint glowed briefly and was passed to

Maxine. To my surprise, she accepted and started coughing.

The moment might have become more interesting had not the lights onstage suddenly gone dead. Even the residual campfires and other illuminations seemed to diminish, as another group was about to play. I could sense the sleek bulk of Sam sitting down next to Cynthia. In the darkness Mauberley's stoned voice muttered, "Fuck it, man." No one paid any attention.

We heard a tingle of chimes as though entering a gypsy's chamber and the mood-riding sound undulated over us. Open sesame, I entreated in the circus of my mind. I give you the world of Ali Baba and the Taj Mahal—inspired by death to celebrate life. . . . Ladies and gentlemen, I give you Woodstock. Let us pray. . . . Let us pray for Southeast Asia and People's Park and the men on the moon . . . and Frank Loesser and Russ Morgan and Brian Jones and Coleman Hawkins . . . and Gabby Hayes and Robert Taylor and Boris Karloff and Leo Gorcey and Judy Garland . . . and Allen Dulles and John L. Lewis and Dwight Eisenhower . . . and 'Little Mo' Connolly and B. Traven and John Kennedy Toole . . . and Jan Palach and Sharon Tate and Mary Jo Kopechne. . . . The night caught the droning rhythms and danced and whined and wound around Yasgur's farm in Eastern enchantment.

"Oh, shit!" Mauberley groaned.

"What's the matter?" My voice lacked resonance against the music.

"I spilled the motherfuckin' grass."

"You have such a way with words," Maxine said.

I pictured Mauberley's eyes, just his eyes, seeking Maxine's voice in the dark.

"When one loses one's grass," he intoned, "it truly *is* a time to lament."

"Oh, so sorry," she answered. "Should I genuflect—modestly of course—or just sit dejectedly with a reverent twist to my mouth?"

"Laaa-deees," Tracy sang. "Play nice now."

"No," Mauberley continued, "I think a flat out supplication would be more in order. Spread-eagled with your face and tits pressing into the dirt—with fervor if possible."

"How about passing out from an overdose of boredom?"

"Fine, but only if you fart three times and take two umbrella steps."

"Aw, c'mon," Sam said, more annoyed than anything else. "We came to see a concert."

"Dalton, give me a cigarette," Maxine commanded, as though she were late for a train and impatiently waiting for a cashier to break a fresh roll of quarters.

"Didn't I just give you one?"

"It went out."

I was annoyed, too. I didn't like it when her hauteur surfaced in front of everyone—expecting me to fall in lockstep. Maxine wants cigarette, Maxine needs cigarette, give Maxine cigarette; I want, I need, give me, give me, give me. . . .

I put a pack of matches inside the Box of Marlboros and handed her the pack. "You should hear yourself. . . . You sound like a sulking princess."

"That's close," her voice was shaky.

"That's close," I mimicked in mock panic. "That's close, that's far, that's nearby, that's neighboring, that's adjacent, that's tangential . . ."

"LADIES AND GENTLEMEN, RAVI SHANKAR." I could feel the words press against my face.

An interested cheer arose. Two shafts of blue poured in upon the stage. A third, red, shot in at a wider angle and merged in a tight oval violetting the musicians. Some of the guide wires now had strings of yellow lights wound around them, and the walking ramp over the road was a humpy path of glowing red matchsticks. In the weak umbra that eddied up half the saucer, I saw Mauberley shrug and slap his pockets for something.

Maxine leaned back and blew away an impatient quiver of smoke. She threw the cigarettes and matches back to me.

Mauberley crinkled papers making a new joint and looked up with a knowing expression. "My, my, how the helicoptered millionaires have kamikazied into the mud."

"What's that supposed to mean?" Maxine said, jettisoning another smoke signal.

"It means anything you want it to mean—that I don't particularly like you; that I think you're a fucking phony; that you're a sad, pathetic, woman-of-a-certain-age trying to stay young and relevant by hanging around people eight, ten, twelve years younger than you. . . . But most of all, I think that you think your daddy's money is the only ticket you need in the world."

"Hey, man," I said.

"C'mon, Hawkes, she's an 18-carat gold bitch. You know that."

"That's enough!" Tracy cried. "Why do you have to turn everything into one of your ugly rants and put-downs?"

Sam looked up from talking with Cynthia, as though she shouldn't have to hear this kind of language.

"No, no, let him go on," Maxine said. "He's stoned. He always is. . . . Although I think we've heard this sermon before."

"You may have heard it before but you've never seem to get it, angel. You'll never be able to see yourself the way everyone else does."

"Profound."

"You fooled me for a while. You really did. And that doesn't usually happen. All your bullshit. You're good. You're very good. But I guess you know that already."

Maxine paused. "Well, again, what pleasant things for you to say. And to think—no one even asked you. How thoughtful and polite."

There was a silence and Ravi Shankar seemed miles away.

"But someone did ask me," Mauberley said.

"Really? Who?

"You."

"Me?"

"That's right. Isn't this what you want? What you *really* want—a confrontation? You love to bring on a good healthy argument, don't you—especially when it happens so wonderfully and spontaneously. It's perfect . . . and it's gotten to the point that you do it without even realizing it. . . . Isn't that what's scaring you?"

"You're mad . . . and you're ordinary and you're mediocre." Maxine's voice was calm and believable. "But let me put it another way, in your *patois*—so even you can understand. . . . Why don't you fuck off? Just fuck off. It's simple—just remove yourself—like flicking away a cockroach."

"Oh, such scathing denunciation. *I'm mad! I'm ordinary! I'm mediocre!* Whoa! . . . But since you put it that way, why don't *you* take all that shit you've been slinging around all summer and shove it up your privileged, Brahmin ass. Savvy?"

"You go to hell," Maxine said, her composure cracking slightly.

Mauberley stood up and it was easy to see his outline against the stage. Sam stood up after him—two, tall gunslingers, their black outlines etched by the effulgence of the stage.

Mauberley smiled. "I guess it had to come to this sooner or later, hah, Hopalong?"

"I've never let an insult like that to a lady pass before, an' I ain't gonna start now."

"Oh, Jesus, you're not kidding," Mauberley laughed. "What am I supposed to say now: 'the lady's a slut—a whore to every dockhand along the Mississippi?' . . . Ah, Sammy how I love ya'. You and your sword are the end of an era. You're dueling life has been a full one, I'm sure. . . . Lay on, McBranch!"

"Don't, Sam, please," Cynthia said quietly, unsure whether she had the right to say it.

"All right, you two, let's take a break," I interrupted. "Let's all take a break."

"I'm sorry, Dalton," Sam said and turned to Cynthia. "This has been building up a ways."

"What's it going to prove?" I asked.

"That he's a man," Maxine said loudly.

Mauberley started to walk away up the aisle and Sam moved quickly to catch up—not to appear that Mauberley was the eager one. I looked after them and sensed Mauberley's fear—a gladiator entering the ring facing almost certain death.

"You know, Hawkes, I think it's good for me to smoke as much grass as I do," Mauberley whispered later on, inspecting the ash on a half-blown joint. "Not only for my health but for my writing, too." He was lying on a battered army sleeping bag that his brother had brought home from Vietnam a few months before he had stepped on a land mine. "Here," he said, passing the joint, "smoke one of these three times a day and call me in the morning . . . if you want the prescription renewed." He laughed his laugh, making his freshly punched face even more grotesque. "Oh, shit, it hurts even when I laugh. . . . Hawkes, honest, do I look as bad as I feel?"

"Worse."

"Are you kidding?"

"You look like you should look."

"Really?"

"Yeah, like someone beat the shit out of you with a monkey wrench."

"Give me a metaphor."

"Your face looks like the relief map of a small third world country."

He laughed and grimaced again in pain. "Great! The place is crawling with poontang and I wind up looking like Quasimodo."

"Well, look on the bright side."

"What's that?"

"You're still alive."

Someone shut a lantern off on the other side of the tent, and one side of Mauberley's face was mercifully cast into shadow.

"Fucking Sam. Hits like a goddamn mule. Talk about all brawn and no brains. Steinbeck's Lenny was only the prototype for someone like Branch. What a dumb fucking yokel. Here, finish it," he said, handing me the joint.

"Why'd you kept pushing him?"

"I don't know? I don't know what I was trying to prove."

I looked over at Maxine. She had gone right to sleep as soon as we had come back from the music after midnight. She was dreaming—her nostrils flaring and her breaths coming in starts. Her hand twitched and stopped.

"How are things with her?" he whispered.

I could feel the hot joint next to my fingers. I took a last hit and pressed the roach into the dirt. I looked back at Maxine.

"I don't know. She's different all right—certainly different from what we're used to."

"Yeah, strange fruit. . . . Tell you though, even after all this—and don't you ever say anything—under other different circumstances, I wouldn't mind tearing a piece off that."

"Go for it."

"Just pulling your chain, man. . . . I don't tread on another man's pussy."

"Since when?"

"Since now."

"Hey, I don't make claims on anyone. I don't ask Maxine to live her life for me and vice versa."

"True—but there's always poon. That's one resource that'll never run out. . . . Yeah, poo-say. I think my next one will be a purple plum," Mauberley looked at me and seemed happy that I wore a quizzical expression. "Black pussy, man. It looks like a purple plum, doesn't it? Check it out next time."

"Yeah, next time."

"And tell her that, too. Black chicks love to hear that shit—say something like, 'Let's hump the plum, mama,' and you'll be in like Flynn."

"I've got enough problems dealing with . . . with a yellow peach right now.

Mauberley laughed and made a wounded face. "You're too good to be true."

"Got any more grass?"

"Didn't you get off?"

"Yeah, but I want to get wrecked."

"Yes, *that's* the Hawkes I've come to know and love. . . . In my shirt pocket. Make a thin one; I'm running low. . . . And with this face, it'll be a major hassle hustling up some more."

"Are you crazy? You can get anything you want in five minutes. There're guys walking around here decked out like Chiricahua Apaches."

"Yeah, but who has any bread?"

"Hey, do it like Davenant—live off the kindness of strangers. . . . They might be able to starve us and make us thirsty, but there's enough weed here to make us forget we even have to do things like eat and drink."

"Okay, you're in charge of our heads from now on."

We were silent as music started up somewhere beyond the tent.

"I'm sorry, man, about tonight."

"Don't worry about it."

"No, I know what a prick I can be sometimes."

"So, what else is new?"

"I hope it doesn't rain again. That'd be a drag."

"I know, but my scars are forecasting big time storms."

"I hope not—I have to meet someone."

"I thought you didn't want to be seen in public."

"I don't but they offered me a gig. They're going to put an organ underneath the stage so I can compose music. No one will have to see me—just hear my haunting melodies. Hopefully, seduce a gamine or two— the Angel of Music," he joked.

"The Phantom of Yasgur's Farm."

"You know, I just realized something—we're probably out of our jobs."

"Right. I don't think there's any more food left? Hey, maybe we'll be able to collect unemployment."

We laughed.

That night Woodstock rested—having feasted on hamburgers, rice and vegetables, and something the Hog

Farm called granola. While we slept, slow persistent rains introduced themselves over Max Yasgur's 600 acres, and in the middle of the night, I awoke with my foot soaking wet from the leak in the tent. My back was cold and I looked over and saw the deflated blankets where Maxine had been. I had been dreaming we were making love in her brass bed in the old stone house, and afterwards listening to the old wooden floors creak.

19

The next morning, my eyes opened onto translucence. The tent was fogged. I remembered hearing the nighttime rain. Raindrops were still tapping the Visqueen. It was cool and the clear-washed Saturday began to crawl into my senses—though my brain was still clouded with alcohol and pot. I looked over for Maxine, still gone. Damn, a new crisis. Someone near me asked the time—nearly ten. He said it was late. For what, I thought? I looked around to get my bearings, then turned and shimmied the foot or so up to the dripping side of the tent and lifted it. The blades of grass were rain-beaded and stood in front of the background like giant sequoias.

"You are General Sherman," I said touching the largest blade and knighting away the tiny beads of water. "You are the largest living thing in the world. It would take four ants with their arms outstretched to encircle your base. At your widest point—two inches from the surface of the earth—you are over a half of an inch thick. From there, you taper to a fine point almost four inches high. . . . You are a perfect creation."

Selectively focusing on the ridge, the blades of grass disappeared and the muddy rise came into view. What once had been freshly worn grass trails webbing up the embankment, were now jagged and irreparably carved mucky-red scars in the earth. Mud everywhere. It surrounded the tents and the temporary shelters where people crouched with blank expressions, staring at the ground and the rain and the passersby with no words spoken—only silent questions. Could the rain drown the innocence from the festival? I was drawn to the ridge where a man was pointing down in my direction, gesturing to a tall, older woman in a blue raincoat, kerchief, and dairy barn mucking boots. It was Mauberley. As the woman looked down at the tent, she brought a cigarette to her face, and the smoke clouded away above them. There was a movement of heads and she began a descent down one of the muddy grooves.

I lay watching for a moment and then I understood. I threw off the covers and looked over to where Sam and Cynthia had slept. Empty. I pulled on my boots and clambered out of the tent with the idea of finding Sam and warning him. Slapping into the mud, I almost ran into the tall Texan standing calmly under a nearby tree—his arm muscles squared around Cynthia's neck, drawing her into him.

"I already know, Dalton. I saw her, too. We were just going to take a walk around. Nice of your buddy to rat me out. . . . Thanks anyway."

Cynthia was silent.

"Don't expect me to apologize for him, Sam."

He understood. He suddenly looked like a kid again. This was a big deal to him—confronting parental authority—the showdown with mommy.

"I don't expect you to apologize for anyone, let alone Mauberley. It doesn't matter. May as well get it over with. Take the bull by the horns."

"Good luck, my friend," I said and turned back towards the tent but stopped. "Oh, Sam, you didn't happen to see . . .?"

"She left last night about two. Woke me up."

"Alone?"

"No."

"You see him?"

"Not really, but she called him 'Cade.'"

Sam's mother was calling him now: "Sam! . . . Sam Branch! . . . Sam Branch!"

I smiled at Cynthia and looked back at Sam. His face was determined—furrows dug in above his eyes and his bare arms hugging Cynthia tighter. Their hair was snaky and pushed back, pasted to their heads. Cynthia was trying to appear brave, watching the mother run down towards them. Sam seemed to know the way it would have to be. I went back into the tent just as the mother arrived. I could hear her heaving for breath. After a moment, the voices intensified.

"What do you mean you're stayin'?"

"Just what I said."

"Are you defyin' me?"

"No, ma'am."

"I'm orderin' you to come back home with me, now!"

"You can if you want, mama, but I've decided to stay up here in New York for a while."

"Over my dead body! . . . An' what do you mean, '*You* decided'? *I* decide, Sam Houston Branch! Don't you *ever* speak to your mama so disrespectful, tellin' me what to do. . . ."

I tried to picture the look on the mother's face. How she looked at Cynthia.

"Is this what you've learned up here—how to disrespect your mama?"

"No, ma'am. I'm not disrespectin' you. I didn't say I wasn't comin' home ever. I just said I won't be comin' home straight away. . . . I'll be home soon enough. Let me put you on a bus back to Lubbock, safe and sound, and that way there won't be any worry?"

"You'll do no such thing!" the mother shrieked in a tone that conjured the rictus of a predatory bird. "Is *she* why you won't come home?"

"Her name is Cynthia."

"I don't care what her name is." There was an abrupt silence—then Cynthia's crying.

Not wanting to be part of a domestic squabble, I dug quickly into Maxine's large shoulder bag she had packed for us. It seemed like ages ago. I remembered a dark blue, long sleeve corduroy shirt I had taken in case of chilly weather. Although I knew if it rained any harder, the shirt would weigh a ton. It was near the bottom, and as I dragged it out, I noticed a roll of bills inside the top pocket. I looked around. Keeping the shirt in the bag, I slid a rubber band off the roll and counted the money. There were fifteen twenty dollar bills. I was disappointed. Had Maxine thought she needed a little insurance policy—enough to whisk her away at a moment's notice? Maybe Mauberley was right. I stuffed the roll back into the shirt pocket and buttoned it. I finished dressing and walked out the other end of the tent away from Sam and his problems.

Maybe I shouldn't have bothered with Maxine in the first place, I thought, as I slapped into the mud up the hill. Whom was I trying to kid? She was always out of my league. When could *I* ever have afforded to leave three hundred dollars in a rumpled shirt in some tent—where any stranger could rip it off in a second? What incredible freedom. People like Maxine really did exist. Rich people really were different from the rest of us. . . . And was I what she'd said? Did I really want to be directed? Did I really want routine and tradition? Maybe I didn't know what I wanted. Maybe I was too accustomed to women falling all over me? Those women I could handle. . . . Maxine knew all along exactly what she wanted—and better than that, she knew exactly what I wanted. No wonder she told me she loved me "in my own way." She knew what I needed to hear. . . . She was a whole new animal to me and it showed, painfully. Maybe she did have Mauberley and me fooled. Maybe she had everyone fooled. Son of a bitch. . . . Who was I anyway, I thought, trudging up the rise. By the time I reached the ridge, my boots were covered with mud.

"Fuckin' disgustin', hah?" a man said, sitting on a newspaper under a plastic lean-to. He was barefoot, and the reddish-brown muck was almost up to the knees of his pants.

"You said it."

"Fuck the boots, man. Get rid of 'em. It don't feel that bad," he said and wiggled his toes.

"Maybe you're right."

"Damned straight. You'll see, man. Soon, it'll feel like you're dragging cement around."

"Well, I guess I shouldn't go walking near the East River."

The man chuckled. "Yep, so long," he called after me. I listened to him laugh as I continued plodding along the ridge.

For some reason, everything seemed to be moving more slowly, as though switching from 45 rpm to 33 1/3. Everyone was walking a bit stooped, looking around for the best place to step into the slough. It started raining harder. Besides finding Davenant's tent gone and coming upon thousands and thousands of people who had slept in the open to keep their places near the stage, the next hour was spent with rumors that Woodstock was about to be declared a disaster area—maybe a state of emergency. Water was dangerously low and for all intents and purposes, there was no food. Then, too, there were the clogged toilets, bogged down service trucks, and wild stories of dysentery and typhoid at an encampment near Philippine Pond. From the stage came fragmented reports and denials. It seemed as though the organizers were as confused as everyone else. I continued wandering through the woods, always in the back of my mind the hope of finding Maxine.

"PLEASE IGNORE THE REPORTS OF MALARIA, LEPROSY AND/OR ANY OTHER EXOTIC MALADIES THAT HAVE BEEN CIRCULATING THIS MORNING. . . . YES, FOOD AND WATER ARE LOW, BUT IT IS TRYING TO BE BROUGHT IN. SO, KEEP THE FAITH, MAN."

Thin distant cheers rose up and died.

"YOU ARE ADVISED TO RATION SENSIBLY WHAT YOU HAVE AND TO SHARE WITH THOSE WHO DO NOT HAVE. HEY, IT'S AS SIMPLE AS THAT, MAN. I MEAN, ISN'T THAT WHAT THIS WHOLE THING'S ABOUT? . . . AND I THINK IT BEHOOVES US TO TRY TO SET AN EXAMPLE TO THOSE AROUND THE WORLD WHO ARE WATCHING WHAT WE DO—READING ABOUT US, SEEING NEWSREELS. . . . WE HAVE TO SHOW THE WORLD THAT A HALF-MILLION FREAKS CAN GET TOGETHER AND NOT HAVE CHAOS! . . . DO YOU REALIZE WE'RE A CITY! THERE'S LIFE AND DEATH HERE. A MAN HAS ACCIDENTALLY DIED, AND SO FAR, TWO BABIES HAVE BEEN BORN. WE ARE REPLENISHING OUR LOSSES . . . GROWING AND CHANGING. . . .

I frowned. Everywhere was mud and people. And because of the sheer inadequacy of trash bins against the onslaught of hundreds of thousands of people, almost everywhere there was garbage—papers and refuse trampled into the sludge or blowing directionless along the ground, as though in the aftermath of a battle.

On the less dense, less filthy ground up by the concessions, I could see the entire saucer and the reddish terrain and the movement of people like a caravan of refugees. What was this now? Suddenly, everything seemed wrong. It was all Maxine's fault.

Feeling the call of nature, I traipsed along a thin network of overlapping boards and sheets of plywood intended to lead one hygienically to the toilets—impossible now as most everything was under the filth. I waited on line as five separate portable toilet compartments were occupied, then available, and then instantly replenished by those on line. It was orderly at least.

"Hey, kid," a short old-timer called to me through the rain from the front of one line, as a booth became free. "I'll meet you after," he said and walked bowlegged into the toilet and disappeared inside.

I nodded congenially, although I had no idea who he was. He looked like someone who should be familiar but I couldn't place him. It was not until I had lined the toilet seat with paper and sat down trying not to breathe the humid stench and do my business as quickly as possible, that I remembered who the funny little man was. Of course, the old socialist hitchhiking to Pelhamville on the way to the Echo Acres Hotel with Kaplan. His name came to me as I walked up to shake his hand—the same baggy pants, same horseshoe of hair, same ever-present friendly smile. . . .

"Nathan Paulding, how are you?"

"Fine, Dalton, thanks. And yourself?"

"I'm doing okay, considering. I didn't think you'd remember me."

He giggled. "The Socialist Workers Brotherhood never forgets a name or a face."

"Nathan, do you know you're the only person I've seen today with a smile. What are you so happy about? This whole damn thing might shut down."

"Nah! They won't shut down nothin'. No one would stand for it. Be the biggest goddamned protest you ever saw. They can't chance that. No, they'll go through the motions and keep their fingers crossed."

"You're crazy but, you know, you're probably right. So, what are you so happy about?"

"What's wrong with happy? Why not be happy? It beats sad. . . . I got a cause and there's a half-million people here to talk to about it. That's happy to me. And your kind of people listen to what I have to say. Yessirree! I love talking to young people about the Socialist Workers Brotherhood."

"You're beautiful, man. I mean it." I put my arm around him and we started walking back towards the stage.

"Now that's a word people don't often associate with me—or the SWB for that matter."

"I mean it—you're incredible. Think about it. You're a guy who's happy because he wants the government of his country to *collapse*. How wild is that? . . . And even though you probably know, deep down, it's never going to happen—at least, not while you're alive—it doesn't matter. You're a completely devoted worker ant."

"Oh, it's gonna happen, Dalton. And there's no better time than the present. The mood is ripe for socialism now. We're ready for it. Doesn't everyone want a better lot in life?"

"Sure, but we've done pretty well for the last two hundred years."

"Yeah, but at the rate we're going, we'll be lucky if we last another two! . . . The administration's pissed off because the kids are making too much noise. Nixon's scared because of the war and he knows we're getting too close for comfort. So, instead of real reforms we get cosmetics and cover-up. No, we of the SWB mean the real thing, my friend. These things take time. People have to be educated. Rome wasn't built in a day. But it will be worth it, believe me."

"Nathan Paulding—the eternal optimist."

"Mark my words. Your generation's bringing back the feeling. Something's happening here. Something's happening in the world. . . . You'll see, your children will complete the process—America will be socialist by 2020."

"I'll be an old man."

"Yeah, well," Nathan replied as though conjuring something beautiful, "as Dr. King said, 'I may not get there with you, but I want you to know tonight that we as a people will get to the Promised Land.' Socialism is the Promised Land."

As we walked along the field, we began to sink into the mud more and more with every step and decided to cross over and sit near one of the boarded-up and abandoned concession stands. One stand was occupied by a few Hog Farmers and some moonlighting cops who had set up a temporary emergency-aid center and were talking people down from bad acid trips. We sat on a railroad tie next to a nearby stand and smoked a cigarette.

"I meant to ask you, Dalton. Do you have any more of that stuff we smoked in your car?"

"The grass?"

"Shhhh!" He gestured to the cops.

"Relax," I whispered. "No one is going to get busted for grass here—and for the same reasons no one's going to close this place down." I shook my head. "Sorry, that stuff is long gone."

"I didn't mean it had to be the *exact* stuff."

I laughed. "You're funny, Nathan," and described to him what our tent looked like, where it was, and that he should come by tonight. I was sure I could get something for him.

His jovial expression changed to concern. "You're not hooked are you, Dalton?"

"Hooked? On what?"

"Marijuana."

"Are you kidding? Nathan, you can't get hooked on grass."

"Psychologically you can, right?"

"You've been watching too much television."

"How do you know?"

"Because I know, believe me, I know. I've been smoking for years, and I still have all my chromosomes." I became serious. "But there is one side effect . . . ."

"What's that?" he asked eagerly—seemingly convinced something so good must have its dark side.

"It's nothing really—except in rare cases after a month or so your dick can fall off."

"IF YOU'VE BEEN HERE AWHILE, YOU'LL KNOW THAT PRETTY SOON YOU START THINKING ABOUT WHOSE LAND THIS IS WE'RE USING. HEY, A HALF-MILLION FREAKS ARE CAMPING ON SOME FARMER'S LAND."

A large part of the audience laughed, another cheered.

"LADIES AND GENTLEMEN, WE HAVE THAT MAN WITH US RIGHT NOW—MR. MAX YASGUR."

Applause.

"I'M A FARMER. . . . I DON'T KNOW HOW TO SPEAK TO TWENTY PEOPLE AT ONE TIME, LET ALONE A CROWD LIKE THIS. BUT I THINK YOU PEOPLE HAVE PROVEN SOMETHING TO THE WORLD—NOT ONLY TO THE TOWN OF BETHEL, OR SULLIVAN COUNTY, OR NEW YORK STATE; YOU'VE PROVEN SOMETHING TO THE WORLD. THIS IS THE LARGEST GROUP OF PEOPLE EVER ASSEMBLED IN ONE PLACE. . . . WE HAVE HAD NO IDEA THAT THERE WOULD BE THIS SIZE GROUP, AND BECAUSE OF THAT, YOU'VE HAD

QUITE A FEW INCONVENIENCES AS FAR AS WATER, FOOD, AND SO FORTH. YOUR PRODUCERS HAVE DONE A MAMMOTH JOB TO SEE THAT YOU'RE TAKEN CARE OF—THEY'D ENJOY A VOTE OF THANKS. BUT ABOVE THAT, THE IMPORTANT THING THAT YOU'VE PROVEN TO THE WORLD IS THAT A HALF-MILLION KIDS—AND I CALL YOU KIDS BECAUSE I HAVE CHILDREN THAT ARE OLDER THAN YOU—A HALF-MILLION YOUNG PEOPLE CAN GET TOGETHER AND HAVE THREE DAYS OF FUN AND MUSIC AND HAVE NOTHING BUT FUN AND MUSIC, AND MAY GOD BLESS YOU FOR IT. . . .

There was a huge applause. Thousands of people jumped to their feet in a time-lapse movement—like a wave at a football stadium. Suddenly, all the obstacles and misfortunes of the festival were gone. It was a new day. There was music. We were required to have fun. We stood and listened and moved to Joe Cocker awkwardly twist and gyrate his way through a song. Without warning, an area in front of the stage compressed into a knot of hands reaching into the air—someone was throwing beer off the stage, as suds spilled out of cans that were tossed to the crowd. The third day had gotten started—so what if it was a little behind schedule.

It was a good time to get high. I remembered the large roach Mauberley had given me and that I had wrapped inside my handkerchief. It was still there blackening a spot, where a few charred seeds and dead embers had fallen out. I stuck the roach between my lips, replaced the handkerchief, and began slapping my pockets for matches. Looking into my shirt pocket with the money, a hand appeared holding a small box of stick matches. I took them, looked up to thank my benefactor, and founded myself face to face with one of the moonlighting cops. We stared at each other—a cigarette in his mouth, a roach of pot in mine. Smiling, I struck a match to light the joint.

"May I offer you some?" I asked, sucking in the sweet smoke and extending the half-joint.

"No thanks."

"Ever try it?

"My kid offered me pot a year ago."

"Like it?"

"I threw up."

I laughed. "I'm sorry, but that just seems funny to me now. I've never heard of that happening."

"Well, it did. Stood at the toilet for two hours. Couldn't move a muscle. Kept thinkin' my heart was going to stop if I moved."

"Talk about a bad trip."

"My kid didn't think so."

I looked at him for explanation.

"When I finally came down, I beat the livin' shit out of him. Told 'im he'd practically killed his father."

"I guess there weren't any more problems after that."

"Wanna bet? . . . He's on methadone now—thin as a rail, looks like he's forty. Costin' me a fortune. . . . The kid's a mess, a total waste. . . . Be better off dead, maybe," the big Irish cop trailed off wistfully and rubbed the back of his neck.

"Tell me something," I said, taking another hit on the roach to keep it alive. "If we were on the streets away from here, would you have busted me?"

"Depends—it ain't that simple."

"What do you mean?"

"Well, like if you get busted for somethin' else, too, okay. Just smokin' grass alone, you're not too likely to get nailed—but then again, it depends on other things. At a sit-in or a protest, definitely yes. Because the whole world's watchin'. Depends."

"Shit, I would've thought you'd bust me in a second—anytime, anywhere . . . other than here."

We looked over the crowd.

"Nah, grass cases are clutterin' up the court calendars—in the city at least. The important stuff— heroin, pills, meth, acid— it's takin' too long. Mark my words, it'll be a long time before marijuana is ever legalized, but you can bet your ass sooner or later we'll stop bringin' those cases to trial at all. A fine or somethin' like that."

"I hope so. That would be very civilized. What would you think of that? You'd hate it like hell, right?"

"What do you think?" the cop replied, looking squarely at me.

"Understood." I looked back to the stage and saw the Old Ford balloons. Maybe Maxine was there. "I gotta go. Take care."

The cop smirked and gave a nonchalant salute. "Catch you on the flip side."

I stopped and turned around. "Oh, good luck with your kid."

"What kid?" he said and walked away.

I made my way over to the left side of the saucer. The broad aisle was no longer there, and I stopped on a piece of cardboard to map out the best way to make it to the balloons. I decided on a meandering channel near Happy Avenue, which only a few days before had known an occasional car and the hooves of Max Yasgur's cows. Now as I looked over, I'd be lucky even to reach it.

Suddenly, I realized I had stopped because walking had become tedious. I had just been enduring it all along, subconsciously—not wanting to take my boots off because there was something distasteful to me about baring one's toes and walking in mud. But there at the ends of my pants were the unbroken sheaths of filth. Almost as a test, I took a step and was able to pull my foot out of the boot quite easily. I stood on one leg with the boot sticking out of the mud like a silent totem on Easter Island. I muttered a curse, pulled off the other boot angrily, ripped away the socks, and triumphantly left everything there in the mud forever. So my feet would be muddy for a day or two longer. I wasn't going to die.

The mood now was that the rains, mud, food, water, and sanitary crises had been tests to measure our devotion. The road to peace and harmony was strewn with the temptations of the complacent, secular world. Weren't clothes, cars, jewelry, houses, money, and life's amenities far removed from life's real values? Job had been put to severe tests—so, too, Anne Frank, John Gunther, and the Kennedys. Who was I? . . . It was a mess only because we didn't want to be disappointed in these messianic affairs. It was bad blood and bad cheese, as Davenant would say.

Even before I made it to the balloons, I could see Maxine there and she was drunk. Uncannily, her stringy, wet hair only made her appear more innocent, more desirable. Somehow, she had not gotten as dirty as the rest of us. As I approached, she called my name. Some in the group looked at me, as though happy I could deal with Maxine myself now.

The music was louder here—visceral, pungent, thudding against my shirt. Maxine was swaying in the center of a loose quorum of Old Ford men who were all faintly familiar from the Cacique. No one seemed more interested in her than any of the others. Above us, a helicopter whisked in and landed behind the hospital tent.

"Hi!" Maxine cheered and flipped her hair back in a rooster tail of water. Her breasts were clearly visible beneath a wet tee shirt.

"Yes," I said.

She hesitated then patted a piece of a wooden pallet and plopped down. "You're crazy. Here, sit next to me."

"Where'd you find this? You know a longshoreman or something?"

"Oh, I have connections. . . . Do I have connections!"

"I'm beginning to see."

"You know, despite *everything,* I'm having a good time, after all."

"Oh, how nice. I'm happy for you. . . . Groovy, what's your sign?"

"Hmmm. . . . I guess you want to talk about last night. . . . My lips are sealed!" she announced loudly and ran a seductive finger along them. "Stoned?"

"A little. Got a buzz on just before I got here."

"Hey, who has a joint?" she called out.

One that was in circulation was passed over and she drew on it, taking mostly air and held it out to me. I declined.

"Wine?"

"Sure."

"It tastes like dishwater but it does the trick. . . . Hey, that's funny—liquor is really the biggest hooker of them all."

"What do you mean?"

"It does the *trick* every time!" Her eyes were bleary but her smile was willing.

"Clever."

"Oh, Dalton," she fell against me. I put my arm around her and felt her warmth. "It's all such a goddamn mess between us, and I'm really a bitch. . . . I think I'm going to throw up."

"Shhh," I soothed, waiting until those who were listening turned away. A slow song started and it was a nice break from the noise.

"No, I'm a bitch," she whispered and her shoulders fell. "I'm the one who keeps talking about not playing games, and I always do most of the playing." She looked up at me with helpless, expectant eyes.

"You don't have to explain to me—I have no claims on you."

"Don't be so noble. . . . I mean, there's such a thing as common courtesy, and I even screw *that* up."

"No one's perfect."

"My god, you're positively insipid! Aren't you going to ask me where I've been? I snuck out in the middle of the night!"

"I know—you woke Sam up. . . . Do you *want* me to ask you where you were?"

"I don't know." She brought the wine bottle to her lips and a thin, rose-colored liquid sloshed into the neck. She gestured the bottle to me and I refused. "I don't know—it's just that I can't help myself. . . . My whole life, I see something I want, I buy it. I see a man I want, I do whatever is necessary to . . . you know."

"Is that what this is for?" I said and brandished the wad of twenties from my pocket.

"No."

"Here then, take it."

"No, you hold onto it. I don't have any pockets with a snap. It's safer with you."

"Anything you say." I put the money back.

"And please don't play the martyr with me. Can't you see that I'm sick?"

"Yes, I can see that you're sick."

"Very funny." She pinched my arm. "It's all really a mess, Dalton. . . . Do you know where I was last night? . . . First, I was with that Cade fella. Turned out to be a five-star liar. . . . Then I was with a guy in one of the groups. A bass player. I don't even know what band he's in."

"I guess you just a groupie at heart. How romantic."

"You don't give an inch, do you?"

"Do you?"

"I think my kidneys are going. Every time I drink, I get pains there. I feel like I'm tensing up. . . . It's all a royal mess, Dalton."

"What's a mess—your kidneys, the conditions, your relationship with Maurice, you, me?"

"Everything. . . . I'm going to see him again—the bass player."

"Why are you telling me this?"

"You know why I'm telling you."

"I haven't the foggiest. I told you—you don't owe me anything."

"I'm just giving you what I'd expect."

"A fucking over?"

"Consideration."

"Consideration? You have some funny ideas about consideration. . . . You just told me you're screwing around with some bass player and you're going to see him again."

"That's right, don't you see?"

"Yeah, I see, but I don't believe it. . . . And while you're being a considerate, thirty-five-year-old groupie, what am I supposed to do—keep the tent warm?"

"First of all, it's not polite to talk about a woman's age. . . . Second of all, it's not as crass as you're making it out to be. I'm telling you because, for the time being . . . I'm going to be incommunicado—that things are changing between us. I'm sorry I drew first blood. . . . But there were no strings from the beginning, you know that."

"Yeah, yeah, no promises, no leases, no fine print . . . no nothing."

"But isn't that what made it good?"

"Sure, but what do I do now—play the fool, the understanding ex? . . . Do I bow out gracefully . . . or hang on until you want me again . . . or just go poof?"

Maxine looked sadly towards the stage.

"Poof," she said softly.

That night the music never stopped and groups came on as they arrived—in invisible helicopters limned in yellow lights shrouded by the rain, rising in and out of the landing fields with the moon. They were beyond the chill and the cold mud and the weather, and it was fascinating to watch the whole panoply.

Despite it all, Maxine and I huddled together and sat listening to the music as if we were alone in the saucer again—the music playing only for us. We kissed and drank and smoked and fell in and out of sleep leaning against each other in the middle of everything.

After kissing me goodnight, she slipped away into the darkness.

20

The next morning Maxine was there when I awoke. The tent had emptied throughout the night. We didn't say anything as we packed and headed for the saucer. I could tell it was going to rain again, as this sky seemed even more determined than the others. People's hair was billowing back in the wind and I knew stronger storms were riding currents only miles away. All the diehards seemed to be waiting for the last rain almost as an excuse to leave, but it had to happen first. In an unspoken way, Maxine and I felt we couldn't leave—we had to be forced away. Looking around, the crowds had thinned considerably.

"Want to stay for Hendricks?" I asked, shifting the weight of the packed travel bag from one shoulder to another.

Maxine looked exhausted for the first time during the festival. Now I could see she really was not a young woman.

"Sure, why not? . . . I feel like I'm just waking up." She looked to the sky and pleaded. "I promise I'll never drink again!" and sneezed twice.

"God bless you."

"You know, I never sneeze more than two times. Never."

"I'm a four sneezer." I looked at her and could not help smiling.

"What's the matter?"

"Nothing."

"Oh, you just like to grin for nothing? How long have you had this condition?"

"No, it's just you."

"What about me?"

"Loving you is dangerous business."

"I warned you."

"Yes, you did."

'YOU CAN LEAVE IF YOU WANT TO. WE'RE JUST JAMMIN', THAT'S ALL. YOU CAN LEAVE IF YOU WANT TO."

Hendricks was at the microphone, his white upside-down guitar looking more like a phallic, deco sculpture than an instrument. He wore a pink headband, festive in contrast to his manicured afro and the dying morning. A white fringed leather tunic swayed to the discordant music. There were wiggly rhythms and sassy chopping chords jellying together so well and so intricately that it was as though the songs were deconstructing themselves on the fly—at times a child's teasing and at other times smartass, boastful melodies forcing us to listen in wonder. His virtuoso musicality demanded, *Watch me, watch me,* over and over, purposely messing with our heads.

"I've never seen him live before, have you?" Maxine asked.

"No." She looked around and moved to the music.

After a few songs, everything ground down to two notes, hovering and playing off one another like a ballerina *en pointe*—calling up some inner guitar creature—an underground voice grumbling earthward, emerging from its subterranean lair. His words, his presence, his uniqueness of expression made me see what everyone saw in him.

And then there were beginning strains of the "Star Spangled Banner"—like five tired yawps of a petulant ghost awakening against its will—the sounds reverberating against each other, incredibly loud, blood-dimmed under shivering desert sands on a faraway continent. He riffed through a passage of seemingly inconsequential, intermittent notes until he reach the phrase, "AND THE ROCKET'S RED GLARE, BOMBS BURSTING . . ." and split the air with his guitar: tremendous rumblings and confusions of liquid sounds; hideous bleating of stricken animals murdered under the parabolas of invisible bombs; sheaths of missiles jettisoning off a fighter wing—always fire and counter fire until the last bomb had fallen and its shock tumbled and trembled and whined down and the explosions were forced out of sync. . . .

"GAVE PROOF THROUGH THE NIGHT . . ." The world was driven downward, always downward, the slow-motion flight of something inexorably falling like the slow, descending debris of the Hindenburg. "THAT OUR FLAG WAS STILL THERE." Everything stopped and there was only the hum of the powerful speakers— until, grudgingly, everything wound back up and the kraken moved on, witnessing our unfurling banner and yearning for freedom. . . .

Maxine and I snapped out of our trance long enough to look at each other desperately and witness the final phrase.

"AND THE HOME OF THE BRAVE," the last note transforming itself into some East Indian wind instrument. The anthem had fallen back reflexively, so completely and totally that it had lost any identity whatsoever, and a new song sprang up from the depths of the old without a break—the plinking sound of a toy that a child might pull after himself—until Hendricks started singing "Purple Haze," and the music engulfed his voice, making him sound trapped in a compartment filling with water. . . .

There was a crack of thunder, so bare and unbidden, that everyone started to panic and run for cover, as rain immediately filled the air and drove into the ground. We turned and hurried up the saucer as people ran by us, the music at our backs, urging us on— impatiently prodding us to safety. I felt water dripping down my back and my corduroy shirt becoming a heavy extra layer of skin. We headed in the direction of the car and tried to speak over the wind as it rode on vicious gusts over the trees and filled the alfalfa field, whipping sheets of rain against the ragged concession stands. Momentarily, we crouched behind one, out of the slanting rain.

As we waited for the storm to slacken, we held hands and watched the fleeing procession before us.

"Thank you, Dalton. . . . You kept your word and saw me through this," Maxine said inside the tempest.

"My pleasure."

"You have every right to feel the way you do."

"How do you know how I feel?"

"I can tell." She smiled. "Whenever your nostrils flare, I know you're worked up over something."

"I don't flare my nostrils."

"Yes, you do. You know you do."

"Well, as long as we're reporting, I should tell you that your hands sweat when you get excited—especially in bed."

"They do not!"

"Sometimes cuddling with you is like holding hands with a dishrag or a floor mop."

"Stop!" Maxine was laughing hard with no sound, holding her stomach, until she gathered herself and sighed, "C'mon, let's get out of this. I don't think we'll be able to get away for a while."

"Okay."

We passed a line of parked trucks, which had brought food and supplies but never had the chance to get out. All of their cabs were full of hippies, their eyes beseeching the skies for a respite from the rain and at the same time sinking deeper into Yasgur's land. As we passed the last truck, two girls jumped out from the cab and ran wildly towards the road, waving their hands and screaming people's names.

"Let's get in before someone else does," I cried.

We ran over, climbed up the step covering the gas tank, and squeezed into the front seat. I eased in behind the big steering wheel and looked around. There was another person inside, a woman, and she nodded gravely. It was Sam's mother. She was wearing the same kerchief and raincoat. The truck smelled stale and funky from years of cigarettes, beer, and untold miles along forgotten roads. I stowed our bag on a little storage area above and behind the seat.

"Wait, there's a dry towel in there. Could you get it out, please?" Maxine asked.

I unzipped the bag partially, pulled out the towel, and handed it to her. I remembered the money. It was still in my pocket, now a wet roll of papers. I threw it into the bag and zipped it closed. As we dried our hair, the rain intensified, pelting the cab of the truck.

"This is insane," I said.

Sam's mother grumbled an unfriendly assent.

The three of us watched the exodus through the drooling windshield. Turning to Maxine, "Where to now?" I whispered.

She hesitated. "I'm not sure," she whispered back.

"Going on tour with the bass player?"

"No. He's just a little boy. . . . I'm thirty-five, Dalton. I could almost be his mother. I sent him on his way. He's not in my world."

"Who is? . . . I'm sorry."

"Don't be. . . . For some reason, I've been feeling the pull of Panama again. My father's old house is still there. I could convert part of it into a studio and paint all day. . . . It could be the beginning of my 'Jungle Period.'"

"It suits you."

"What about you?"

"I don't know. Mauberley thinks we should 'tour Europe in the grand style'—hole up in different places and finish things we're working on. Get a proper continental education."

"Sounds lovely. Send me a postcard."

"Will do. Paint me a picture of a sunset."

"Will do."

We moved against each other, and she rested her head against my shoulder.

"We made some good memories," I said.

"Yes, we did. . . . Oh, Dalton, why did everything always seem so life and death between us?"

"Maybe that was the problem—life and death can make everything look like love."

There was a frightening crack of thunder. We watched people running by, and after they passed, the garbage remained behind on the saucer. A young black woman stopped, as one her three little girls fell into the mud, crying, struggling to get up. The other two children stood by scared. The woman stared at us briefly through the windshield—before gathering her loved ones and searching for safety.

"My God," Sam's mother said slowly, "someone should've taken a hatchet to all that long before it came alive."

We stared at her soberly.

"Guess you don't like hearin' things like that up here, do you?"

"No," we said in unison.

"Well, what do you know 'bout people? What do you know 'bout anythin'? Who are you anyway?"

"We are stardust," I said.

THE END

Meet our author

Russell Paul La Valle is a New York-based writer and screenwriter—having had previous incarnations as a teacher, songwriter, and marketing and advertising executive, where he wrote for many of the country's top companies and corporations.

His work has appeared in numerous newspapers and magazines such as The Washington Post, The New York Times, New York Daily News, The Village Voice, Newsday, as well as online opinion sites, including The Federalist, American Thinker, The Daily Caller, and The Hill.

His cable features have appeared on HBO, Showtime, Cinemax, The Movie Channel, and The Playboy Channel. He is also the author of the 2017 novel Underground Dreams. In addition, he is a former contributing editor to The Atlas Society, a philosophical think tank, where he wrote on issues of the day from an ethical and rights-based perspective. His work has been picked up nationally, internationally, and anthologized.
Born in New York City, he lives with his wife in the Hudson Valley.

Here Comes the Sun is Russell Paul La Valle's second novel.